An Exchange of Souls

An Exchange of Souls

Barry Pain

With an Introduction by S. T. Joshi

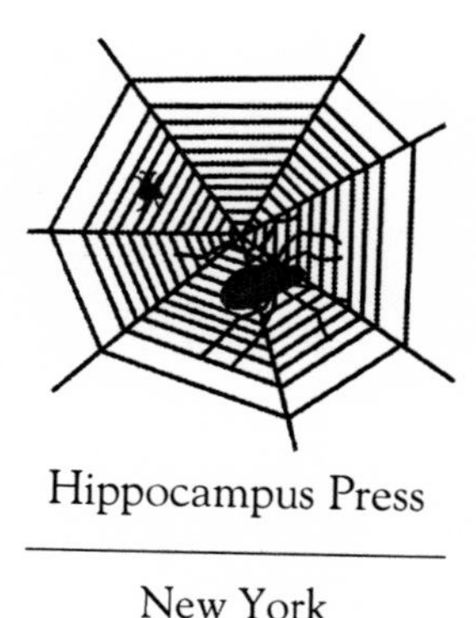

Hippocampus Press

New York

Published by Hippocampus Press
P.O. Box 641, New York, NY 10156.
http://www.hippocampuspress.com

Cover art for *An Exchange of Souls* is from the first edition (London: Eveleigh Nash, 1911) and provided by Raimondo Biffi. Regrettably, the artists's identity could not be determined. Cover design and Lovecraft series logo by Barbara Briggs Silbert.

Hippocampus Press logo designed by Anastasia Damianakos.

First Edition
1 3 5 7 9 8 6 4 2

ISBN: 0-9771734-4-5
ISBN-13: 978-0-9771734-4-0

Introduction

Not a great deal is known about the British writer Barry Pain (1864–1928). As John D. Cloy, the author of a recent monograph on him, states, "Pain in particular, and [W. W.] Jacobs generally, were private men who hated being interviewed."[1] Born in Cambridge, Pain attended a preparatory school, Sedburgh School (1879–83), to whose literary magazine he contributed. Entering Corpus Christi College, Cambridge, he edited a school magazine, the *Cambridge Fortnightly,* and contributed to other college publications. This early interest in writing would set the stage for an immensely prolific literary career as a short story writer, novelist, poet, and essayist. Pain graduated from Cambridge in 1886 and in 1890 moved to London, where he at once began contributing to some of the leading middlebrow publications of the day—*Punch, To-day, Black and White,* the *Idler,* the *Sketch,* and numerous others. He, W. W. Jacobs, and Jerome K. Jerome were quickly branded the New Humourists—a term initially coined in derision because it was believed by highbrow critics that these writers (all of whom, curiously, wrote the occasional weird tale) were deliberately seeking to satisfy the lowbrow tastes of the rapidly increasing British middle class. As a result of the Education Act of 1870, the middle and lower-middle classes were achieving a level of literacy previously unheard of; at the same time, they were not inclined to sample the literary and artistic work of such highbrows as Oscar Wilde, Aubrey Beardsley, Max Beerbohm, and others who made the "Yellow Nineties" so memorable. Essentially conservative in their tastes, these readers sought a literature that was accessible, entertaining, and unthreatening to their political, moral, and sexual predispositions. The New Humourists, among others, were on hand to satisfy them.

Pain's first book, *In a Canadian Canoe* (1891), was largely a collection of humorous tales, although—as with almost every other story collection he published—it included at least one or two weird specimens, whether of supernatural or psychological horror. It was the first of sixty books he would publish in a career spanning nearly four decades; his

1. John D. Cloy, *Muscular Mirth: Barry Pain and the New Humor* (Victoria, BC: English Literary Studies, University of Victoria, 2003), p. 12.

uncollected tales and sketches (the great majority of them humorous, but with apparently a few weird items buried among them) number in the hundreds. The overwhelming mass of this material is, probably, deservedly forgotten: it was written for its day and could scarcely be considered a "possession for all time," as Thucydides wrote of his history. There is a grim irony in the fate of such writers as Pain, Jacobs, and Robert W. Chambers, who experienced immense popular success for work that is now rightly consigned to oblivion but who live on, if they do at all, for a slim but distinguished body of weird fiction that appears to constitute their most serious output.

One wonders if Pain did not write more extensively in the weird because such items were poorly received. When *Stories in the Dark* (1901), a collection almost exclusively devoted to horror tales, appeared, it was almost entirely ignored by the press. *Studies in Grey* (1911) was not ignored, but reviewers complained that the book was regrettably uncharacteristic of the comic work that had won Pain such celebrity. After twenty years of humorous writing, he had been definitely typecast.

What therefore Pain him to write (in conjunction with James Blyth) *The Shadow of the Unseen* (1907), a capable witchcraft novel, and *An Exchange of Souls* (1911) is a mystery; perhaps we are left with Lovecraft's possibly whimsical notion, in "Supernatural Horror in Literature," that the tenacity of the inclination toward weird fiction is evidenced by "the impulse which now and then drives writers of totally opposite leanings to try their hands at it in isolated tales, as if to discharge from their minds certain phantasmal shapes which would otherwise haunt them."[2] In Pain's case, it might be inferred that his several novels and tales about bold and resourceful (but not exactly feminist) female characters—notably his "Eliza" novels, *Eliza* (1900), *Eliza's Husband* (1903), *Eliza Getting On* (1911), *Exit Eliza* (1912), and *Eliza's Son* (1913)—led to his conceiving, in *An Exchange of Souls,* a more intimate fusion of the male and female life-principle than was possible in comic stories intended for a lowbrow audience.

Lovecraft's reading of *An Exchange of Souls* is circumstantial; he had the book in his library and clearly knew that it was a weird tale, as he

---

2. H. P. Lovecraft, *The Annotated Supernatural Horror in Literature,* ed. S. T. Joshi (New York: Hippocampus Press, 2000), p. 22.

lists it in his "Weird &c. Items in Library of H. P. Lovecraft."[3] That the fundamental plot of Pain's novel—a man exchanges his soul or personality with that of his fiancée—bears an uncanny resemblance to that of "The Thing on the Doorstep" (1933) is undeniable. Lovecraft has, however, indicated that the prime influence on that story was H. B. Drake's *The Shadowy Thing* (1928; published in England in 1925 as *The Remedy*). Entry 158 of his commonplace book supplies a plot synopsis of Drake's novel: "Man has terrible wizard friend who gains influence over him. Kills him in defence of his soul—walls body up in ancient cellar—BUT—the dead wizard (who has said strange things about soul lingering in body) *changes bodies with him* . . . leaving him a conscious corpse in cellar." At the end of the entry is the laconic notation, written later: "Thing on Doorstep."[4]

What should be evident is that Lovecraft has made a fundamental change in the plot of *The Shadowy Thing* in adapting it for "The Thing on the Doorstep"; and that change—whereby the "exchange of souls" (or bodies) is between a man and a woman with whom he is intimately related—could well have come (if it had a literary source) from Pain's novel. In his story Lovecraft has infused the character of Asenath Waite with features deriving both from his mother and his ex-wife, Sonia H. Greene, while the character of Edward Derby is a fusion of traits from himself and such of his friends as Frank Belknap Long, Clark Ashton Smith, and Alfred Galpin;[5] so a literary influence for this use of male-female personality-exchange may not exist; but it is likely that Pain's novel gave Lovecraft some suggestions as to how this exchange could be effected and what its ramifications might be.

There is, indeed, some ambiguity in both works as to exactly what has been exchanged. Pain speaks of the "transference of an Ego to a mind and body other than that [*sic*] with which it had previously been associated," but makes it clear that this Ego does not include the brain or mind (or, more specifically, the contents of the mind): the scientist Daniel Myas, who has conducted an experiment in which he has exchanged his "Ego" with that of his fiancée, Alice Lade, finds that he no

---

3. See S. T. Joshi, *Lovecraft's Library: A Catalogue,* 2nd rev. ed. (New York: Hippocampus Press, 2002), p. 152.

4. *Miscellaneous Writings* (Sauk City, WI: Arkham House, 1995), p. 99.

5. See my essay "Autobiography in Lovecraft," in *Primal Sources: Essays on H. P. Lovecraft* (New York: Hippocampus Press, 2003), pp. 59–60.

longer has the knowledge that had allowed him to construct the apparatus that effected the exchange—an apparatus that, in a fit of madness, he destroyed when he found that he was in the body of Alice and that his own body had died in the experiment. In Lovecraft, it is a bit clearer that Edward's mind (or its contents) has been transferred when he finds himself in the body of Asenath; indeed, Lovecraft the materialist does not speak of the "soul" at all, knowing it to be a vestige of an archaic religious worldview. Neither Pain nor Lovecraft addresses the potentially bizarre possibilities of gender-switching; if anything, Pain is a bit more forthright on the subject than the sexually repressed Lovecraft could allow himself to be. One final detail that may clinch the hypothesis that Lovecraft did indeed read Pain's book and learn from it is the strikingly similar use of the telephone at the conclusion of both tales (see section 4 of the postscript of *An Exchange of Souls*).

Barry Pain's bountiful works of humour may be justly forgotten, but his weird work deserves to survive. Lovecraft himself jotted down Pain's masterful tale of a monstrous birth, "The Undying Thing" (from *Stories in the Dark*), for discussion in a revised version of "Supernatural Horror in Literature," although he did not in fact cite the work when he came to revise his treatise. How much more of Pain's work Lovecraft read is open to question; certainly, some of Pain's best weird tales appear in a late, untitled collection in the series Short Stories of Today and Yesterday (1928). In spite of such a volume as *Stories in the Dark* (1989), a collection of tales by Pain, Jerome K. Jerome, and Robert Barr, edited by Hugh Lamb, the totality of Pain's weird work remains uncollected. One can only echo the sentiments of John D. Cloy: "It is a pity that Pain didn't expend more energy on his serious fiction; he might have made a more lasting mark as a teller of strange tales."[6] As with so many other writers, from F. Marion Crawford to Thomas Burke, we can only be grateful that Pain did choose, with surprisingly frequency, to broach the weird in the midst of a career devoted to work of a very different kind.

—S. T. JOSHI

6. Cloy, p. 41.

An Exchange of Souls

CHAPTER I

I met Daniel Myas first in the winter of 1905, at Hamilton's house, in Paris. Hamilton married a Frenchwoman, and they lived in Paris for the greater part of the year. They were both terribly musical, and musicians of many nationalities came to the house. Conversation, on the days when Madame received, was tryingly polyglot for a plain Englishman like myself.

As often happens at a first meeting, one received an impression which was in part erroneous and in part short of the truth. Until he spoke to me, I thought that Myas was a Frenchman. His necktie was aggressively French. It was bulgy and droopy and black silk. He used a little gesture. He had been speaking French to my hostess, and with a perfection that in an Englishman was almost unpatriotic. But he spoke English to me, and as only an Englishman can ever hope to speak it. It was not only a question of a perfect accent; he knew the latest phrases of the society in which he was moving. His talk with me was principally on the subject of the Paris restaurants; he seemed to have made a special study of the art of dining, and as a result of the experimental work he had slightly sacrificed his figure. He gave me the impression that I had much to learn. He was rather under the medium height and powerfully built. His eye was vivacious and his expression kindly. I noticed his hands particularly; they were rather too white and well shaped.

Just as I was leaving I had a few words with my hostess about him. Madame was always amusing, but not always accurate. She told me that I had been talking to a great savant. No, he was not always so sweet-tempered as he appeared. For example, he always swore at his manicurist; but then he sent her sweets from Rumpelmayer's to make up for it. If he interested me, would I not meet him at dinner there on the following Wednesday? It further appeared that somebody with a name like a tropical disease would be playing the 'cello.

I accepted, and in this way began an acquaintance which I wish that I had never made. I say that deliberately. I liked Myas. I hope that this story will show that when he became my friend I accepted the duties of friendship. But he led me into a track where I was mazed and lost.

In the course of the next month I saw Myas frequently. He knew Paris well, and showed me much that I had not seen before. He was generally interesting, and sometimes astounding. One day he happened to speak, with a flash of that temper which Madame had led me to expect, of the extreme narrow-mindedness of medical men.

"Well, you are a medical man yourself, aren't you?"

"Oh, yes," he said. "As a matter of fact I am an M.D. of London, and at one time had a practice—a beastly practice in a beastly Somersetshire village. But as soon as I was in a position to give it up, I did so, and that was two years ago. I came into some money on my father's death."

"I see," I said. "And as soon as you became independent, your interest in medical science ceased."

"Goodness, no! You might almost say that was when it began. It is that which has kept me wandering round the foreign hospitals for the last two years. Research is absolutely lovely work. As a rule, it leads to nothing; when it does lead to anything, you get punished for it. You think you have found out something, you send a communication to the scientific press, and you metaphorically get your head bashed for your pains by your distinguished and learned colleagues. But don't try to look as if you were interested in science. You can't be, you know. You belong to the leisured classes. Come along, and we will lunch at Ledoyen's."

"If I belong to the leisured classes, that is more my misfortune than my fault. I'll tell you all about that one of these days. What was your line of research, and who jumped on you?"

"Somebody or other on the *Lancet*. I should imagine from the style and knowledge displayed, that the office-boy is allowed to do a little reviewing in his spare time. Well, well, it's a lesson to me. Never show children or fools half-finished work—there's no better proverb than that."

He was by way of making a joke of it, but it was quite obvious that in reality he was very sore about it, and for this reason I did not press him further on the subject.

It was my last day in Paris, and as we were smoking the post-luncheon cigarette, Myas asked me when we could meet again.

"Don't know. Soon, I hope. Do you ever come to London?"

"Of course. Everybody does. I am not quite sure, but I think my work will send me there in the spring."

We arranged that he should come to see me then at my little flat in St. James's Place.

"And by that time," he said, "I may be able to answer you more explicitly about my work."

"Quite likely," I said. So far of course, he had not answered me at all.

The day after my return to London, I happened to meet at the club an old friend of mine, Dr. Habaden. He is a mighty physician, with a right to put a decoration on his evening coat on suitable occasions. I asked him if by any chance he knew a Dr. Myas.

"Daniel Myas?"

"That's him," I said, with the usual disregard of grammar.

"Yes, I know of him. As a student he did rather brilliantly. Got a resident appointment at his hospital. Quarrelled with everybody about everything, and had to go. Then he bought himself a practice, and that was how I came across him. He brought a patient up from Somersetshire to see me. I don't mind telling you that it was a devilish difficult case, and I found that Myas had diagnosed it correctly and treated it correctly."

"Did the patient recover?"

"No; died. But that's got nothing to do with it. He impressed me at the time as a very able man, quite beyond the run of the ordinary general practitioner. He's given up practice and taken up research now, and he's gone absolutely off the lines. You should see the kind of stuff that he's been writing. A ghoulish business, I call it."

"Ghoulish? How do you mean? What is it he does?"

"Dr. Daniel Myas is making a special investigation of the moment of death. You understand? He makes observations of dying people. When the thing is practically over, and a decent man would go away, down swoops Myas with his ophthalmoscope and his electrocardiograph and all the rest of his bag of tricks, like a scientific vulture. I should suppose he's watched more deaths than any man living. Does his work abroad principally. And if the truth's told, he has tried some rum-funny experiments, too—things that would never be tolerated in any hospital this side of the Channel."

"I met him in Paris, you know, just the other day. He didn't tell me that he was interested in death, and I should have said he was much more interested in his dinner. In fact, he didn't impress me as a ghoul at all."

"Oh, I don't say he's a ghoul in ordinary life. He probably wouldn't talk shop to you. It's the man's work that is ghoulish."

"I thought that science had declared all research to be good, and that in the sacred cause of truth nothing was to be considered horrible or disgusting?"

"Yes, that may be so if the research is directed to any useful end. But what good do you suppose Myas is doing? He is simply wasting time. We know what life is and what death is."

"Do we?" I asked.

I knew the question would irritate Dr. Habaden, and it did.

"If you think you're going to lure me into one of your profitless metaphysical discussions, you're mistaken, my friend. The medical man knows when life ends and death begins, and in the case of a patient who is past remedial aid that is all he needs to know. There is plenty of good work to be done, and as Myas has the time and the means he might just as well devote himself to it. What is the ætiology of disseminated sclerosis? What's the morbid anatomy of paralysis agitans? That's the kind of thing he ought to be telling us. Cancer isn't settled yet. I could name fifty things that might employ him usefully. He prefers to worry the last moments of poor devils for whom neither he nor anybody else can do anything. It's sheer perversity, and I hate to see a man of his abilities so much misled."

"Well," I said, "Myas will be coming to town in the spring, and I shall be seeing him. Shall I tell him what you think about him?"

"Do. Mind, it won't be any news to him. He's been rapped over the knuckles already. But I suppose he has some respect for my opinion, since he brought a patient to me, and I dare say he will believe that I am well disposed towards him."

"Very well," I said. "I'll tell him, and it's my belief that it won't make a pin's head of difference to him."

"Oh, that's very likely," grunted Dr. Habaden, and went on up to the billiard-room.

CHAPTER II

I had expected that Myas would write beforehand to tell me when he would arrive. But it was not his habit to do what was expected. He called on me at my flat one morning early in the following March. He had already been in London some days, and said that he had got his work in Paris finished sooner than he had expected.

"At least 'finished' is not the word. I had gone as far as I could safely go there. There are some very brilliant gentlemen in Paris, and they have an inquiring turn of mind."

He still wore flowing and abominable neckties, and his silk hat had a perfectly flat brim. In fact, as I observed to him, he looked more like a French charlatan than an English gentleman.

"Possibly," he said, quite unperturbed. "I am thankful to say that I am neither."

He was energetic and vivacious, and there was a distinct note of triumph in his talk. When I asked him what he was so pleased about, he became vague in his expressions, and said that things had gone rather well with him in Paris. Then he changed the subject and began talking about the Hamiltons. They had received a serious blow. The Italian gentleman who played the 'cello like an angel had been shown to be a trigamist. Morals had triumphed over music, and the Hamiltons had blotted him out. They had now gone to Rome for Easter, he told me.

He refused to stay at my little flat. He said that his plans were too undecided, and his temperament was too erratic; and that he did not wish to make himself a perfect nuisance.

"But," he said, "I will come and feed, if you like. Food is the one subject to which you have given any serious study."

That statement, by the way, is, as I told him, a grotesque untruth. I took him off to the club with me, and gave him a quite simple and unpretentious luncheon. He was pleased to be enthusiastic about it, and I told him that he was making a deal of unnecessary and unseemly cackle.

"Don't say that," he said. "I know what the enthusiasm of your life is. You are not one of the illogical and nervous weaklings who are ashamed to eat and drink."

"Are there such people?"

"Of course there are. They're a feature of the age. They browse on breakfast cereals and drink ginger-beer. The way the consumption of alcohol is decreasing in this country is perfectly appalling."

He paused to take a cup of black coffee. He refused the liqueur and proceeded:

"I have dined out a few times since I have been over here, and I have noticed things. One of the best wines is never drunk at all. It is always offered—apparently as a kind of ritual—and always refused. Although dinners have been made very much shorter, most women and some men refuse the joint. Dinner is becoming a farce. The really tragic thing about it is that these dyspeptic duffers seem to have the idea that their physical incapacity makes for refinement and mental improvement. It does nothing of the sort. Food for the body is food for the mind; the two are inseparably associated. Tell me now, what period in English history produced the finest men—the finest statesmen, generals, admirals, artists?"

"Well, I'm not an historian, but I suppose there is no dispute about that. Roughly speaking, the period would be the latter part of the eighteenth and the early part of the nineteenth centuries."

"Of course. And that was a hearty age. It was an age of beef and beer, and it was also an age of courage and inventions, which is precisely what one would have expected. Pitt drank his two bottles of port, went into the House of Commons, and spoke magnificently. There was oratory in those days, and there was consequent enthusiasm. The modern member of Parliament sips barley-water and stutters statistics, mostly wrong, and national enthusiasm is at a low ebb, which is also what one would expect."

"I wonder if there is anything in all this?" I said.

"It can hardly be otherwise. After all, the stomach is the one fundamental thing. It exists in the very lowest organisms, which have neither limbs nor brain. It is practically the first part of a man to get into working order. Its function is correct, before the baby can speak, or walk, or co-ordinate his movements. In fact, if I wanted to determine the Ego, I might be more likely to find the clue in the stomach than in the brain."

"Look here," I said. "What on earth do you mean by determining the Ego?"

"Well, in what does your 'self' consist? You would probably tell me that it consists in the association of your mind and your body. Now does it? When the mind has practically vanished, and no longer suffices even for a man's simplest needs, his life is still carefully preserved in an asylum. This would not be the case if it were not believed that the man's self was still there. When the man's body is dead and has decomposed, it is held by all religious people that the man's self still persists—that his personality is continued in another world; and perhaps science has rather more to say for this view than most men of science are aware. All of which is abominably dull talk after luncheon, isn't it?"

"Not to me," I said. "I have been getting rather interested in your work lately."

"You flatter me. And what do you know about it anyhow?"

"I know what that great and good man Dr. Habaden has told me."

"Dr. Habaden is a perfectly sound man in his own line, which is rather a terrific thing to be. It is quite detrimental to a sense of proportion. He sees a few blades of grass and he misses the landscape. I suppose my distinguished and learned colleague damned me as usual?"

"Oh, yes. Damned you very heartily, and told me to tell you so."

"Why?"

"He thinks you are a man of great ability, wasting your time out of perversity. He says you ought to be studying the ætiology of insanity, or the cure of cancer, or some other problem which really does need solution. He also suggests that you worry the last moments of dying patients, when they ought to be left in peace."

"Seems to have been saying a lot of sweet things about me," said Myas grimly. "Well, I needn't bother you with it. It's not your business. You belong to the leisured classes."

"You accused me of that before. It is true that I have no profession, and the only profession I ever wanted to have was not medical. But all the same I——"

"Hold on," said Myas. "What was it you wanted to go in for?"

"Army. The doctors wouldn't pass me. Ten years ago my people tried to get me to go into Parliament, but I had no ambitions that way. Still, I've got lots of friends, and I'm keen on lots of things, and I do occasionally think. Of course, I don't know what your work is, but if it lies in the direction of the determination of self——"

"That is precisely it."

"Then it must be very interesting. Every man who thinks at all must ask himself sometimes, 'What am I?' And he has not got the answer."

"Look here, you should ask my esteemed colleague, Dr. Habaden, that. Put it in another form, and ask him what life and death are."

"I did," I said, "and he was pretty sick about it. He said that he knew when life ended and death began, and that was all we needed to know."

"Well, I deny that. I say there is no limit to what we need to know. I say, too, that the very first things which we need to know are the great elemental things. Let me know exactly in what 'self' consists. Let me be able to isolate 'self' from its usual concomitants of mind and body, by which alone it has hitherto been cognizable. To isolate the 'self' is to add to the dignity of humanity; it is to exhibit humanity with the sources of all human frailty left out. You must surely see that this is fine work. If I can do that, then all the minor points, about which Habaden is so desperately anxious, will be added unto it. It seems to me that he wants me to begin at the wrong end of the stick. He calls my attention to details of more or less importance, when I am looking for first principles."

"Let me understand you," I said. "It comes to this. You are trying to comprehend—to capture—to isolate—the human soul."

Myas glanced at his watch. He shrugged his shoulders.

"That is the theologian's name for it," he said. "Names matter much less than facts. I've got my appointment at the hospital, and I must be off now. But if you are really interested, we can discuss the matter later, and I can tell you how the thing goes."

"Do," I said. "I want to hear about it."

CHAPTER III

For a fortnight I did not see Dr. Myas, and heard nothing from him. I had not got his address, or I should certainly have written to him. I was extremely annoyed about it, and not merely because his neglect seemed to me unfriendly. He had promised to let me hear more of the very curious and interesting work on which he was engaged, and I was anxious to hear more. The matter had haunted my mind a good deal.

I am not an erudite man, and I am not a philosopher, and I had been puzzled by a point on which neither the erudite nor the philosophical seemed to help me at all. I refer to the way the mind acts on the body and the body on the mind.

A small piece of paper is placed on the hand of a man who has been hypnotized, and he is told that this will produce a blister. The blister does actually appear, but it is mind, and not a piece of paper, which has caused it. Every doctor knows how important in some cases the mental attitude of a patient is. With a fixed determination to recover, and a belief that he will recover, recovery does take place. Without this determination and belief, the man sinks and dies. The whole secret of the occasional successes of "Christian Science" lies here. It is as true that body acts on mind. A certain state of the liver produces unfounded melancholy. A certain state of the lungs produces an equally unfounded hope—the characteristic *spes-phthisica.* The hypodermic injection of a drug produces the full feeling of happiness. Everybody knows these things, but so far I had found no satisfactory explanation of them.

I asked a physiologist what was the connection between mind and body, and where was the bridge between them. He told me that they were not connected in any way, but merely associated, much as the shadow is associated with the thing which casts the shadow.

I put this view before a well-known metaphysician, a man who spoke of all practical science with gentle contempt. "Yes," he said, "that is about right. But which is the shadow?"

This was not very illuminative, but if, as Myas had confirmed, both mind and body were but concomitants of the soul and self, it was easy to see how through the soul the one might affect the other. A man at

Knightsbridge, wishing to speak to a man in the City, does so through the Telephone Exchange. It seemed to me possible that the soul might constitute a somewhat similar exchange. It might receive from the body and convey to the mind, or it might receive from the mind and convey to the body. Of course Myas had proved nothing, he had given me no details, he had narrated no special discovery of his which had led him to his conclusions. And there was one other point which made me cautious. Myas had already shown me, in the way in which he discussed the question of diet and in other conversations I had had with him, a distinct preference for the unaccepted view; and this preference was often a source of weakness. There is a type of mind which always falls in love with the minority, and suffers in consequence from that blindness to facts which is supposed to be incidental to those who fall in love. Still, I was intrigued. I wanted to hear what the man had to say. I wanted to go into the matter further.

I hope that the above does not give any false impression of myself. I am no profound student of such questions. I pretend to be no more than just an ordinary man of the world. But even to the most ordinary it seems to me that such things must occasionally offer both an interest and a perplexity. It does not destroy one's interest in politics or in bridge; it does not spoil one's fondness for sport, or upset one's convictions as to the way a man should deport himself; but it does occur to the mind now and again at odd moments. Ordinary men like myself rarely speak of such things, it is true, for we talk mostly trivialities. But I fancy that most of us do sometimes think of such things.

Consequently, I was rather glad, as I was walking down Piccadilly one Monday afternoon, to hear behind me the deep and sonorous voice of Dr. Myas calling me by name. He looked more abominably French than ever.

I shook hands with him, and told him—I trust with cheerfulness—that he had treated me disgracefully, and that on the whole he had better go to the devil.

"My dear Compton," said Myas, "if I have treated you badly, it is only because other people have treated me much worse. You see before you a martyr to science, or rather to the men of science. A grievance occupies one's mind to the exclusion of everything else. I confess that I had forgotten you, but I am glad to be reminded again. Now then, I am going as far as the fruit-shop, and then across the parks, and you may just as well come with me."

"I shall not," I said. "I am going on to Knightsbridge."

But as a matter of fact I did go with him as far as St. James's Park Station. At the fruit-shop opposite the Green Park he purchased roses and strawberries. I heard the address to which they were to be sent, and I told him that he ought to be ashamed of himself.

"You have an absolutely evil mind," said Myas. "She was by way of polishing my nails, and incidentally she polished off the whole of the first joint of my fingers with wash-leather and pumice. If you like that kind of thing I don't. It hurts. I swore and she wept. Hence the strawberries."

"That's a very silly story," I said. "I'd sooner hear who has been ill-treating you scientifically, and how."

"You remember that when I last left you I was going to keep an appointment at the hospital with which I was at one time connected. I wanted to obtain there certain facilities for my experimental work. I was refused. At any rate I was so hedged in with conditions and qualifications that the thing became impossible for me. I have tried other hospitals with a similar result. That is the way the scientific investigator is treated in this rotten country."

"All right," I said. "If you don't like it, why don't you leave it? Who's stopping you? Skip back to Paris again. That hat of yours would feel a good deal more at home there, and so would your nostalgic necktie."

"No," said Myas decidedly, "I am not going. Here they take no serious interest in my work, but in Paris they take just a little too much. Everything I do is watched. Inquiries are frequent. If I went back to Paris, some man would take advantage of my preliminary work and would possibly get to the goal before me."

"I wonder, Myas, that you have the cheek to talk like that. You were quite right when you told me that men of your profession were narrow-minded. You are a case in point. What on earth does it matter who makes a discovery, so long as the discovery is made? You are not a scientific martyr at all. You are only selfish and greedy. What do you say to that?"

"I don't pretend to transcend human nature. If somebody managed to sneak your watch, you would not say that so long as somebody enjoyed the watch it didn't matter who it was. You also would be selfish and greedy."

"But then I'm not posing as a scientific martyr. Hospitals are not established solely for research, and I have not the least doubt that you wanted something which was quite improper and illegitimate. I gathered from what your friend Habaden told me——"

"He's no friend of mine. Damn him, anyhow. He was one of the men who wanted to put the drag on the wheel."

"Well, what are you going to do about it? Have you got a plan at all?"

"I have—a very definite plan. Some time ago I made the mistake of showing children and fools half-finished work. I think I told you about it. I published the results of some of my investigations and the deductions I had made from them. Really I ought to have known my learned and distinguished colleagues better. I had broken the first commandment, which is that you shall make no new departure. You may continue work which has already been begun, and may make fresh discoveries in it, and be complimented and K.C.V.O.'d. But originality and imagination are the unforgivable sins. Very well, then. I shall publish nothing further at present. In spite of the hospitals, I have found a way by which I can continue my work here, and I intend to do it. But nothing more will be published until I can give an absolute demonstration of my determination of the Ego. The fact which they can see and test must convince."

"When you spoke of this before you said that mind and body were but the usual concomitants of self or soul, and that neither separately nor in association did they constitute self or soul."

"Something of the kind," said Myas. "Extraordinary that you should have remembered it."

"Not at all. Now if science had chosen to deny, say, the existence of sheep, I can understand that you could produce the sheep and demonstrate it. But I do not see how you are to demonstrate the existence of the human soul."

"Don't you? I have given up explaining my work now. I will be judged by results. And I tell you this definitely—before this year is out I will demonstrate the existence of the soul to you personally."

"If you mean that seriously I'm quite content."

"I do. And here, by the way, is my station."

Before we separated, I asked him for his address. I was not quite sure which of our hotels could reach the high standard of luxury that Myas had habitually demanded. Myas smiled whimsically.

"I am living at 121 Knox Street. Know it?"

"Oh, probably, but I don't recall it for the moment."

"It is a back street in the Walham Green neighbourhood."

I said sardonically that he seemed determined to be right in the centre of things, and that I hoped he was comfortable.

"The place suits my purposes. I have four rooms over a little shop that sells newspapers and tobacco, and I have made them a little more possible than they were when I took them. The shop is kept by a widow, Mrs. Lade, and her daughter, and they wait on me—so far as a man of my simple habits requires any attendance at all."

I was astonished, of course. The best hotels of Paris had struggled in vain to be good enough for Dr. Myas. He had pointed out their defects to courteous and long-suffering managers. I had never known a man who required more attendance or was more particular as to the character of it. And now he had taken lodgings in a back street in Fulham, with a widowed tobacconist to wait on him. I supposed it was some fantastic whim of his, and I do not encourage fantastic whims. People who try not to be like other people are very tiresome. As I was sure that Myas expected me to ask many questions about his extraordinary selection, I would not gratify him by asking any at all.

CHAPTER IV

When I accepted Myas's invitation to dine with him at the Ritz a few days later, I did so with my eyes open.

"I ought to tell you," his letter said, "that I am bringing with me a Mr. Vulsame, a young surgeon who is in practice not far from here. He will be having a great treat, and I can remember that I once expressed agreement with your dictum, that the young man who is having a great treat is always a great nuisance. Briefly, Vulsame, though he is useful to me, will not suit your fastidious taste. At the same time, I shrink from spending a whole evening with him by myself, and you can help me considerably if you will. I believe that under a highly conventional exterior you conceal some slight kindness of heart, or I would not venture to ask it. Do come and lend a hand with the beggar."

I replied that I should be charmed. One meets so many bounders that one more or less does not greatly matter. Besides, I was interested in Myas.

Myas himself was at his very best and perfectly delightful, but frankly, it was rather an awful evening. Vulsame had good looks, of rather a coarse and common kind, and his dress and manners were enough to make angels weep. He called me "Sir" previous to the champagne, and "old cock" afterwards. He bragged absurdly. Somewhere about nine o'clock we got him to some stupid music-hall, where he was particularly anxious to see that appalling abomination, a "female impersonator." We came too late for this particular turn, at which he was very angry and I was very pleased. His comments on women and life were distinctly Rabelaisian, and Myas had to get him to speak in a lower tone. Throughout the evening Myas showed much tact in his management of the man. I think it was my good fortune to please Mr. Vulsame; at any rate, he asked me to drop in some evening in a friendly way. I cordially accepted the invitation, and to make the thing more realistic, put his visiting-card in my pocket. But it can hardly be necessary to say that it was not my intention to let the thing go any further. I fully expected that that night I was seeing Mr. Vulsame for the last time. As it happened, I was destined to see him many times. Myas took him on to supper somewhere or other afterwards, but I thought I had done enough philanthropical work for one night, and pleaded an engagement.

During the whole evening Myas made no reference of any kind to his work, though he talked with a good deal of wit and acumen of most other subjects. I did not gather why he had taken lodgings in Fulham, nor why he was so desperately anxious to give this Mr. Vulsame a great treat. However, it was none of my business, and I made no attempt to get any information. It was for him to make the next move, if he cared about it.

One day in the following week, while I was at lunch in my rooms, the telephone bell went. My man, who attended to it, brought me word that Dr. Myers wished to speak to me. "I said I would inquire if you were in," the man added. He is a discreet fellow.

I guessed, of course, that Myers was telephonic for Myas, and went to hear what he had to say. He told me that he was very much depressed and worried, and that it would do him good to see some normal and commonplace person like myself? Would I come and see his new rooms?

As it happened, I had a blank afternoon, and I said that I would come with pleasure.

I had never seen Myas depressed or worried, and I gathered that information was awaiting me.

I told the driver of the taxicab to take me to Walham Green. There I dismissed him, and proceeded on foot in search of 121 Knox Street. I wanted to take a leisurely view of the neighbourhood, with which I was unfamiliar.

Knox Street is dull, and grey, and narrow. It contains many shops, and most of them look as if they were on the verge of bankruptcy. Everything in the windows seemed to be offered at sacrificial prices and far under cost. And apparently trade was possible in the things that one generally throws away. Curious and obscene rags were being sold as second-hand clothing. Soiled and aged back numbers of magazines had a price put upon them. As long as you got a lot for a penny, it did not seem to much matter what you got. Each shop displayed notices of a familiar and even slangy character. "Stop that cough!" shrieked the chemist. "Here's a Sunday dinner for you," cried the butcher. Mrs. Lade seemed to be doing rather better than some of her neighbours. She offered for sale many different things. The solid basis of the trade was apparently penny novelettes and Woodbine cigarettes, but it also branched out into sweetmeats and mouth-organs.

There was no private door, and I entered the shop. Had I been dishonestly inclined, I might have snatched up a couple of mouth-organs and made a bolt for it. Nobody was there to prevent me. But from behind a door, which was half a window with a red curtain over it, at the back of the shop, there came voices. The first voice was, I diagnosed correctly, the voice of a fat and elderly woman.

"It may be all right, and I expect it is all right, for you're a good girl, Alice; but what I say is, that it don't look right, and sooner or later other people in the street will be bound to notice it, and if I was doing my duty, I shouldn't allow it to go on."

The second voice was much younger, and rather plaintive. Despite a London accent, it was not unpleasant in quality.

"I'm sure he always treats me with respeck—with most perfeck respeck. And why I should miss a chance of improving myself I can't see. It's most kind of him. And I can tell you this, he's not a gentleman that will stand much interference—not from nobody. If you want to lose the rent, paid regular as it is—"

"Setting up there for hours with him like that!" said the fat voice indignantly. "I don't call it—"

I thought the time had come to rap sharply on the floor with my umbrella. Through the red-curtained door came Mrs. Lade. She looked a conscientious, kindly, rather worried woman. She was fat and moved slowly. With a fold of her grey apron she concealed her red hands from the glance of the curious.

"Dr. Myas?" I said.

"Were you wishful to see him?"

"Yes," I said. "That was the idea. I am Mr. Compton."

Mrs. Lade opened the red-curtained door again and called to an invisible Miss Lade: "Gentleman to see Dr. Myas. Just take him up, Alice, will you?" Then she raised a flap of the counter and turned to me. "If you'll step this way, sir."

I stepped that way, and behind the red-curtained door I found a very beautiful girl. Her hair reminded me of the days in my extreme youth, when I kept silkworms; it was just the colour of the natural silk, and she had any amount of it. Her eyes were a greyish-blue. Her face was well cut and delicate. When she saw an actual stranger and spoke with him, it was apparently her habit to blush slightly. She was rather above medium height, with a slight graceful figure. Her dress was plain and quiet. She took me up some rather dingy stairs, and tapped at a door which had been newly painted. The deep voice of Myas bade us come in.

Myas flung down the book that he was reading, and shook hands with me. I noticed, by the way, that the book was "Alice in Wonderland." I took one of his cigarettes, and sat down to talk to him.

"Before we go any further," I said, "tell me how is our dear friend, Mr. Vulsame?"

Myas grinned in a melancholy way. "I managed him beautifully. I gave him supper. I brought him back here in a taxicab. I kept him here for an hour, and took him to his own place in another taxicab. And it was really not until he reached home that he was actually drunk."

"It seemed to me that he was rather nearer that blessed condition than I cared about most of the evening."

"No, I assure you," said Myas. "Even when he got to his own home he was not incapable, and he was very, very happy. Speaking seriously, I'm awfully obliged to you for helping me with him. He's rather a useful man to me."

"Useful? How?"

"Hadn't it occurred to you? I should have thought it would have been fairly obvious. I have still a little experimental work that I must do. And the hospitals refuse to give me the opportunities that I want. Vulsame has a practice—quite a large practice—in a poor neighbourhood. You see he inspires no sense of shame, and people are sure they can tell him everything. Frequently he has cases which are of interest to me and have a bearing on my work. When that happens, he lets me know, and I come in as Mr. Vulsame's assistant. Mark you, I get none of the qualifications and conditions that the hospital wanted to lay down. As Mr. Vulsame's assistant, I do just exactly as I think right. Naturally I remunerate Mr. Vulsame. I also at times think it expedient to remunerate the relatives of the patient. When I came here, my friend, I did not do it merely to surprise you. It was essential that I should be living and working in a poor neighbourhood. With the expenditure of a very few sovereigns, I can get what I want. The relatives actually like it; it gives them so much money to spend on the funeral baked-meats."

"You're a gruesome beast, Myas," I said. "If you're not careful, you'll make this place too hot to hold you, and Vulsame's practice will go pop."

"Very likely," he said, with indifference. "At present I am being careful."

I looked round the room. The walls were newly papered in a flat tint. The furniture was all new, not strictly artistic, but fairly good and comfortable.

"You didn't find all these things here when you came, did you?" I asked.

"Lord, no! The rooms were empty. I went to Tottenham Court Road, gave them a rough idea of what I wanted and the price I would pay, and Tottenham Court Road did the rest. As long as the stuff was comfortable, and none of the things had any pattern on them, I did not mind much."

"What's your objection to pattern?"

"All pattern is an abomination. It annoys you because it is repeated. And then, where it has to stop because there is no more of the blessed curtain or wall-paper, it annoys you because it is not repeated. It reminds me too much of my fellow-men—so many of them and all just alike. Now you, of course, would suffer patterns gladly."

"I don't worry. I'm not particularly cracked about anything of that kind. Why should I enjoy patterns?"

"The thing's obvious. Your one aim in life is to resemble as closely as possible every other man in the same position in life, and their aim is to resemble each other and you. Any one of you would sooner commit a murder than wear the wrong necktie. Not cracked? Of course you're cracked."

"And you're quite sane, I suppose."

"Absolutely," said Myas, with conviction.

"Very well, then. How's that girl getting on with her lessons?"

"Go to the devil!" said Myas.

"And I suppose the girl can go to the devil as well?"

Myas smote the palm of one hand with the fist of the other. "My word," he said. "How absolutely wrong you sordid and worldly people can get in your judgment. However, there is just this to be said for you. You live and learn. You'll get to know that girl better. Now then, let's speak of other things."

CHAPTER V

"Look here," said Myas. "You must see the rest of my bachelor establishment." He opened the folding doors at the end of the room. "Here, for example, we observe my dining-room—furnished by Tottenham Court Road for £35, and looking exactly like a dining-room which has been furnished by Tottenham Court Road for £35."

"What do you want a dining-room for?" I said. "You can't possibly feed here."

"Can and do," said Myas.

I walked to the window, which opened down to the floor. From it an iron staircase led down to a narrow slip of ground, which was by way of being a garden. A gardener would call it a back yard. It was a weary, cat-haunted spot between high and blackened walls, but I noticed that there were two fine old mulberry trees in it. There was also a newly erected building, looking somewhat like a studio. This was raised a little from the ground, with three steps up to the door of it. I asked Myas what it was.

"That's where I do my work. That door in the wall at the farther end of the garden opens into Durnford Place. Durnford Place runs parallel to Knox Street, and I'm not quite sure whether Durnford Place is at the back of Knox Street, or vice versa."

"Both, I should imagine."

"Anyhow, it's a very useful door, for it enables me, and incidentally my friends, to get up to my rooms without going through Mrs. Lade's part of the house. When you come to see me again, as I hope you will soon, you must come in that way. I've had a new lock fitted to it, and I'll give you a latch-key."

I pocketed the latch-key, and said that the confidence he showed in me was pleasing. "What I shall do, of course, will be to let myself in and burgle your work-room. There I shall reap the fruit of your researches, anticipate your discoveries, and subsequently enjoy the fame which you wrongly suppose is coming to you."

"You couldn't do it. You are far too much of a duffer at that kind of thing. What you found inside the work-room would be incomprehensible to you. For that reason I won't trouble you with the work-room at present. Could you be bothered to climb up more stairs in order to see the most absolutely ordinary bedroom that Tottenham Court Road has ever achieved?"

"Certainly not."

"Well, there is one thing more you must see, just across the passage." He opened a door. "This is my kitchen—electric as you observe."

"And does she cook here?"

"No, idiot. The cooking which is done here I do myself."

It was easy to believe this. Cooking was one of the things which he took seriously. He was doubtless acquainted with the practice as well as the theory of it.

"Well," I said, "I confess that I don't see your game. I suppose you built that place in the garden. You have redecorated these rooms. You have put in electric light and heating, and a telephone. You have filled them with a lot of fair-to-middling furniture. Now in six months you'll be sick of this, and will start off on your travels again. Do you suppose you'll ever see your money back? There is probably nobody on the face of the earth, except yourself, who wants to live over a tobacconist's shop in Knox Street."

"No, my practical friend, I don't suppose I shall see my money back, but I wanted to live here for reasons which I have already given you, and I had to make the place possible; but it is by no means certain that I shall be leaving in six months, and I might quite possibly remain here for the rest of my life. After all, living here is absurdly cheap. It cost me twenty times as much in Paris. Oh yes, I am quite satisfied with what I've done, so far as expenditure is concerned. I wish I had nothing else to worry me."

He seemed quite pleased with the electrical toys in his kitchen, and insisted on showing me how they worked, although I told him that he was talking like a man at an exhibition and becoming very wearisome. Then we went back into the sitting-room, and he rang the bell for tea.

It was Miss Lade who brought the things in and arranged them on a low table by the fire. She did not look once at either of us. Myas stopped her as she was turning to go.

"Do wait and pour out tea for us," he said. "I want to present to you a great friend of mine, Mr. Compton."

She murmured something unintelligible, and seemed a little in doubt whether she should shake hands. I settled the question for her. Her hands did not look as if she did much rough work.

I believe it is said to be the test of a gentleman that he is at ease under all circumstances and in all society. If this be the case, I am emphatically not a gentleman. At this extraordinary tea-party I was not at my ease at all. I did my best, but it was poor. I wanted to talk to Miss Lade—and not only because she was a very pretty girl—and the only mutual ground that I could find on which we might meet was the mulberry trees in the garden. At the time of the Revolution French exiles came to London and there planted mulberry trees, notably in St. John's Wood, and to a lesser extent in Fulham. So I told her, and I dare say it may be true. I heard with great interest that the mulberries did actually ripen, and I made her promise to send me some of them in due season. She was certainly very shy, but, I should say, appeared considerably less of a fool than I did. She poured out tea very nicely. Myas said little, and did not help a bit.

After a while things went more easily, and I got her to talk about herself. She spoke of a theatre to which Myas had taken her. She told me that at one time she had been very fond of lawn tennis, but that she could not find time for it any longer. She had a very pleasant voice, and great simplicity—two things which I have always especially admired. She was absolutely free from affectation. There was not the slightest attempt to make an impression of any kind. I should think she was with us for about half an hour. Then she rose, and said that her mother was going out, and that she would have to attend to the shop. I tried to help her as she was taking away the tea-things, but she would not let me do anything. Myas did not even attempt to do anything. He had sat back in his easy-chair all the time, and watched us through the smoke of his cigarette, as if we were doing an interesting scene in a play for his benefit. It was scandalous behaviour.

"Well?" he said, when she had gone.

"Leave her alone," I said.

Then he spoke, with a good deal of emphasis, almost with excitement.

"Look here, my dear fellow, you misunderstand this altogether. I don't blame you for that. You take the ordinary view, and any other man of your blessed pattern would take the same. I'll go further than that. If you were in my position, I should give you exactly the same advice that you have just given me. But, as it happens what you say is absolutely beside the point. The things that you imagine are not concerned in the question in the least. I'm not going to make love to that girl. Understand that definitely. I told you over the telephone that I was worried and depressed, and so I am; and that girl is principally concerned in it, but most emphatically not for the reason which you would suppose."

"I'm no good at mysteries," I said. "If the trouble is not what I think, I don't pretend to understand what it is. But I do profess to know something about human nature. Your intentions are excellent, of course. But in a case like this there is often a marked difference between a man's intentions and his conduct. I will flatter you so far as to tell you that you're not an ordinary man. Still, you're a human being."

"Admitted. I do not profess to have lived the life of an anchorite hitherto. But I am telling you the exact truth when I say that nothing exists now for me but my work, and that this girl troubles me only in so far as she is connected with my work. And if I do as I wish, she will be very intimately connected with it."

"Oh, very well!" I said. "But there's another thing to think about. For the last half-hour or so I have been watching that girl in here. If she is not very much in love with you, I'm mistaken, and I know nothing."

Myas seemed to reflect for a minute. Then he said, with conviction:

"I hope she is. I hope to goodness she is. If she is not, she is not likely to be of much use to me."

"I give it up. I don't understand you."

"No," said Myas. "But you will one of these days."

"How?"

"How?" echoed Myas. "Well, you will understand, because either that girl or myself will give you the explanation."

As I rose to go I pressed him to come and see me some time. He said that he would if he could, but that he was very busy now, and it was a long way to come.

"It is," I said. "But I should like to point out that the distance from Knox Street to St. James's Place is exactly the same as the distance from St. James's Place to Knox Street, which distance I have covered this very afternoon."

He said that I was a man of leisure, and that time, distance, and taxicabs were all as nothing to me. I was to come again. He generally knocked off work for an hour or two in the afternoon. I had my latch-key.

I left him with the uncomfortable feeling that I had been spending the afternoon with a friend of mine who was by way of being a blackguard. I did not suppose that he was a typical deceiver and seducer, but he did seem to me to be a man absolutely without scruple where his work was concerned. I did not like his business with Vulsame. I did not like the way he was treating Alice Lade. What business had he to make use of her fondness for him for his own purposes? That she was fond of him I had no doubt whatever. She looked at me with candid and friendly eyes, but when her eyes met his they became timorous and perturbed, and the long lashes flickered. The one saving grace of the man was that he was really worried about what he was doing. If he was indeed without scruple, it was with great difficulty that he had brought himself to that point.

About a month later I rang up Myas on the telephone, and suggested that I should come to see him that afternoon. He replied that he was very sorry, but that work which it was impossible to leave would occupy him the whole of that afternoon. He would come to see me.

But he did not come to see me. It was in June that I received from him a rather curious letter, in which he announced his engagement to Alice Lade.

CHAPTER VI

Myas said in his long letter that the news of his engagement would probably give me a comfortable feeling of superiority, I having always known, of course, what would happen. With this would be mingled a certain regret that he had not allied himself more advantageously from the world's point of view. And both feelings, he assured me, would be quite out of place.

"The fact is," he wrote, "that it had become necessary for the purposes of my work for Miss Lade and myself to be frequently together for long periods. Knox Street shook its respectable head, and Mrs. Lade did not like it. The proclamation of an engagement, and the purchase of an absurdly valuable ring, have changed all this. Knox Street smiles upon us, and dreams confetti. Mrs. Lade is quite happy. Briefly, the engagement is simply the price we pay to Knox Street for permission to continue our work as before. So if you have any impression that you ever foresaw anything you should correct it. It is quite probable that we shall never be married, but that depends to some extent on the result of my great experiment.

"Meanwhile, as I require the whole of Miss Lade's time, I have provided a domestic substitute, to Mrs. Lade's considerable, but rather tremulous, satisfaction. For her Knox Street is the voice of society, and almost the voice of God. It is a street filled with people who have kept themselves respectable. Think of all the poignant meaning of that phrase. With insufficient means for the purpose, and with countless temptations to be otherwise, these good people are still respectable. Beside their hard-won respectability, your own, facile and cultured, is no more than sounding brass and a tinkling cymbal. Mrs. Lade is tremulous, because she has advanced one step up the ladder. There is a definite line of demarcation here between the people who keep a girl and the people who do it all themselves. Mrs. Lade naturally fears lest she should be thought guilty of that quality, which the Greeks called 'hubris' and Fulham calls 'swelled head.' She therefore sighs, and explains to her friends that it was all on account of the lodger, and that she hopes it may be for the best.

"My work has gone on very rapidly, and the day is not far off now.

I have little doubt that I shall be able to redeem a promise that I once made you. I wish you would come and see me to-morrow afternoon. It is too bad of you to have neglected me like this."

The man was astounding.

On looking into the matter, I found that I had made two appointments for the following afternoon. I had promised to go with the Hamiltons, who were in town for a few days, to the Queen's Hall, and I had also promised to play bridge with some other people. That made it all quite easy. I excused myself from the bridge-party on the ground that I had forgotten about the Hamiltons, and from the Hamiltons on the ground that I had forgotten about the bridge-party. These two appointments being safely and easily cancelled, I got into a taxicab and drove to Durnford Place.

I let myself in with the latch-key that Myas had given me, and went up the strip of garden. As I passed the work-room, I heard within a chink of glass and a light footstep. I hesitated a moment, thinking that Myas might be there; but I remembered that when he showed me the rest of his establishment, he had rather made a point of not showing me the work-room. So I went on up the iron staircase, and tapped at the window. Myas himself let me in.

"Come to deliver your congratulations?" he asked.

"No. I've come to ask you to explain yourself."

"But, my dear fellow, what is there to explain? It all seems to me so simple and natural."

"What do you mean by saying that it had become necessary for you and Miss Lade to be together for long periods? The thing is absolute nonsense. What possible use can she be to you in your work? She has certainly had no scientific education. She has probably had precious little education of any kind."

At this moment the door opened, and Miss Lade entered. She addressed herself to Myas, speaking eagerly and quickly: "The variation is three seconds and two-fifths."

As she spoke she saw me. She greeted me cordially enough, and shook hands, but instantly turned back again to Myas.

"Yes," said Myas, "that's too much, isn't it?"

"I thought," she said, "of trying again with ether alone."

"Yes," he said, "you might certainly try that. Do. You'll be through with it by tea-time."

"I expect so," she said, and went out of the room again. I think I have never before in my life experienced more completely the sensation that I did not matter in the least. I felt like a small boy who remains quiet and orderly, while his superior papa and mamma discuss questions of finance, or the morals of the parlourmaid, or anything else which is "not for little boys," in indifferent French.

"Let's see," said Myas, "you were beginning to talk about education, weren't you? Sorry for the interruption. I've got views about education."

"Oh, you've got views on everything under the sun."

"The London season's telling on your nerves, Compton. You incline to be irritable. I do not think, speaking quite dispassionately, that Alice Lade is exactly what you would have expected from her parentage and position in life."

"Obviously she's not. I admit all that."

"It is true, as you say, that her education was of the very slightest. That was all the better from my point of view. I had no rubbish to clear away. Nothing on earth is quite so easy to understand as what is popularly called Science. The only way that men have been able to make it at all difficult is by inventing a very frantic terminology which they habitually mispronounce, and by carefully suppressing all habit of simple and lucid speech. Education for the child means a march into the unknown. He is told that he has to do quadratic equations, but nobody ever dreams of telling him why. He has to know the name of the capital of Portugal. He has, in extreme cases, to know the names of the kings of Israel and Judah. The patience of the child is remarkable. He really does consent to lumber up his mind with all this nonsense, merely because papa, or the governess, or the schoolmaster wishes him to do it. It is a wonderful thing that any horse consents to draw any cart, but it is still more wonderful that any child consents to acquire knowledge, on the lines on which knowledge is now generally imparted. When you start on a journey, it is advisable to know where you're going, and you do not journey with much purpose or enthusiasm if you do not know it. One of the very first things I did with Miss Lade was to show her what I was aiming at, and how she could help."

"I see," I said. "You told her that you were aiming at the determination of the Ego, and she understood all that at once. Naturally, she would."

"Don't be an ass! That was, of course, what I told her, but equally, of course, those were not the words which I used. I asked her what she was, why she was here, and what would happen when she died. She told me that she was a girl, that she was here to do her duty, and that she would go to hell if she did not do it. As soon as I began to show her how far from satisfactory these answers were she became interested. These simple elemental things interest everybody, even you. We know, of course, very little about them at present, and the prospect that she and I would be able to discover more naturally attracted Alice. But I am not taking all the credit for my way of teaching. She is intelligent, plastic, receptive, to a very unusual degree. Many things she seems to acquire unconsciously. For instance, her talk—you noticed it?"

"Yes, I noticed it. The London accent has been eliminated."

"Yes, she now talks just as you do."

"There you are wrong. It is your own accent which she has copied. There is the faintest possible foreign note in it, which has come to you, I suppose, from the fact that you have been speaking French for so long. How did you get her to acquire it?"

"I did not. I have just told you that it was one of the things that she picked up unconsciously. I have never corrected her speech in any way. The fact of the case is that in some respects Alice is singularly childlike. If a child is given a nurse with a Cockney accent, the child will soon talk Cockney. If he has a French *bonne,* he will soon talk French. The influence of the person in authority, with whom the child is on intimate terms, always works, and always unconsciously."

"Well now, my friend, suppose we look at this engagement from Miss Lade's point of view. Does she understand that the whole thing is merely a farce, and that you have no intention of carrying it out?"

"But that is not the case. You must have misunderstood something I said in my letter. I have every intention of carrying it out, if it is possible. But the result of my experiment may make it impossible. It all turns upon that. I don't want to go into the question with you just now, but I admit there is a very grave risk in the experiment."

"And yet she is to take part in it."

"Well, yes. Why not? She wishes it. She is absolutely devoted to me, and for that reason alone she would do it, and by this time she is quite as keen about the work as I am. I own that I felt some reluctance first. I was worried and depressed about it, as you remember. I still feel that I should be wrong if I put any kind of compulsion upon her—if, for instance, I told her that it was of supreme importance to me that she should take this risk. But I have not done that, and she is a free agent. What she is going to do, she has volunteered to do. And, mind, she runs no risk which I shall not share equally with her. That seems to me to make it all right. Don't you think so?"

"Of course I don't. It's all wrong. It seems to me that what I ought to do is to go downstairs and have ten minutes' talk with the poor victim's mother."

"You can have ten minutes' or ten hours' talk with Mrs. Lade, if you like. It would make no difference. She is not the dominant factor, and Alice is. Of course, the consideration which you are leaving out in your own mind, is really the consideration which best justifies me. There is no advance without sacrifice, and in this case the advance is tremendous, and the sacrifice, if it is needed, is justified. However, the last thing I wish to do is to quarrel with you just now, more particularly as I want to ask a favour of you. I have just made my will."

"Don't for goodness' sake say that you want me to be a trustee. I am trustee for three people already. They all liked me once, but they all hate me now. And they're all convinced that if I were not a curious combination of knave and fool, I could get them seven per cent. out of trust securities."

"Well, I do want you to be a trustee. I am leaving everything in trust for Miss Lade. I promise you that she will give you no trouble whatever. You will find her perfectly reasonable and docile."

After some discussion, I gave way and consented. And then Miss Lade came in again from the work-room.

"Well?" said Myas.

She shook her head. "No use at all. Worse than before." And then she turned to talk to me.

Certainly, the change in her in a very short time was remarkable. She was self-possessed, and only blushed once—when I congratulated her on her engagement. It was easy to talk to her. Her voice was pleasant and musical, and I thought her perfectly charming.

Myas came down the garden with me when I left. I said to him: "Do you mean to tell me you're not in love with her?"

"Undoubtedly I shall be if all goes well. At present there is too much to think about. I haven't the time for love. Why, I've never even kissed her."

"If I were you, I should go back now and do it. Believe me, it doesn't take long."

"It would be absolute ruin," said Myas.

CHAPTER VII

During the next fortnight I saw a good deal of Myas and Miss Lade, and got to know the latter much better. I did not go to Knox Street every afternoon—Myas asked me to do so—but I went very often. One afternoon Miss Lade spoke with some interest of a forthcoming play. This seemed to me to offer an opportunity, and I asked her if she and Myas would dine with me on the first night and come with me to the theatre afterwards.

"I'm afraid I couldn't," said Miss Lade. "I have not got any evening dress. But it's very kind of you."

"That kind of thing must come later," said Myas. "When we've finished our work we'll come to you as often as you like."

"Good," I said. "I'll tell the theatre to postpone the production."

"Don't get angry with us," said Myas. "At present, except for an hour or two in the afternoon, we are horribly unsociable. There is a kind of interest in life, that shuts out all other interests. But the end will come soon now, won't it, Alice?"

"Very soon," said Miss Lade. She was standing against the window, and the pure beauty of her profile was a delight to one's eyes. Suddenly she exclaimed with ecstasy: "Carter Paterson! They've sent it at last."

"Good!" exclaimed Myas, and flew down the stairs.

Miss Lade turned to me rather apologetically. "It is some apparatus," she said. "We have been kept waiting a long time for it. Scientific instrument-makers seem to be the slowest people in the world."

Myas came panting into the room with a large box in his arms. They did not unpack it completely, but they took out one or two pieces and fitted them together. Miss Lade's joy over the contents of the box was quite real and unaffected. I doubted if her first evening dress would give her so much pleasure.

The more I saw of Miss Lade, the higher my opinion of her became. She had great abilities, but even so her acquirements and her advance during the last few months seemed to me miraculous. She still kept that almost childlike simplicity which from the first I had appreciated in her. Her devotion to Myas was obviously of the most exalted kind, and her enthusiasm in the work was not less than his own. I could understand now what he meant when he told me that it would be absolute ruin if he began to make love to her. Afterwards, he would have been unable to continue his work, or to conduct any experiment in which the least risk to her was involved. Nature would have forced its way. Passion was not suppressed, but it was postponed. When the work was done, there would be dinners and evening dresses, and there would be time for love. I got an impression that she understood all this.

One afternoon I returned to St. James's Place on the top of a motor omnibus. On the seat in front of me were two old women with strident voices. They were discussing Mr. Vulsame. "I wouldn't go to him," said one of them, "and I wouldn't call him into my house, not if there wasn't another doctor in England."

"Bit too fond of lifting the elbow, eh?" said the other.

"Yes. That's true enough. But that's not all."

She became confidential and dropped her voice. I was not greatly surprised. I knew that Vulsame drank, and my curiosity as to what else he did was not very keen.

It was at the end of this fortnight, in the middle of the London season, and with countless engagements on hand, that I gave the whole thing up and went away. It was a sudden and overmastering impulse, which had occurred to me before, and will probably occur to me again. To my friends and acquaintances I suppose that I seem a normal and cheerful bachelor of forty. That, perhaps, is what I am most of the time. Still, I have been through things of a kind that leave their mark. I was quite a young man when the doctors cut me off from the only profession that I could ever have loved. They stopped polo and hunting as well. For a while I was a good deal of an invalid, and that I dare say, was a sound enough reason for the girl who threw me over and married a better man. My health is fairly good now, and I do most of the right things at the right time. I enjoy the society of my fellow-men, and I think I can hold my own in any of the sports that my health has left open to me. I am not broken-hearted, and I am not a sentimentalist, but occasionally I get a sudden revulsion against the kind of life that I am leading. Its pleasures become an unmitigated bore. Its absolute uselessness and selfishness disgust me. Then I remember that, but for a whim of fate, I might have been engaged in an active profession, and possibly doing some good in the world. Just at this time too, I recalled the girl who broke her engagement with me. Alice Lade reminded me of her a little. I was not in the least in love with Alice Lade, but yet I regarded Myas with envy. He had at any rate managed to make some woman care very much for him. My mood at such times is not cheerful, and there is no reason why I should ask my friends to put up with it. Besides, I have found that quiet and solitude are the best cure for it. That is why some years ago I bought for half-nothing a little cottage far up on a hill in Gloucestershire, ten miles from the nearest railway station. When I find that solitude and the simplicity of life there no longer please me, my cure is complete. I can go back and mix with my fellow-men again.

I never take my valet down with me to the cottage. An elderly couple have the charge of it, and they can do all that I require. When I am down there I want nothing that reminds me of London. I keep a small car, and have learned to drive it. The distance from shops and the station make it a necessity. I have the fishing rights over three miles of river. If I ever needed it, I could get some golf, but so far I have left it alone. I go down to my cottage to avoid my fellow-men, not to mix with them.

It may have been partly, perhaps, because I had seen so much lately of the work which Myas was doing, that this fit of disgust of my own life came on me. I got tired of taking so much care of such unimportant things. I got tired of hearing so much worthless talk, and of contributing my share to the sum of it. For an hour or two I was busy with telegrams and telephone, and by that time my man had packed my things and the cab was ready to take me to Paddington. I did not, of course, let my friends know where I had gone. The cottage was my harmless secret. If I let my friends know, they would probably wish to come down and cheer me up, and that would be too depressing. I said that I was going to Paris.

I took with me two books, or rather pamphlets, which were all that Daniel Myas had so far published. The first of these was entitled *A Clinical Study of the Physical and Psychical Phenomena of Somatic Dissolution.* Myas had often laughed at scientific jargon, but he admitted that he was a master in the use of it himself. This work had appeared originally in the American *Journal of Abnormal Psychology,* and had attracted some little attention. The *Lancet* had dealt dutifully but severely with it. Much of it was simply Greek to me. I was never taught any science at school, and I did not know what a good deal of the jargon meant. But there were passages in it, notably where he summed up his conclusions in more popular language, which were wildly interesting. The other pamphlet had been privately printed since his arrival in England. It was called *Experimental Observations on the Continuity of the Ego*. I got on better with this. It was a most amazing little pamphlet. It was Science plus Religion, and Religion plus Poetry. As any reader must have gathered, I am not much of an author myself, but I have read a good deal, and I think I do know good writing when I see it. I read that pamphlet more than once, and it increased my respect for Myas's abilities.

I had a week of the most delightful quiet at my cottage. I did a good deal of gardening under the direction of old Welsford. He is rather severe with me, and I think I like it. At any rate, it makes a pleasant change from the cat-like obsequiousness of my man in town. Welsford is a great Nature student, too, and tells me and shows me much that is interesting. Everything in the garden has for him a distinct personality, and he speaks of flowers and vegetables very much as he would speak of human beings. I have heard him accuse potatoes of being obstinate.

At about eleven one morning, as I was working in the garden, a telegram was brought out to me which had been forwarded on from St. James's Place. It was signed "Lade," and there was nothing to tell me whether the mother or the daughter had sent it. It said: "Please come here at once."

I hesitated for a moment. I thought of telegraphing for further particulars, but the message seemed so urgent that I decided not to waste time on that. I sent Welsford to get the car out, and hurried indoors to change my clothes. There was an express that I should just be able to catch. I drove myself, and left the car in a garage near the station. Shortly after four I was in London.

I went first to a telephone office to tell my people at St. James's Place to expect me that evening, and then, as I had my latch-key with me, I drove to the entrance in Durnford Place.

My taxicab could not get quite up to the door, as a dog-cart was standing there. It was a seedy-looking dog-cart, and apparently had not been washed for a week. A wretched old horse stood dejectedly in the shafts. At the horse's head was a groom in dusty and ill-fitting livery. He was eating nuts, and he stared at me curiously, as if he wondered what I was doing there. Durnford Place was very quiet that afternoon, and the crack of the nutshells rang out loudly. I was just about to pay my cabman, when it occurred to me that after all he might perhaps be useful. I told him to wait. At this moment the garden door opened, and Mr. Vulsame came out. He was drawing a pair of excessively ugly yellow gloves on to his fat hands. He had changed if anything for the worse since the night I met him first. His clothes were shabby, and he looked unwashed and unkempt. His expression was grave and troubled.

He spoke to me at once, without offering to shake hands. "So you've come at last, Mr. Compton?"

"I came as soon as I got the telegram. It was forwarded to me from London. I was away in Gloucestershire."

"I see," he said. "Well, I suppose I had better go in with you."

"Can you tell me what is the matter, Mr. Vulsame?"

"Matter? I thought you knew. They should have told you in the telegram. Daniel Myas is dead."

CHAPTER VIII

Inside the garden I paused for a moment. "It seems almost incredible," I said. "A few days ago, when I left him, he seemed in the best of health. When did he die?"

"I was telephoned for at a quarter to eight this morning, and was here by eight. So far as I can tell, death must have occurred at least six hours previously."

"And the cause of death?"

"The direct cause was failure of respiration under an anæsthetic. The anæsthetic was chloride of ethyl, and it was automatically administered. It was in his work-room there that he died. I gave notice to the coroner at once, of course. It will be for the inquest to settle whether the death was accidental or not."

I did not much like the man's tone. It was at once truculent and suspicious. "Dr. Myas was about the last man in the world to commit suicide," I said.

"I didn't say suicide. There's a sealed letter waiting for you up at the house. You would probably prefer to open it in the presence of the police, and to show them what it contains."

"Very well," I said. "And what about Miss Lade?"

"I haven't seen her. In fact, she won't see me. Well, I can understand that. She is shut up in her room alone, and I don't for a moment suppose that she will consent to see you either, Mr. Compton."

"I don't want to bother her," I said. "It is all perfectly natural. She was devoted to Myas, and this must be a terrible shock to her."

"Possibly. It may be so. Do you by any chance happen to know the terms of the will?"

"I do. Why?"

"Oh, nothing. Mrs. Lade knew them. I have had that definitely from her own lips. So presumably her daughter knew them too."

"I don't see what bearing that has on the question."

"Don't you?" sneered Mr. Vulsame. "Perhaps you will see it at the inquest. It is a point which will probably be raised. You seem to be singularly innocent for a man of your years."

I loathed the fellow, and I was getting more and more angry with him. "Wouldn't it save trouble," I said, "if you were to say quite plainly what you mean? Or are you afraid to say it? What is it you are trying to insinuate?"

"I am afraid of nothing, and I am not trying to insinuate anything. Perhaps everything is all right. There is no doubt whatever that Myas made frequent experiments upon himself. He had also experimented with Miss Lade. I found a record of many of the experiments, and I tell you frankly I cannot see for what purpose they were conducted." He jerked his thumb in the direction of the work-room. "I should say he had every known variety of anæsthetic in there, and some very neat apparatus for administering it. Clockwork can go wrong, and the medical man may make mistakes. That may have been the reason why, when already under the anæsthetic, he received double the amount of the chloride of ethyl that he intended. In that case I suppose the death would be considered accidental. I can't say. I have an open mind on the question."

I felt instinctively that this man might do some mischief, and that it would not do to lose one's temper with him. I decided to handle him a little more carefully. "I was told by Myas," I said, "that I was to be his sole executor and trustee for Miss Lade. Myas was a great friend of mine. You see I am very deeply interested in this, and I hope you will help me to get to the bottom of it. Could you perhaps spare me an hour or so at St. James's Place, if you are not too busy?"

"Busy?" he said savagely. "Plucky lot of business Myas left me! Well, he's dead. I'll say no more about that just now. Yes, I can come if you like."

"Thank you very much. Perhaps you would like to send your cart away. I've got a taxi there, and I don't suppose that I shall keep you waiting more than a few minutes."

"All right," said Vulsame. "There's the inspector, if you want him."

A friendly looking man in plain clothes had just come out of the work-room, locking the door behind him. I introduced myself to him.

"This is a terrible business," I said. "Have you any idea how it happened?"

"That's not for me to say, sir," said the inspector. "Not at present, at any rate. I'm just collecting the facts. So far as I have gone, I have found no motive for suicide, and it is quite possible that the death was accidental. I have been looking at the apparatus in there, and it's easy to see how a mistake could be made. It's a clockwork thing, actuating a little pump.

You can set it to deliver this anæsthetic stuff once and then stop, or twice and then stop, or any number of times. He was playing a very dangerous game, and there is the evidence in his own writing that he had played it often before. I suppose he was studying the nature of these different anæsthetics. However, something else may turn up yet. Mr. Vulsame will have told you that there is a sealed letter waiting for you."

"He did."

"Well, we haven't been into that yet. Would it be convenient?"

"Quite. If you will come on up to the house, we can open it now."

We went up the iron steps, and Mrs. Lade's servant admitted us. She was a young girl—very frightened, stupid, and tearful. Somehow it seemed strange to stand there in Myas's rooms, and to know that he would never enter them again. What had become of his proud boast to me that he would demonstrate to me personally the existence of the human soul? The news of his death had been an unexpected shock to me, but I felt the necessity to put personal feelings aside and to keep very keenly on the alert. It was obvious that Mr. Vulsame meant mischief, and I had promised Myas, in the event of his death, to do the best I could for Miss Lade.

The letter contained Myas's will, properly executed, and a short note for myself. The note merely said that Myas was engaged in a line of research which presented certain risks, and that if anything happened to him he wanted to take that opportunity of thanking me for my great kindness to him in the past, and for my promise to look after Alice for the future.

"Had he any near relations?" asked the inspector. "I see he leaves this girl everything."

"No, he had no near relations. He has told me so more than once."

"I see," said the inspector. He made a few notes, including one of my name and address, and then left.

I saw Mrs. Lade for a few minutes. The poor woman was rather incoherent. It was clear that she regarded the presence of any policemen on the premises as a disgrace, and an inquest as a stain on her own personal honour. On these points I did my best to console her. Of Myas she spoke with great enthusiasm.

"A better and a kinder man no one could wish to see, if only he could have been kept from messing with chemicals, as I often told him. And now I must look forward to seeing Alice go the same way, she being of age and with a will of her own."

"How is she?"

"Seems like a person dazed. She is alone in her room, and been there the best part of the day, and perhaps it's as well. But, oh, she's quite strange to me."

"How do you mean, Mrs. Lade?"

"Well, not like my daughter. That's the bitterness of it. It's no fault of hers, mind. It's just this education that's done it. I often think that girls nowadays would be happier without it."

"What did you mean when you said that you must look forward to Alice going the same way?"

"Well, she has told me already that the work must go on, and when she is once determined on a thing there is no moving her. But to my mind it is simply disregarding the warning that God has given us. Of course, she may still think better of it. We can but hope."

It was true, as Vulsame had told me, that she knew the terms of the will, and that Alice was now comparatively a wealthy woman. I will do her the justice to say this did not seem to affect Mrs. Lade in the least, except in so far as it removed the terror of funeral expenses. "By which so many have been crippled," she added feelingly. "The money will be little good to Alice," she said, "for she will never marry now. There never was but one man in the world for her, and that was Dr. Myas." I was entirely of her opinion.

I left word with her that Miss Lade could see me at any time. She had only to send a telephone message, and I would come at once.

I now went back to Vulsame. I found him seated in my taxicab, and smoking one of the very worst cigars I have ever had the misfortune to smell.

"You've kept me waiting a hell of a time," he said angrily.

"Sorry," I said. I persuaded him not to talk to me in the cab, on the grounds that the traffic made it difficult for one to hear, and while he remained silent I could think over the situation and make my plans. I studied his physiognomy very carefully. It struck me that, if necessary, Mr. Vulsame would probably be purchasable at a moderate figure, provided, of course, that he was allowed to save his face.

At St. James's Place he watched me as I paid the cabman. "My word!" he said. "You toffs don't think much about keeping them waiting, ticking up twopences all the time. But it runs up, doesn't it?"

"Yes," I said, "it runs up."

"But I suppose," he added tactfully, "you take that out of the estate."

He accepted with alacrity the offer of a whisky-and-soda. "I don't mind admitting," he said, "that I'm simply parched. A thing like this knocks one over a bit too, though of course I'm a doctor and used to it. I can tell you it wasn't a very pretty sight when I went into that laboratory early this morning."

I had the whisky left by Mr. Vulsame for purposes of reference. The more talkative he was, the better he would suit my purpose. I told him that I should be glad to have his opinion on some cigars of mine. I struck a match and handed it to him. In fact, I waited on the beast. For a moment or two he jabbered nonsense about the cigars, and then I struck in.

"There was one thing you told me this afternoon, Mr. Vulsame, that surprises me very much."

"Ah," said Mr. Vulsame complacently, "I dare say. I've surprised a good many people in my time. What was it?"

"Well, I don't see how poor Myas can possibly have interfered with your practice. I should have thought that was quite secure. Myas always spoke of you as an able man; for that matter, I could see as much for myself. If I may say so, I am sure your genial manners would make you popular in Fulham or anywhere else. I was sorry as well as surprised to hear that business was not very good with you."

"The competition is pretty keen everywhere," he said. "It doesn't take so very much to put a man wrong. What I have told you is quite correct, and my books will show it. If you doubt my word you can see them."

"But, my dear fellow, why on earth should I doubt your word?"

"Very well, then. I suppose you know the lines Myas was working on. I did permit him to make certain observations and carry out certain experiments with patients of mine. It was all quite legitimate, mind you, or I wouldn't have allowed it. Not for a moment. But it got talked about, and, of course, it got exaggerated, and it did me a deal of harm."

"By the way, do give yourself another drink, Mr. Vulsame. And it is solely to this that you assign the falling off in your practice?"

"Solely. I'm as good as ever I was. Better." He took the other drink.

"Well," I said, "this, of course, is a thing which ought to be looked into. If it's not too delicate a question, did Dr. Myas make you any payment for these important services that you seem to have rendered him?"

"If you can call it payment."

"Oh, I didn't want to know the exact amount. That, of course, I shall get later, because, as his executor, I shall have his bank-book in my hands." I wished to spare Mr. Vulsame the humiliation of telling lies which would afterwards be discovered.

"Quite so," said Mr. Vulsame. "I knew that. Well, as a matter of fact, he did pay me what was agreed upon between us, before I knew what the result would be. It is the result that makes all the difference. What we've got to look at is the injury to the capital value of my practice. You understand what I mean by capital value? Quite so, I thought you would. If he had left me in his will a matter of two hundred—or, say, three hundred—pounds, I should never have said a word about this to anybody. But I understand that I'm not so much as mentioned."

"You are not. And you consider that you have really a moral claim against his estate."

"Moral claim. You've hit the phrase exactly."

"Then, of course, it becomes my duty to consider this. I must turn it over in my mind, and see what ought to be done. Naturally, you wouldn't expect a decision off-hand."

"Not at all. I'm a reasonable man. Your time is mine." And he took another drink.

"There's one other point," I said. "What is your real opinion about the death of Myas?"

"Between ourselves?"

"Quite."

"The thing's as clear as mud. It was murder. And either the old woman or Miss Lade did it, though almost certainly it was Miss Lade."

"This," I said, "is very interesting."

I was pretty certain that it was not a case of murder. I was absolutely certain that, if it was murder, neither Mrs. Lade nor her daughter had anything to do with it. But I did not want any suspicion of Miss Lade to be stated publicly. These things cling to one and do harm, even when the suspicions are shown to be baseless. There is always some idiot who has read half the newspaper report of a sixteenth of the evidence, and thinks himself justified in expressing his wonder afterwards whether there was anything in it. There are some offences, of which the mere accusation is enough to produce something like ruin. My interview with Mr. Vulsame began to be, as I had frankly told him, very interesting.

CHAPTER IX

Mr. Vulsame waved a soiled and impressive hand at me. "Now, Mr. Compton," he said, "I'm going to tell you. I'm going to put all my cards on the table."

"That's very good of you."

"I dare say you thought me a little short in my manner with you up at Knox Street just now. I have been a good deal worried of late, and worry—especially financial worry—gets on one's nerves. No offence was intended."

I murmured something consolatory.

"As a matter of fact," Mr. Vulsame continued, "I have very great confidence in you, Mr. Compton, and I'm going to be quite candid with you. I think you had a high opinion of this Miss Lade, and from something poor Myas once let drop, that was what I gathered."

"Quite correct."

"So, naturally, you are not inclined to believe in her guilt. Still, one must do one's duty. One has got to face the facts."

"Undoubtedly. And the facts?"

"Some of them are known already. One of them—the most serious of all—is at present known only to me. I didn't mention it to the inspector, or to anybody else. I'm going to mention it now. Let us see what happened. Mrs. Lade, her daughter and her servant, all went up to their respective bedrooms at a few minutes past ten last night. They are agreed upon that. They left Myas at work in his laboratory in the garden as usual. He often worked very late. It is said that they did not leave their rooms until the following morning. The servant, who rose at six, discovered that Myas had not been in his bedroom all night, and then called up Mrs. Lade and her daughter. Now, as it happens, I have got a latch-key to the garden entrance in Durnford Place. Myas gave it me at a time when I was seeing him frequently, and often had to fetch him away to cases of mine—sometimes after the rest of the household were in bed. For the last three weeks I have seen much less of him. He told me that he had completed his observations, and that he did not think I could be of any further service to him. When I met him casually in the street, he was rather inclined to snub me. And that's not a thing I take from anybody. Last night, soon after twelve, I was coming back home. I'd been spending the evening with a few friends in a convivial sort of way. That is a most unusual thing with me. Doctors have to be temperate men. But the fact of the case is that I had been a good deal bothered by a patient of mine—a woman. She jabbered about malpractice and neglect, and threatened an action. There was nothing whatever in it. I shall have her signed up and planked into an asylum in a week. But it was a disturbing thing, and when some of my friends thought that I wanted cheering up, I didn't say no. Well, let's see what I'm talking about."

"You were coming back after being cheered up."

"Exactly. I took Durnford Place on my way. It occurred to me that I might as well go and look up Myas, and have some explanation with him. I wanted to talk to him about the way my practice was going downhill. He was a generous man, and I felt quite sure he'd be prepared to meet me. I don't mind owning that I wanted another drink too. And it doesn't do for a man in my position to be seen passing into a 'pub' just before closing time. People might think I'd been called in professionally, or they might not. See?"

"Naturally, Mr. Vulsame. You showed your customary good judgment."

"As soon as I let myself into the garden, I saw that the laboratory was brightly lit up. Funnily enough, Myas had never shown me his laboratory, though I had dropped a hint or two about it. He was secretive about his work. I don't know to this day what it was that his particular line of research was aiming at. That garden path, as you may have noticed, is all grown over with grass and moss. Your footsteps make no sound upon it. I got close up to the window, which was partly open, and was on the point of calling to him, when I heard within the studio two voices. I could not catch what was said; but one was the voice of Myas, and one was the voice of a woman. What would any gentleman do under those circumstances?"

"Go away and hold his tongue."

"That," said Vulsame, with conscious pride, "is exactly what I did. I put myself in his place. I asked myself how I should like it if I were sitting in there with a girl, all cosy and comfortable, and somebody came and interfered, or dropped hints about it afterwards. However, we needn't go into that. I suppose you see the point. If Miss Lade says that she went to her bedroom shortly after ten last night, and did not leave it till somewhere about seven this morning, Miss Lade lies."

"You are sure it was her voice?"

"Pretty sure."

"Do you think it enough to be pretty sure?"

"Well, there is what might be called corroborative evidence. What had Miss Lade to gain by the death of Myas? Absolutely everything—he had left her every penny he possessed, and she knew it. What had any other woman to gain by his death? Nothing. It can have been no other woman than Miss Lade, though I dare say her old mother is mixed up in it as well. We will go on a little further. This morning I am called in and find Myas dead from an anæsthetic automatically administered. Now no medical man in his senses would dream of giving himself an anæsthetic in this way without having somebody present qualified to watch him, and to do anything that might be necessary. Miss Lade had been working as his assistant for some time, and was fully competent. I have definite proof in his own handwriting that on another occasion he had placed himself under an anæsthetic with Miss Lade in attendance. This time, either she deliberately altered the regulator of that mechanical pump, or she saw that things were going wrong and did nothing. Murder in either case."

"Well now, Mr. Vulsame, I'll give you my point of view. I know that Miss Lade did not murder Myas. I know it definitely. I have seen them together frequently, and I cannot be mistaken. Miss Lade's devotion to that dead man was a very real and a very beautiful thing. She would have given her life for him cheerfully. If your evidence before the coroner is on the lines that you have just shown me, that is some of the evidence with which I shall meet it. You see, my friend, that it is of no use for you to say that no medical man would dream of administering an anæsthetic to himself unless there was some competent person with him. It is no use to say it, because that automatic pump proves you wrong. If Miss Lade were present and if she were competent to watch the process of anæsthesis, she was also competent to give the anæsthetic, and there was no necessity whatever for any mechanical apparatus. Myas had made many experiments upon himself with anæsthetics. You have told me there is a record of them. Probably he had found out exactly what he thought he could do within the limits of safety. He may have been exceptional in taking the risk, but the apparatus proves that he took it. You say that Miss Lade lied, and I fully agree with you. It was natural that any woman should lie under those circumstances. If she was with him alone in that laboratory so late at night, after the rest of the household had gone to bed, and this became generally known, her character would suffer for it—though in this respect as in the other I believe her to be entirely innocent."

"Put like that, it does, of course, look different," said Vulsame.

"Quite so. Now you and I are reasonable men, and can talk this over. You did not find me unreasonable when you spoke, for instance, of your moral claim against Myas's estate. I am somewhat more than the trustee for Miss Lade. I was asked by Myas to look after her. I give you my word of honour that I'm absolutely convinced of her innocence. If you mention before the coroner that Miss Lade was, or may have been, alone in the laboratory with Myas after twelve last night, I have no doubt that she will have an explanation to give. That explanation would go along with my evidence, which I tell you frankly would be dead against you. But though this preposterous charge of murder will be shown to have nothing in it, in the eyes of the pious and evil-thinking people of Knox Street Miss Lade's reputation will be gone. I do not think it necessary for you to tell the coroner anything whatever about your visit to the laboratory last night. Remember, I was more the friend of Myas than I was of Miss Lade, and I wouldn't say this if I believed there had been the barest possibility of foul play. The reasonable thing and the chivalrous thing for you to do is to say nothing whatever about this incident. And if you are reasonable, you will also find me reasonable."

"In what particular way do you mean?"

He shot one quick glance at me from his small and furtive eyes, and I saw that he understood exactly. I had to put the thing plainly enough, but not too plainly. I trust that I appeared to be more at my ease than was really the case.

"Reasonable in every way, I hope. To take one instance—the first that happens to occur to my mind—there is your moral claim against the estate of which I am trustee. You know, of course, that a moral claim is not a legal claim. I cannot pay you one penny out of the estate; if I had the best will in the world to do it, the law does not permit me to do it. This does not mean that I do not recognize the force of your moral claim. I am quite sure that Myas never wished you to be a loser by any transactions which you had with him."

"That's absolutely certain. If I had done what I intended to do last night, and what I was prevented by the natural delicacy of a gentleman from doing, I shouldn't be talking to you like this. As things stand, I am sacrificed to my feelings of chivalry."

"Well, now, Mr. Vulsame, the consideration of what Myas would have wished has great weight with me. If I wrote you a cheque on my account for, say, three hundred pounds—I think those were the figures—it would not inconvenience me in any way, and it would indeed give me a great pleasure to do this small thing for my dead friend. Naturally, I should not wish to act less chivalrously than yourself."

"If that is the way you look at it, I'm agreed—perfectly agreed. Why not? The reputation of the girl and the memory of the dead man both gain from the transaction. But if you put it to me that I'm to take three hundred pounds to hold my jaw——"

"My dear fellow, my dear Mr. Vulsame, please make no such preposterous suggestion as that. Do you think I'm not aware that I'm dealing with a gentleman? No, you may be assured that the arrangement between us will never be represented in that light. It is a matter purely between ourselves, and concerns nobody else. You will come to me after the inquest, and we will complete the matter, and not another word will be said about it."

"Very good. These cigars are first class. I'll just take another and one last little drink, with your permission, and then I must be off. But I tell you candidly—there are some queer things about this case, and they beat me entirely."

"You are quite right. There are several things in it which I cannot understand in the least. What were you referring to particularly?"

"Well, I'll tell you one thing. In a corner of that work-room this morning there was a whole lot of apparatus. What it was I can't say, but it was a big elaborate thing, and must have cost a pot of money. I should imagine it was electrical. Now that was all smashed to bits, just as if it had been broken up with a hammer. What's more, I found a hammer there that might have done it."

"Yes, it's strange. But I can't see that such a thing should have any bearing on the death of Myas. For all we know, Myas himself may have smashed the thing. He had a nasty temper when his work disappointed him, and he was never very patient with anything ineffective. By the way, before you go you might give me your latch-key to the garden in Durnford Place. I am returning my own key to Miss Lade, and I'll send yours with it."

"Myas gave it me—he didn't lend it me. Still, I don't want to make a fuss about it. Anything that you say is right is good enough for me. Besides, the damned thing is no use to me anyway. Here you are, Mr. Compton."

He laid the key down on the table. It appeared that he had his cigar-case with him, and was willing to pay me the great compliment of filling it with my cigars at my suggestion. He had not, however, brought his purse with him, and borrowed a couple of sovereigns for what he described as incidental current expenses. He then, to my great joy, drew on his absurd gloves, picked up his hat, and demanded a taxicab.

When he had gone, I reflected at length on my own position. I knew Miss Lade to be innocent. I knew definitely that she had not murdered Myas. I knew that if she was in the laboratory after twelve the night before, it was merely on account of the work that Myas was doing, and that she had made the visit secretly for obvious reasons—to prevent servants or Vulsame from misunderstanding her. This being so, it seemed to me the thing to do was to save her as far as possible even from the shadow of suspicion.

But one fact remained—I was about to pay a man three hundred pounds to suppress evidence at an inquest, and I did not quite like the thought of that when I went round to see my solicitor at his private house that night. I liked it so little that I did not say a word to him about it. Otherwise, it would have interested me to have asked him how many years' penal servitude I was likely to get if I was found out. Certainly, for a respectable, law-abiding, middle-aged gentleman I had gone rather far. But I thought the circumstances justified me.

CHAPTER X

The coroner's jury returned a verdict of Accidental Death, and there was little or no suggestion during the inquest that any other verdict was possible. Mr. Vulsame was quite at his best. He had a frock-coat and his professional manner. He was omniscient, but he was also sympathetic. He spoke of Myas as a singularly gifted man, who had at one time come to him for advice. Myas, so he told us, was interested in medical psychology, and made many experiments upon himself; he (Vulsame) had given him a warning on this point on a previous occasion. In fact, Vulsame was very impressive and magnificent. Possibly with a view to earning his money, he mentioned that Myas was very happily engaged, and that Miss Lade's devotion to him was a real and very beautiful thing. The echo of my own words made me squirm.

I had not seen Miss Lade before the inquest. She was dressed entirely in black, of course, and kept her veil down. She spoke in a low voice, and seemed perfectly self-possessed. There was even a vague suggestion of dominance and decision about her which I had not noticed before. She was not required to say much. If Vulsame's story of the two voices in the laboratory was a true story—and certainly I believed it—then Miss Lade lied, and she lied simply, firmly and well.

My own evidence was merely to the effect that Myas had no financial trouble, and no other cause so far as I knew for taking his life. I confirmed Vulsame's opinion of the happiness of his engagement, and I mentioned that to my knowledge Myas had been anticipating a considerable success in his line of scientific research.

The coroner had a few wise words to say on the distinction between eccentricity and insanity. The jury might reasonably come to the conclusion that Myas was slightly eccentric, but they could not go further than that. Many medical men, he reminded them, had tried experiments upon themselves. Mr. Vulsame, who had given his evidence admirably, had told them that he himself had found a record of similar experiments in Myas's handwriting, and had given him a very proper and judicious warning against them.

Altogether it was a great day for Vulsame. As we left the court, I handed him an envelope, and he thanked me. "Pulled it off all right, eh?"

"I think you gave your evidence admirably, Mr. Vulsame."

He tapped the breast-pocket in which he had placed the envelope. "Not a word about this to anybody, you know."

"Much better not," I agreed. "It could be so easily misunderstood."

The envelope contained three hundred pounds in Bank of England notes. I had not thought it advisable to pay by cheque. I had even taken the trouble to get the notes from four different sources. In fact, I was not prepared to trust Vulsame quite so far as I could throw him.

In accordance with the directions contained in his will, the body of Daniel Myas was cremated and no religious service was held over it, and I was the only person present. Mr. Vulsame had expressed an intention of being there, but was prevented by a professional engagement. I think it was Miss Lade who was responsible for the absence of herself and her mother. Old Mrs. Lade spoke to me about it and seemed to regret it. She had the deep interest in funerals which is characteristic of her class. "But we mothers have to do what we're told nowadays," she said. She also expressed a hope that friends in Knox Street would not think the funeral arrangements shabby. She admitted that Myas's directions for simplicity and his prohibition of floral tributes had to be observed.

That year, for the first time in my life, I spent August and September in town. I was engaged in clearing up all the business of Myas's estate. Fortunately, it proved to be a very simple matter; Myas had always been in the habit of consulting a solicitor as to his investments, and very few of them had to be changed.

I called at Knox Street on the day after the funeral, but Miss Lade was not to be seen. I did see her once in the following week, for a few moments only, at her solicitor's office, on matters of business connected with the estate. And I noticed then that her manner to me had changed completely. She said as little as possible, and she got away as soon as possible. She told me nothing as to her future plans. She asked for no advice. I noticed further that she avoided meeting my eye directly.

I met her again by chance, and rather curiously. I had received a letter from old Welsford. I was meaning to run down to my cottage for a week-end, and there were certain things which Welsford desired me to bring with me. He wanted a rain-gauge of a particular kind, and his letter reminded me that I had promised him his blessed rain-gauge. He also described the garden thermometer as being now "past work," and suggested that it should be replaced. That was how I came to visit the shop of Denville & Moore, the instrument-makers in Holborn.

In the shop was Alice Lade, talking freely and even urgently to a managerial and dignified person on the other side of the counter. She had her back to me and did not see me. As I waited for an assistant at the other counter, I could hear what was said. People do not tell their secrets in the shops of the scientific instrument-makers, and I felt no scruples about it.

"You must have got Dr. Myas's original specifications," said Miss Lade.

"We have, madam," said the man. "We always keep everything of that kind. Our difficulty is that while this piece of apparatus was being constructed, Dr. Myas modified those specifications and in some cases departed from them altogether. It was a very delicate piece of work indeed, and very complicated. We could construct the apparatus again according to the original specification, but we feel sure it would not give you satisfaction. He supervised every detail of the construction himself."

"That's all right," said Miss Lade. "I can understand that. Then let me see the workman to whom he gave his verbal instructions. Only an intelligent man could be employed for work of that kind, and he would be certain to remember any instance in which the specification was not followed."

"Probably he would. But there we are brought face to face with another difficulty. Dr. Myas's orders were given to our foreman. He was a very able and well-educated man, but unfortunately he was intemperate, and for that reason we had to get rid of him. We cannot say now where he is."

At this moment my assistant produced rain-gauges, and my attention was for the moment diverted. But as he was packing up my purchases, I again heard Miss Lade:

"That's what you must do, then. You must advertise for this man. At any cost I must have this apparatus reconstructed."

And then she turned and saw me.

She seemed startled and embarrassed, but what struck me most was that she looked very ill. She shook hands with me in a perfunctory sort of way, murmured a silly word or two about the weather, said good morning, and turned to go.

But almost immediately she turned back again. Her eyes beckoned me, and I followed her out to the cab which was waiting for her.

"Get in, please," she said.

As she spoke, I looked at her, and saw that her face was contorted with pain. She seemed suddenly to have grown many years older. I followed her into the cab. The driver apparently already had his directions. Alice Lade sat with her elbows on her knees and her hands covering her face. Then suddenly she touched my arm.

"Can you get me some brandy?" she said. "I have a kind of neuralgia that gives me such intense pain, that I'm afraid of fainting."

By the direction of my doctor I always carry with me a tiny flask of brandy, though for the last two years I am thankful to say I have never wanted it. It was useful in this emergency.

She drank eagerly. Her colour returned slightly, and her face became more tranquil.

"Thank you very much," she said. "If you will stop the cab, I won't keep you any longer. I have to go on to some chemists in the City that are doing some work for me."

I was angry, of course, but I trust that I only appeared firm.

"You are not fit to go on to the City, or to do any further business this morning, Miss Lade. If you insist upon it, I shall certainly come with you. If you will promise me to go straight home, I will leave you. You will probably think me very officious and interfering, but you must remember that I promised to look after you."

"I don't think you officious or interfering. I am really grateful to you. It is only that just at present I cannot bear to have anyone at all with me. I must be alone. But I will do as you say, and will go home at once."

I stopped the cab and got out without shaking hands. As I stood with the door open, I said: "To Durnford Place or Knox Street?"

"To Durnford Place, please. Thank you again. One day perhaps——" She did not finish her sentence, and once more covered her face with her hands. I waited a second or two, and then closed the door and gave the driver his order.

I had a good deal to think of, as I sat alone after lunch that day. Try how I would to prevent it, Vulsame's suspicions of Alice Lade would come back to my mind. I told myself that these suspicions were unworthy of me. Miss Lade had seemed somewhat ungrateful; she had snubbed me and discarded me for no reason of which I was aware. Neither of those things should have made me suspicious, and I have always considered it rather low class to be wounded and resentful. But it was in vain that I tried to bully myself into a better frame of mind. The horrible and astounding fact was this—if Miss Lade had really been responsible for the death of Daniel Myas, I should have expected her to behave very much as she had behaved. She looked to me like a woman tortured with remorse and sleepless nights.

CHAPTER XI

Naturally, Myas was a good deal in my mind during these months. Again and again I recalled his definite and boastful promise that before the year was out he would demonstrate to me the existence of a human soul, of which mind and body were but the concomitants. Great had been his enthusiasm. Everything had been made to give way to his work. He had risked both life and love for it. He had looked forward with the utmost confidence to the day of his experiment. He had told me that it would revolutionize thought—that it would make a new heaven and a new earth. Had the experiment succeeded, his claim would perhaps have been justified. And now all the years of work, all the ambition and ability, had ended in a little heap of dust in an oak casket. And things went on as before. I still insisted upon believing in Miss Lade's innocence; and if she were indeed innocent, then it seemed bitter that so much should have been wrecked by so little—by a flaw in a piece of mechanism, or by one careless moment in Myas himself.

One or two obituary notices had appeared. That in the *Lancet* was brief, but peculiarly admirable. Without taking back one word that had been said about Myas's pamphlet, it still found much to praise in him, and its expression of regret that he had not lived to complete his researches, seemed both decent and genuine. It has occasionally been my lot to read obituary notices of those whom I have known personally, and I have read them always with a kind of surprise. I have never recognized in them the men that I knew. This may be because it is the important part of them which figures in the obituary, and the characteristic trifles which one has grown to like or dislike are omitted. Certainly no one could have reconstructed Daniel Myas from his obituary notice. His work was there, but the man himself was not. After all, it would have been difficult to give a picture of him; the strange blend of serious strength and amusing weaknesses is common enough and human enough; but it is difficult to make it seem real.

There was much that was rather morbid in this business of Myas and Alice Lade, and I was not sorry when, early in October, another subject occurred to occupy my mind. An old friend of mine, coming rather late in life into possession of the family archives, chanced upon a manuscript diary relating in part to the Peninsular War. The rather absurd idea occurred to him that I was just the man to edit it for publication, and I'm afraid I was too vain to put the idea aside at once. I said that I would at any rate read this diary. I did read it, and I found it extremely interesting. It was filled, however, with things which I did not understand, and allusions which I could not follow. I thought I had just an average knowledge of eighteenth-century history, but average knowledge was of very little use here. I was driven to the British Museum and to other libraries. I think I may say that I consider the joy of clearing up a difficult point in an old personal history to be one of the purest and noblest that I have known.

One sunny day, more like midsummer than October, I had spent the whole morning in the British Museum, and afterwards had lunched at the club. I had been rather successful that morning and had several excellent notes to add to my edition of that diary, if ever I undertook it. I went back to St. James's Place immediately after luncheon, in order to get to work again.

I let myself into the flat with my latch-key, and found on the table in the hall a registered letter in a foolscap envelope. It was addressed to me in a handwriting which, if I had not known him to be dead, I could have sworn to as the handwriting of Daniel Myas.

One obvious explanation occurred to me. It might actually be his writing; it might be some letter which he had left in the care of Alice Lade with instructions to forward it to me at this interval after his death.

I was on the point of opening it, when my man came out and told me that a person giving the name of Mrs. Lade had called to see me.

"Is she here now?" I asked.

"Well, yes, sir. She said that she knew you very well, and seemed so insistent that I allowed her to wait. Will you see her, sir, or shall I send her away?"

"I'll see her. Show her into my study."

I put the letter down on the table in my study with the address downwards. Mrs. Lade would also have recognized the handwriting, and would probably have found it very upsetting. She was easily upset.

She was well dressed in deep mourning, and seemed rather embarrassed by her clothes and by the situation in which she now found herself. As she struggled towards speech, I told her I was sorry I had been out when she called, and that she had had to wait.

"That did not matter in the least, sir. I had expected to wait. I have been made quite comfortable and had *The Times* newspaper."

"What's more to the point," I said, "is, have you had any lunch?"

"Oh yes, sir," she said. "Yes, Mr. Compton, I've lunched."

Here, suddenly and without warning, Mrs. Lade burst into tears. I dislike tears. I have the feeling, which is perhaps rather selfish, that people should not weep when I am present. However, I tried to be sympathetic and to find out what was the matter.

The flood-gates of her speech were now wide open. But some little time elapsed before I could rescue anything like a coherent story out of the torrent. She repeated over and over again that nothing had been the same since the death of Daniel Myas. She asked tragically what daughters were for. She said that she had always been respectable, as anybody in Knox Street would tell me. Friends in Knox Street had been kind to her under trying circumstances. She informed me that she was not a good sailor, far from it. She gave me, with more minuteness than delicacy, the details of the disease of which poor Willy's wife died, long before I found out that Willy was her brother in New York.

Gradually and patiently I drew out all the facts and pieced them together. The thing which was affecting Mrs. Lade most was the great change which had taken place in her daughter. In the matter of money Alice was apparently generous. "I can buy what I like and go where I like. Cabs I take frequently. If it wasn't for this sacred time of mourning I might be sitting in the theatre every evening in the week. And I should enjoy it too. For it takes you out of yourself."

But it appeared that Alice showed her mother very little affection, and was seldom with her. During the greater part of her time she was shut up in the work-room in which Myas died. She refused to see any of her friends in Knox Street, and Mrs. Lade was tired of making one excuse after another to them. She spoke very little to anybody. And, although she caught cold, sitting late in that laboratory, and although it had affected her voice, she had refused to allow her mother to nurse her at all. "Different altogether, she is," sobbed Mrs. Lade. "And ammoniated quinine she simply refuses to look at."

At this juncture a letter had arrived from Mrs. Lade's widowed brother in New York. He had a house and children, and he needed someone to look after them. His experiences with paid housekeepers had not been encouraging. Some of them, he said, were sniffy and superior and incompetent, some of them drank, and some of them desired him to marry them. He appealed to Mrs. Lade and her daughter to come over and live with him. Mrs. Lade showed me this letter, and I was rather surprised that it could have been written by her brother. In spite of the fact that she was a bad sailor, the idea had appealed to Mrs. Lade. She had relinquished her shop now, because there was no necessity to keep it on. I should imagine the income derived from it had never been very attractive. At the same time, Mrs. Lade was a woman who liked to have an occupation. "Added to which," she said, "they tell me America's a nice place." She had put the matter before her daughter, and her daughter's decision had grievously distressed her. Mrs. Lade was certainly to go to live with her brother. It was her duty. All the money that was wanted for her outfit and passage would be forthcoming, and on her arrival in New York she would receive a sufficient income to provide for her in comfort and independence. Thus, if she and the widowed Willy did not happen to hit it off together, she would be free to employ her activities elsewhere. Alice had urged—almost ordered—her to go. But at the same time Alice definitely refused to accompany her. She said that she was continuing the work which she had begun with Daniel Myas, and that this made it impossible for her to leave England. Tears and persuasions had seemed to have no effect on her.

I tried to get Mrs. Lade to see the thing from another point of view. Alice's resolve to continue that work was really a kind of loyalty to the dead man. But Mrs. Lade was not to be convinced.

"If she would promise to come out a year after me, or even two years, I could be satisfied. It's the separation for ever that is hard for me to face. But when I speak to her about it, she gives that quick little wave of the hand, same as the poor doctor always did when you annoyed him about anything; and I don't know that I've told you the worst yet."

The worst proved to be that for three days Mrs. Lade had not even seen her daughter.

"Do you know where she has gone?" I asked.

"Gone? She's not gone. She's still there. She has the rooms that were his now, and her time is spent between them and the workshop, and most of it in the workshop. Do you know, Mr. Compton, that I've had doors locked against me in my own house? Do you know that she doesn't even take her meals with anything like regularity? A few words scrawled on a scrap of paper—that's all I've had from her these last three days. I'll tell you what I think about it."

"Well?" I asked.

Mrs. Lade tapped her forehead significantly. "That, to the best of my belief, is what is the matter with her. There has been no history of it in my family, but, as Mrs. Porter was saying to me in Knox Street only this morning, grief may overturn the mind. If I had had any feeling of confidence in that Vulsame, I should have called him in, expense being no longer a consideration. But there, what use would it have been if I had? It's twenty to one she would have refused to see him."

I thought this extremely likely. The conduct of Alice was becoming more and more inexplicable to me. However, the absurdity of Vulsame's suspicions seemed to be demonstrated by it, and I was rather ashamed that the same suspicions had occurred to my own mind. A woman who had murdered Myas would not care to shut herself up in the rooms which he had occupied, and in the laboratory where he had died. Alice Lade had always had a simple natural affection for her mother; this had apparently vanished. The desire for solitude was remarkable. There were points in her behaviour when I met her at the instrument-makers', which had seemed to me curious. I knew, too, how great her devotion to Myas had been. It was quite possible that, as a result of his death, her mind had given way.

I sympathized with the poor old woman, and did the best I could to console her. I promised that I would myself go and see Alice. I would talk things over with her, and, if I found that she was ill, I thought I could use my authority sufficiently to persuade her to see a doctor. I think that when old Mrs. Lade left me, she was much comforted by what I had said. In my own mind, I felt far from sure that Alice would see me, and wondered what my next move ought to be in that case.

When my visitor had gone, I picked up that letter from the table and tore open one end of it. Something fell from it with a metallic little tinkle, and I picked it up. It was the latch-key to the garden entrance in Durnford Place.

CHAPTER XII

The letter which accompanied the latch-key covered several pages of foolscap, and was written entirely in the characteristic handwriting of Daniel Myas. It seemed to have been written freely and firmly, and gave not the slightest suggestion of a laboured imitation of his writing. The sheets were fastened together by a staple placed, as he always placed it, in the middle of the top of the page—not in the corner, which is a more usual custom. My eye fell on the date under the address, and I was astounded. It was the same date as the postmark. I will give the letter in full:

"Dear Compton,—It is not a coincidence, a chance similarity; it is I, Daniel Myas, who write this, though the hand that holds the pen is the hand of Alice Lade. And I shall redeem my promise to you—to prove by demonstration that the Ego, the soul, the self, exists independently of mind and body, though it is only by mind and body that it becomes cognizable by man under his present conditions.

"I had hoped to redeem that promise differently and more fully. I assure you I write now with no pride in what I have done, but even with an intense horror of it. I have reached the end to which I devoted so many years of labour, and I would gladly give all that I possess—yes, and life itself—if it could be undone again. I do not write to you to boast of any achievement. I write to ask your help.

"Do you understand? I am supposed to be Alice Lade. I am possessed of her mind and her body, but with some modifications that have already taken place, and with others, I think, imminent. I am not Alice Lade and I am Daniel Myas. Yes, I know it is incredible, and I know what facile explanation will leap to your mind at once. But that explanation of madness plus a considerable gift for forgery is wrong. I am Daniel Myas. I want your help. I want you to come to the laboratory in the garden. If you do that—if you see my face and hear my voice—you will need no other evidence. You will know that I am Daniel Myas."

At this moment the door opened. I was absorbed in what I was reading, and the opening of the door made me start up, but it was merely my servant.

"The gentleman who was with you here, sir, some months ago, Mr. Vulsame, has called, and wishes to see you particularly."

The man hesitated. "Well?" I said.

"He is not sober, sir."

"Very well. I'm not at home. He is not to wait."

"Very good, sir."

I picked up again the pages in the handwriting of Daniel Myas, and I read on:

"I have to tell you what happened on the night when my soul, the soul of Daniel Myas, became cognizable only through the mind and body of Alice Lade. I will tell it as clearly as I can. But you must make allowances for me. You saw what I was like at that shop in Holborn, and you can believe that I am rarely free from actual physical pain. For months too I have lived in an agony of fear and remorse, working without hope of success, and with the fixed intention to commit suicide if I failed. It was only a few days ago that something happened to make me give up that intention. I still suffer, though with a flicker of hope that I may yet undo the evil that I have done. Remember, too, that the mind at my disposal is not my mind. There are things which I knew once and know no longer. There are abilities which I once had, but no longer possess. Some of these things may come back to me, for some of them have already come back. At the moment, for instance, I can write with equal ease the handwriting of Alice or my own. Other modifications have occurred. Still I write as one not in full possession of my own powers, but limited by the medium through which my Ego becomes cognizable. The Daniel Myas of some months ago could have explained in the smallest detail what his intentions were, and how he proposed to carry them out. I have not these details, and am left with generalities.

"I know that it seemed to me that there was but one way in which the independent existence of the Ego could be demonstrated, and that this was by a transference of an Ego to a mind and body other than that with which it had previously been associated. I put it clumsily. Simply, the aim was that Alice Lade and I should for a while exchange our selves—or souls, as I think you preferred to call them. Many years of experiment and observation had convinced me that this exchange was possible. There were limitations, of course, and some of these I cannot recall. But I know that the exchange could only take place between two persons of opposite sexes. I know that it had to take place when these two persons were anæsthetized. I have a recollection of a piece of very complicated and elaborate mechanism. I know what firm made it for me. It was in their shop that you saw me. I recollect that there was the necessity for most accurate timing, and that the whole experiment hung, so to speak, on a sixth of a second. Further than that my memory has not helped me. I have seen the specifications of that mechanism written with my own hand, and I cannot understand them. I have by me many volumes of manuscript notes that I made from time to time for my own assistance, and they are as much Greek to me as if I were a first-year student. However, as I have said, a few days ago there came a flicker of hope that my knowledge will come back. In one particular it has already returned, and most wonderfully. You noticed, when we met in Paris, that I spoke French just about as well as I spoke English. I knew the language thoroughly, of course, and therefore the compliment meant nothing to me. The only people who like to be flattered on their French are the people who cannot speak it. I am glad, though, that you noticed it, because it gives me further evidence with which to convince you. In my new incarnation, in the body of Alice Lade, I had practically no knowledge at all of French. I could not read a French book, though I knew what a word here and there meant. I knew what Alice knew exactly, and nothing more than that. A few days ago, quite suddenly, I found that I was actually thinking in French. The whole thing had come back to me. That is why I hope more important knowledge than that may yet come back."

I paused a moment as I read this. To say that the only people who cared for compliments on their French were the people who could not speak it, would be quite characteristic of Daniel Myas, but Alice Lade would certainly not have said it.

"On the night of my supposed death," the letter went on, "Alice came secretly to the work-room, as she had often done before. The righteous and evil-minded people of the neighbourhood made such secrecy a necessity. An hour or more was spent in preparation for the experiment, but I cannot remember in detail what was done. When I try to recall it now, I seem to see myself handling different pieces of apparatus, but I seem to see with the eyes of a person who does not in every case understand the why and the wherefore of what is being done. My last recollection of the moment when we both were passing under the influence of the anæsthetic is the tick-tack of the machinery, seeming to grow intolerably loud and then dying away as if it had vanished into some distant grey mist. My recollection only becomes perfectly clear at the moment when I recovered from the anæsthetic. It was a sudden recovery. I stood up and rubbed my eyes, trying to recall where I was and what I was engaged upon. Then I looked round, and saw, huddled in a chair close to me, my own dead body. I turned and looked into a mirror, and from the mirror the face of Alice Lade looked back at me. Half of the experiment had succeeded and half had failed. My own Ego was transferred to the body and mind of Alice Lade, but where was she? What had I done with her?

"Then followed a short period of panic and madness. I had the feelings of a murderer, and was possessed with the idea that, to save myself, it was necessary to remove all evidence of the actual experiment which had taken place. I found a hammer and broke up the delicate apparatus which I had employed, and no longer understood. I burned in the stove papers which I think now should have been kept. Remember, I had become a frightened woman. I did things for which there was no reason whatever. I began to make everything neat and tidy. I put drugs away in their place. I swept the broken bits of apparatus into one corner of the room. I hid the little automatic pump which had administered the anæsthetic to the brain of Alice Lade. The other automatic pump I did not dare to touch, because it was too near to the dead body. That, perhaps, was as well.

"I wanted to get out into the open air. I left the dead man lying there, closed and locked the door, and went into the garden. A breath of wind sprang up and shook the dark trees, so that they seemed to be living things that were trying to get at me. I fled up the staircase. The body and mind of Alice seemed to work automatically, doing actions which she must often have repeated, actions which were no longer controlled by the higher centres. I found my way in the dark through a part of the house where I had never been before. I stepped aside to avoid obstacles. At one point I was very careful to tread very quietly on tiptoe. I found the handle of the door easily, without fumbling for it, knowing just where it would be. It was Alice's bedroom door.

"It sometimes happens that one comes upon a scene which is really absolutely new, and yet seems familiar. On a road where one has never been before, one seems to expect every bit of it as it comes into view. It is, I suppose, the memory of a dream. My feelings in that room were very much like that. I slept there. It seems a wonderful thing, but for two hours I actually slept. And after that came hours of horror, on which I do not wish to linger. You are not an imaginative man, Compton, but I think you'll suppose pretty well what I went through. I was not able that night to make any plan of action for the future. All that I thought of was to keep the secret and to save myself at the inquest. I remained alone as much as possible, and said as little as possible. At the inquest, as you know, I lied.

"After the inquest, I tried to get to work again. It was a hopeless business. I was working with the cortex of Alice Lade, not of Daniel Myas. At every step I found that I did not remember and did not know. I tried to get the apparatus reconstructed, which I had broken up in my panic. This has been done in some sort of a way, but I do not think it is right, and in any case I do not understand its use. I suffered tortures from insomnia and from headache and neuralgia. I was filled with fears that Mrs. Lade, or someone else who had known Alice, would see something strange in me, and would guess my secret. Suicide appeared to be the only thing left for me.

"Then, a few days ago, as I have told you, I suddenly recovered one branch of knowledge which I had lost. Who knows that in time the rest may not come back to me? The nature of Alice was plastic and receptive. The dominant force of my own Ego is even now working upon it. It has modified her mind. It has even produced physical changes. Let me become Daniel Myas with the knowledge that he had before, and with some of the ability that he had before, and I will undo some of the harm which I have done. The soul of Alice Lade shall once more become cognizable by her own mind and body. And my own soul shall go out into whatever it may be that awaits the lost.

"I know that my own feelings before the experiment were feelings of triumph. I felt that I, and I alone, had the secret of life and death. As I write that now, with my present defective knowledge, it looks like the raving of a megalomaniac, but it all seemed logical to my mind then, based on science and working out inevitably. Is there not a faint possibility that I may find myself again in the same position, not with the same feelings of triumph, for these can never come back, but with the same confidence in myself and with the same certainty that what I have done I can also undo?

"I cannot stop here. There are many people in this neighbourhood who knew Alice Lade, and will notice the changes that are taking place in her. Much of her special knowledge is slipping from me. Mrs. Lade speaks of things which she expects me to know all about, and I know nothing of them. The strain of fencing with this is becoming too much for me. An opportunity has now arisen to get Mrs. Lade away to America. I feel a great deal of pity for her. I want to spare her as much as possible, and for that reason alone it is best that she should go. There, perhaps, you will be able to help me. But there are many other ways in which I need your help.

"I had intended to cut myself adrift from you altogether. You probably noticed that I had intended to let you think that Alice Lade still lived, and that I was dead. I was ashamed to let you think the truth. I am ashamed still, but I am compelled to appeal to you. What was done must be undone. You must help me to get away from Knox Street, and you must find for me some place where I can be absolutely alone. If necessary, you must help me in the work. I think circumstances will arise which will require me to give you a power of attorney to deal with all financial business. You understand what I am asking, Compton? I am asking you to help me to bring Alice back again. You must do it.

"It cannot all be arranged by letter. You must come and see me, painful and shocking though this will be to you. I enclose the key of the garden entrance in Durnford Place, the key which you returned. Come to-night after ten, when there will be no fear of interruption."

There was no signature to the letter. By the time that I had finished reading it, it was beginning to grow dark. I switched on all the lights in the room. I locked the letter away in a drawer, so that I might not see it. I picked up a review and began to read, and found that the words meant nothing to me. I felt sick with horror and disgust. I could not bear to remain alone in my room. As I rose to go out, I heard a loud voice in the passage outside. It was the voice of Mr. Vulsame.

CHAPTER XIII

I had never expected that I could hear with pleasure the voice of Vulsame, even in his more sober moments. But now this crude and material brute was almost a relief to my mind. My servant came in and appeared to be agitated. Mr. Vulsame had not only returned, but had definitely refused to go again. He was sitting on a chair in the hall, using the most awful language, and saying that if I was out he should wait there till I came back again.

"I think," I said, "it might amuse me to see this man for a few moments. Let him come in here."

Mr. Vulsame lurched into the room. His gait was slightly more intoxicated than his speech, and his speech was not strictly sober.

"Glad to see you've got more sense than that damned fool of a servant of yours, Compton," said Mr. Vulsame aggressively.

"Sit down," I said, "and tell me what your business with me is."

"You'll know that fast enough, just when I like and how I like. You'll find I'm top dog this time. Don't issue orders to me, because I won't take 'em. I can sit and I can stand."

"The latter," I said, "seems to be an over-statement."

In illustration of my words, he sat down hurriedly and dropped his hat.

"Now then," he said, "don't give me any of your damned superior airs, because I'm sick of 'em. I don't want 'em. What I want is a three-finger whisky and a little soda-water."

"On a superficial observation I should say you are mistaken. But if you really think so, you had better go out and get it."

"Did I say something just now about your damned superior airs? because if I didn't, I meant to. Don't let me have to speak twice. If you offered me a drink, I wouldn't take it. I'd throw it in your face. I can buy a drink if I want one. I've got money, and I'm going to get more. I'm going to get it before I go home to my dinner to-night."

"Then I'd better not detain you. Go and get it by all means."

"That's where you slip up, my friend. That's where you come down and hurt yourself. I'm going to get that money out of you, unless you want to do time. You wouldn't look very pretty in a suit of clothes with broad arrows all over it."

"No," I said. "And what is it exactly that I'm going to do time for?"

"For bribing an honest man to suppress legal evidence at an inquest, and letting a murderer go free."

"I have no recollection of anything of the kind. There has been no murder, so far as I know. The last time I had the pleasure of any conversation with you, you pointed out that you were incapable of taking a bribe, but were willing to receive some slight compensation for damage to your practice caused by the late Daniel Myas. That is correct, isn't it?"

"It's your way of putting it. I've got my own way. Why are Mrs. Lade and her daughter going to bolt to America? Does that look like innocence? You seem to think I know nothing. I was called in to attend a family in Knox Street this morning, and I picked up a thing or two, I can tell you. If I don't go straight off to the police and tell them everything I know, I run a risk of getting into a good deal of trouble myself, and I don't run risks for nothing."

"What is the figure," I said, "at which you do run risks?"

"One thousand pounds," said Mr. Vulsame solemnly.

"It is a large sum. I have not so much money at my bank at present. I should be compelled to realize securities."

"Can't help that," said Vulsame. "You've brought it on yourself."

"Suppose I paid you this sum, what security have I got that you will not come here to-morrow demanding another thousand?"

"You've the security of my word of honour. You're dealing with a gentleman. You seem to me to be continually forgetting that."

"Well," I said, "of course that would make a difference. If I could have your word of honour given me definitely in writing, I might be prepared to pay this sum, without admitting that I have been in the wrong in any way, but simply in order to save a public scandal."

"Quite so," said Vulsame. "I see your point. You're a sensible man, Mr. Compton. I said so when I came into your room, and I say so again. You don't want any public scandal. Give me this sum of money, and you'll get no public scandal. You'll never hear of it again. Nobody will. And I'll write anything you like. But as a matter of business, you don't get my undertaking in writing until I've got your cheque—see? You say you haven't got a thousand at the bank, but I suppose they might cash your cheque for that amount."

"Of course they would. They hold my securities."

"Very good. Sit down and write the cheque now. Make it payable to G. W. Vulsame, Esq., M.B., or bearer. Not order, mind, and don't cross it."

I sat down meekly and wrote the cheque as directed. Then Vulsame came to the writing-table and gave me a receipt and his written undertaking that he would not molest me further, either with regard to the death of Myas or in any other respect. I locked up the receipt and the undertaking, and he put the cheque in his pocket and prepared to go. Really, it was all so easy that I was almost ashamed to do it, but the man was very drunken and disgusting, and had made me angry.

"One moment before you go, Mr. Vulsame," I said. "I do not recommend you to present that cheque for payment at the bank tomorrow morning, as the money will not be paid and you will be immediately arrested."

"What for? What are you talking about?"

"Don't be childish. You must see. You have threatened to charge me with being an accessory after the fact in the murder of Daniel Myas, and have withdrawn the charge in consideration of receiving a sum that you have demanded. You have given me evidence in your own handwriting that you have done this. If I remember rightly, this particular offence is punishable with penal servitude for life. The law does not encourage blackmail, you know."

This sobered him. He took the cheque from his pocket and tore it in half. "Give me back that undertaking of mine," he said.

"My dear Mr. Vulsame, you cannot suppose I shall do anything so silly as that. Behave nicely and you will hear nothing more about it. That's all I can do for you."

"I'm just going to tell you what I think of you, Mr. Compton. I'm going to say it in plain words. You've played a dirty trick on me. You——"

"Stop that," I said, "and get out!"

Rather to my surprise, he did exactly as he was told. The alcoholic collapse had followed on the alcoholic courage. I congratulated myself that I had seen the last of Mr. Vulsame. I congratulated myself prematurely. As it happened, I saw him again that very night.

In one respect I felt grateful to the blackguard. For a few minutes, at any rate, he had taken my mind from that letter and the handwriting of a man whom I knew to be dead, summoning me to come and see him in a few hours' time. I was determined not to go to Durnford

Place. I changed my clothes and walked round to the club for dinner. I had meant to look in at a telegraph office on the way and send my excuses. In my own rooms I had gone to the telephone, but had stopped short; I was afraid of what I might hear on the telephone.

I did not go into the telegraph office. It would be easy enough to send a telegram from the club. But of course the thing that really stopped me was the conviction that, however much I might hate it and however great my horror, I should have to go to Durnford Place that night. There was the direct appeal for help. Whether it came from a man or from a woman, it came from a friend of mine, and to disregard it would have been to lose my most precious possession, my self-respect. Once I had determined that I should have to go, my mind became much easier. I played billiards for half an hour after dinner, and gave my whole attention to the game. And then it was time to have a taxicab called.

CHAPTER XIV

I have occasionally seen, when for my sins I have been taken to a music-hall, a performance which is, I believe, intended to be amusing and funny—the impersonation of a woman by a man. It is a thing which always disgusts me. The more cleverly it is done, the more loathsome it is. If I happen to see that item on ahead in the programme, I take care to be out of sight and sound of it. I do not know if this is a special peculiarity or weakness of my own, but it helped to add to the difficulty of what I had to do. I had been the friend of Myas, and I had been the friend of Alice Lade. Whatever was waiting for me behind the door of the laboratory had a claim upon me. I, plain, conventional, and unimaginative man, as Myas had described me, had by sheer force of circumstances been drawn into a very whirlpool of horror and morbidity. I had to go through the mud.

Now that I had made up my mind to it, I went through the thing pretty steadily. There was an electric light in my taxicab, and on my way to Durnford Place I read the evening paper assiduously. Whoever this creature was that had appealed to me in the undoubted handwriting of Daniel Myas, it was a person desperately in need of my help and advice. Help and advice cannot be given intelligently by the perturbed and terror-stricken. By the time that I had read the last advertisement of the latest hair-restorer, I had brought myself, I think, to my normal frame of mind. At first I had some trouble with my key; the lock of the garden door had not perhaps been much used of late, and had rusted. I began to think that I should have to go round to Knox Street, but at last the thing went back with a click and the door stood open. In a dark corner, from a mass of dusty laurels, a cat began to cry like a child. The place was very dark. The blinds were drawn down over the windows of the work-room, and only a faint glimmer of light shone behind them. I groped my way to the door and knocked—my usual brisk, social knock.

I had expected it, of course, and I think it should have had less effect upon me than it did. The voice which bade me enter was deep and resonant. It was the voice of Daniel Myas. I knew it to be his voice, and yet I had seen his dead body as it lay in the coffin. I'm afraid that I hesitated for a second or two before I could bring myself to turn the handle of the door.

The work-room was, perhaps, thirty-six feet in length. Near the door by which I had entered there was one electric light, heavily shaded. I could see rows of bottles and retorts, and stands of test-tubes. Books were scattered about. The farther end of the work-room seemed at first to be in complete darkness. Then, as my eyes got accustomed, I could distinguish something moving. It came a very little nearer to me, and now I could distinguish a man's dressing-gown, with the sleeves turned back, because the arms within were too short for it. The collar of the dressing-gown was turned up, and there was a veil over the face.

Again the voice of Myas came out of the darkness:

"I know exactly what you're feeling, Compton. You needn't shake hands. I understand."

"Nonsense," I said; and, advancing, took in my own the small hand of Alice Lade. Through the veil I could distinguish dimly the face of Alice Lade, but through her eyes the eyes of Daniel Myas looked out. That was, perhaps, the supreme touch of terror—the eyes of the man looking from the woman's face.

He thanked me for coming, and motioned me to a leather-covered chair by the lamp. I notice that I have written the word "he"—it conveys the impression made on me. He himself sat at some distance from me, in the dusk.

"My voice must have been a shock to you," he said. "You know, of course, that the organs of the voice are peculiarly susceptible of variation, and there my dominant personality has made a great change. I can still write in the handwriting of Alice—I made the experiment just before you came in—but I cannot speak with her voice. When I try to do it, I produce an absurd falsetto. There are other changes that you may have noticed."

"The colour of the hair seems to me darker," I said. "I noticed it when you came into the light just now."

"Yes, the pigmentation of the hair and of the iris of the eye have changed. Do you see what this means? Sooner or later, with all my care and precautions, Mrs. Lade will be definitely certain that there's something wrong. I only dare to speak to her in whispers, making a pretence that my voice is affected by a cold. But that kind of thing cannot go on indefinitely. This afternoon she knocked at the door and asked me if I would not see Mrs. Porter. I have not the faintest notion who Mrs. Porter is. Probably Alice knew her very well. You see the trouble, don't you? As I get back some of the knowledge that Daniel Myas had, I lose some of the knowledge that Alice had. The first thing I want you to do for me, the very first thing, is to get Mrs. Lade to go away to America. I don't want to be cruel to her, I want to spare her. If she found out what is going on in me, I think it would kill her. Can you get her to go?"

"I can," I said. "I think I can promise that definitely. I saw her this afternoon, and she made a suggestion then as to your mental state, which I shall be able to make use of."

He began to thank me, and broke off abruptly, and groaned as if in extreme physical pain. Then he took up a hypodermic syringe and I saw the heavy sleeve of the dressing-gown pulled back, and a small and feminine white arm.

There was a moment's pause, and then he apologized for the interruption. "Acute pain," he said. "It is part of the price I pay for what I have done. When the Ego of a man becomes cognizable by the body of a woman, that body must suffer. If it should happen again, don't take any notice of it, please. When can you get Mrs. Lade to go?"

"The idea that occurred to me was to make her believe that your restoration to health absolutely depended upon her departure. If she can be made to believe that, she will go by the end of the week. Can you get along until then?"

"Yes," he said. "I shall see her very little, and never in a room that is brightly lit. You will tell her not to prolong the last scene, when she says good-bye to me. You can say that the strain might be dangerous for me."

"Yes," I said. "I think you may consider all that as settled. But that is only the beginning of things. What are you going to do, my friend, after she has gone? What is to become of you?"

I remained for over an hour longer, talking with this ghastly hermaphrodite. Part of the time he spoke in French, and I dare say he did this with intention. To me it was entirely convincing. Alice Lade may have known a few words of French, but certainly she could not have spoken it like that. Very few men in England could have spoken it quite like that.

He had his scheme quite ready. His one aim was to bring Alice Lade back again. It was to that end, and to his own self-obliteration that he now meant to devote himself. He believed, though the belief seemed to me instinctive rather than reasonable, that if he could recover the knowledge he possessed before the experiment, this would become possible.

As soon as Mrs. Lade had gone, he meant to get to some place where he was not known, and there to continue his work.

I told him of my little cottage, standing all by itself on a hill in Gloucestershire. I was ready to put this cottage and my two servants there at his disposal. He accepted this with great gratitude. When I warned him that the place was desperately lonely, for the first time he laughed—a short, grim laugh. He wanted nothing better than to be quite alone now. Mrs. Lade was to leave for Southampton on the Friday, and on the Saturday following he would go down to Gloucestershire.

Then he told me something which, after all, did not greatly surprise me. He had made up his mind that he would no longer even try to pass as Alice Lade. He would not go down to Gloucestershire as a woman at all. Already, so he said, he felt it would be more easy to pass as a man than as a woman. As a man he would have more freedom and independence. He would be able to go about alone. He needed, of course, a complete outfit of man's clothes, and he had already taken all the measurements, so that I might get these for him. They were to be ready made, of course; there was no time for anything else. The power of attorney had also been prepared beforehand. He dealt with the necessary financial arrangements in a business-like, matter-of-fact way. And somehow every one of these prosaic touches seemed to add to the ghastliness of the whole thing.

"I am taking a great deal from you," he said, "and I am giving you a deal of trouble. I know that the sight of me must disgust and distress you. If it can possibly be managed, we will not meet again."

"Don't say that," I said. "I am sorry for you, and glad to be able to do anything for you. It does not amount to very much, when all is said and done. And certainly I intend to see you again. I am not going to leave you to go mad in solitude. I admit that I find the whole thing horrible. You would not believe me if I said I did not. You have done something which is against Nature."

"That is it," he said. "That is exactly it. And Nature punishes."

I shook hands again with him when I left. I hope he did not feel how much I hated to do it.

CHAPTER XV

I had not kept my cab, and started to walk until I found one. I had only gone a few yards from the garden door in Durnford Place, when I heard a man running after me, and turned sharply round. I found myself face to face with Mr. Vulsame. When he left me in the afternoon he had been a collapsed wreck, but he had been drinking again and had recovered his spirits. He seemed to be extremely excited, but he was no longer unsteady on his legs nor thick in his speech.

"I've got you," he said, shaking a clenched fist. "This is a fair knock-out. This explains everything."

"I don't know what you mean, Mr. Vulsame, and I don't want to know. I have had a great deal to try me to-day, and I do not think it would be wise for you to try me any further. You had better go home. If you want to communicate with me, you can write, you know."

But he would not be stopped. "I'll say what I've got to say. I'm not afraid of you nor of twenty like you. You were mighty particular that I should give back my key to the garden gate, weren't you? You were ready to pay out your money to save the girl, and you did it. Now I know why. It's a bit indecent, seeing Myas has only been dead a few months."

"Well," I said, "if you will have it, you must." I gave him a good punch in the face, and he went down on the pavement. Very slowly, and breathing hard, he collected his hat, which had fallen off, and replaced it, and struggled to his feet. I had waited to see if he wished to attempt the usual form of retort, but as he did not, and merely babbled solicitors, I told him to go to the devil, and left him. Apparently sobriety brought wisdom, for I never heard from Mr. Vulsame's solicitors.

I spent rather a horrible night. I slept, but the creature that I had talked to in the laboratory haunted my dreams.

Next morning there was a great deal to do, and no time to be lost. I went to see Mrs. Lade, going to the Knox Street entrance. I had telegraphed to her to expect me, and found her waiting and rather too well dressed. I said that I had seen her daughter, and I quoted the opinion of a non-existent medical man. I said that her own theory had been quite correct, that Alice's mind had been affected by her profound grief at her loss. The doctor recommended that she should be taken away into the country at once, and I undertook to see to that myself. It was expected that in time she would recover, and then doubtless she would regain her old affection for her mother and wish to go out and join her in New York. One has to tell these kindly lies, I suppose. To Mrs. Lade the voice of a doctor was as the voice of a god. Once the medical authority was quoted, it was easy to do anything with her. When I left her, she was going round to fetch Mrs. Porter to help her with the packing. I was to book her passage, and I offered, if she cared about it, to see her off. But I was rather glad that the offer was refused. She said that Mrs. Porter had been a great friend to her in her time of trouble, and would expect to accompany her to Southampton. I gathered that, not only would Mrs. Porter be gratified by being able to render this service to her friend, but that also it would be to her somewhat of a jaunt at the friend's expense. My last words to Mrs. Lade enjoined her to make as much haste as possible, and to keep out of her daughter's way. The doctor, I said, had insisted upon that. She might see her just for a moment, to say good-bye, but no more than that. I felt quite sure that Mrs. Lade would be far too agitated at this last interview to notice any of these slight changes which had occurred in Myas-Lade's appearance. I cannot say that any of this was work which I liked doing. Frankly, I hated it, but it had to be done, and quite as much for Mrs. Lade's own sake as for the sake of Daniel Myas.

In the afternoon I went to the stores where I was to buy the outfit. I gave the assistant the measurements, and he found me at once some suits of clothes which would do well enough. The only trouble was about the boots.

"You see, sir," said the assistant, "it is quite an unusually small size for a man. Ladies' boots, of course, we could do in that size, but that's not what you require."

Ultimately I succeeded in finding boys' boots which would do. The assistant's words had rather put me on my guard. I paid for the things, and he asked me to what address they should be sent. I was on the verge of giving the name, and then stopped myself. "I'll take them myself. I have a cab waiting outside. Let them be packed up and taken down to it."

In the cab I scribbled a brief note to Myas on a leaf from my pocket-book, telling him what I had done so far, and asking him to speak to me on the telephone at nine o'clock that evening. I stopped at a stationer's and bought an envelope for this. I addressed it to Miss Lade and put the note in the envelope underneath the string of the package. I drove to Knox Street and found that Mrs. Lade was out; she also had an outfit to buy. I directed her servant to take the things just as they were to Miss Lade, but I did not myself go in.

Punctually at nine o'clock that night my telephone bell went. I had a long conversation with Myas, pausing at intervals to prevent the exchange from cutting me off. We spoke principally about the house and laboratory. He wished these to be left exactly as they were. I was to find a caretaker for them, and it was to be a caretaker who had never seen himself or the Lades. He wanted me to order for him a portmanteau and a suitcase with the initials M. D. stamped on them. I asked him how he was going to pack the rest of his things, his books and his apparatus. He surprised me rather by saying that he was not going to pack them at all. He was going to take nothing of the kind with him to the cottage. He gave me his reasons. His knowledge of French and his ability to speak it had come back to him quite suddenly, and without any effort on his part. He believed that his special scientific knowledge would come back to him in the same way without effort or struggle. All he had to do was to remain quietly up there in the cottage, reading my books, wandering over the country, trying to think of other things.

Somehow the voice no longer inspired me with any feeling of horror. It was exactly like the voice of Daniel Myas. It created the illusion that it was Myas himself, with no change in him, who was speaking. It struck me that as far as possible he avoided any but the most commonplace subjects. He took common-sense views about the house in Knox Street. He wondered if it would be worth while to let it, but on the whole decided that a caretaker would be preferable. He asked me, almost as if it were a matter of real importance, what I thought the wages of a caretaker ought to be.

So little disturbed was I by this conversation, that I asked him to come and see me in St. James's Place on the Saturday morning before his departure. I went to bed, well satisfied with my day's work, and with my peace of mind restored to me. But no sooner did I fall asleep than the old horror returned to me in the form of a dream.

In my dream I was wandering very late at night over a Yorkshire moor. I knew the place well, I had been to a shoot there. It was a stormy night, and the violent wind tore my cap off. I could not find it, and I went on bareheaded, a few drops of cold rain splashing in my face. Already a feeling of imminent horror had begun, though I did not know what form it would take. Suddenly I saw a bright light. It was an electric lamp like those that they have in Hyde Park. I ran towards it as fast as I could go. I clung to it panting. I was glad to be there in the circle of light, and afraid to go out into the dark again. Suddenly, at a little distance, where the light was at its faintest, I saw a figure moving. It danced about fantastically and came nearer. It was a small white figure of a woman, wearing a man's heavy dressing-gown. Her long hair streamed in the wind. The wind caught the heavy folds of the dressing-gown, and tossed them hither and thither. With a quick rush the figure slid up to me, and put two small and cold hands on my throat. It whispered in my ear, and the voice was a husky falsetto, as if Daniel Myas had been trying to imitate the voice of Alice Lade.

"That's exactly it," said the voice. "It is against Nature, and Nature punishes. It is said that there is no place for me, neither in this world nor elsewhere."

I woke with a start, and switched on the reading-lamp by my bedside. I fetched a book from the library. It was one of the Badminton volumes. I got back to bed again and read, studying the subject of punt-racing, as though I were getting it up for an examination. I was determined not to fall asleep again. At last there came the early morning sounds, the twitter of the sparrows and the clatter of a milk-cart. I felt with relief that after all the ordinary world was around me. I put down the volume, switched out the light, and almost instantly fell asleep again.

I got up at my usual hour, unrefreshed by the sleep, haggard and worn out, and depressed by the feeling that there was something to come—something hanging over me. I recalled what it was. Myas was to leave by an afternoon train from Paddington on Saturday afternoon, and I had asked him to come and see me in the morning. There would be time to stop that. I walked across to the telephone and took down the receiver.

"Number, please?" said the girl at the exchange.

"It's all right," I said. "It's a mistake, I don't want anything."

After all, I could not do it. It was too absolutely selfish and cowardly.

CHAPTER XVI

"A Mr. Daniel is asking if you will see him, sir."

I knew that Mr. Daniel was Daniel Myas. He had told me of his intention to use another name. I directed that he should he shown into the library where I was sitting.

The first impression he made upon me was one of strangeness. I thought I had never seen him before, and did not know him in the least. There was really nothing about him which reminded me of Alice Lade. The hair had been quite short and was of a reddish-brown in colour. The eyes were the eyes of a man. Indeed, the general appearance, though it suggested an undersized and nervous little man, ludicrously out of keeping with the deep voice, had nothing that was feminine about it. His face was very white, and he looked as if he were ravaged by disease, but he no longer appeared, as on that night in the laboratory, to be in actual physical pain. His expression was one of distinct relief. He no longer inspired me with horror, but for the first few minutes, at any rate, I felt as if I were talking to a man whom I did not know.

He took a cigarette and began to say commonplace things. He had left his luggage at Paddington, where he would pick it up in the afternoon. He wondered how long it would take him to drive to Paddington. As he spoke, I noticed that his manner with the cigarette was that of Daniel Myas exactly. When a little ash fell on his coat, and he flicked it off, he swore just as Myas always did, with set teeth and without a sound beyond the initial letter. It was characteristic of Myas that the trivial things in life made him much more furious than the great disasters. I began to feel that, after all, I did know this young man in the blue serge suit, sitting opposite to me and watching me anxiously to see how I was taking it.

"How did you manage to effect this transformation?" I asked him. "I should have thought it was impossible for anyone anywhere in London to take on the dress of the opposite sex, without taking somebody into the secret, or without being found out."

"As it happens," said Myas-Lade, "it was simple enough. That old woman, the caretaker, wanted to go out to do her shopping. I told her that she could be away for an hour, if she liked, and that I should probably have left before she returned. I had everything ready in the laboratory. My clothes were all packed, except those which I meant to wear. The hair gave me some trouble. I cut it short myself, as well as I could, but not very short, and burnt it in the laboratory stove. After I had changed, I went first to Paddington, where I left my luggage, and then to the nearest barber. I told him that I had been living for months in a lonely spot in the West Highlands, away from the resources of civilization, and had to cut my hair myself. He seemed quite satisfied, and not much interested. Of course, someone who knew me might have seen me coming out with my luggage to the cab that was waiting in Durnford Place. Even if anyone did, it does not matter in the least. No one would have recognized me. You yourself, Compton, look as if you were hardly sure who it was who was speaking to you."

"That is very likely," I said. "I knew Daniel Myas and Alice Lade. When I saw you that night in the laboratory, there was something of each personality in you. Now, in appearance at any rate, there is nothing that suggests either. Only the voice and the manner recall Daniel Myas to me. You look as though you were no longer in any pain."

"I am not," said Myas. "Last night, for the first time since the night of the experiment, I managed to get four hours' continuous sleep. Somehow it seems almost worth while to have suffered as I did, in order to get the ecstasy of being free from suffering. It is almost difficult for me to understand how it is, that people who are not in bodily pain do not experience constant and conscious pleasure from their freedom. I do not suppose that it is all over. On the contrary, the pain is almost certain to return, but that I do not mind. I have had my breathing-space. If it comes back ten-fold, I can bear it now, and go on bearing it until the work is finished."

"Until the work is finished," I repeated. "You seem confident."

"I am confident. Yes, Compton, I shall not come to see you again, but Alice Lade will. It is only a matter of patience. What happened in the one case will happen in another. Because the knowledge of a language came back, therefore most certainly the other knowledge will return."

"And then?"

"That knowledge will form the means for my release. I use the word 'release' intentionally. My Ego, my soul, is detained here like some poor animal that has one foot caught in a trap. My body is dead. The apparatus of my mind contained in that body is dead. It is only, as it were, by murder and theft, that I, Daniel Myas, am cognizant to you now. I am due elsewhere."

I have known people who were very old or very ill to have that same curious feeling of being due elsewhere.

He told me much that was very curious. The knowledge which belonged specially to Alice had not entirely left him. Before the caretaker's arrival, he had gone through the rooms in the house in Knox Street, and in one of them had found the cheap foreign piano on which Alice used to play. To own a piano and to give Alice music-lessons had formed part of the laudable ambition of Mrs. Lade. Alice had some slight gift for music—nothing very remarkable. Myas was perhaps more of a musician *au fond*, but he played no instrument and had never had a lesson.

The sight of the piano seemed to awaken something which had been dormant in him. He sat down and began to play. What he played was part of a movement, very tinkly and simple, of one of Mozart's sonatas. Suddenly, he became conscious of what he was doing, and stopped abruptly in the middle of a phrase. He could not go on playing. The subconscious mind of Alice Lade made it possible. The conscious mind inhibited it. He told me that when Mrs. Lade spoke with him about things that Alice would be supposed to know, he always found it easier to answer if he closed his eyes and tried to keep his conscious mind on some other subject.

In one trifling respect, he showed the personal taste of Alice Lade still. Daniel Myas had been an epicure and a judge of wine. Alice Lade hated the taste of it, and otherwise cared very little about what she ate or drank. I noticed that at luncheon Myas-Lade drank water only. He saw that I had noticed it.

"Yes," he said, "it is so. The other day I went into a confectioner's shop and bought sweets to eat. Perhaps after all it is not so strange that something still lingers, as that so much has already gone."

I did not go with him to the station. Much time is wasted in a very wearisome manner by kindly people in seeing other kindly people get into a railway carriage. I had promised to run down for a week-end at the cottage in a fortnight's time. Meanwhile I thought I was to have a rest from a trying and rather revolting business. I turned to that manuscript diary of which I have spoken, and resumed my work on it. I must have become rather absorbed in it. I have a faint recollection of telling my servant that I would not take tea and did not want to be bothered.

It was seven o'clock before I finally put down the thing and went to dress for dinner. The window of my bedroom as usual stood open. Outside in the street I could hear the newspaper boys crying, "Disaster on the Great Western Railway."

CHAPTER XVII

I could learn very little more that night. I got all the evening papers, of course, but the notices were very scanty, and did not in details agree with one another. The train in which Myas-Lade had travelled had been wrecked. He might or might not be dead. My first impulse was to go off at once to Paddington and see what details they had, but I did not go, and I think my second thoughts were the wiser.

The morning papers gave fuller information. The accident had been due to the error of a signalman. The human machine, however near perfection, is never quite perfect. Considering the nature of the accident, the number of those actually killed was very small. Among the headlines of the account I read, "Sensational Discovery—Unknown Woman Disguised as a Man." Myas-Lade had been killed, his face being rendered unrecognizable. The railway authorities were doing their best to trace his identity.

What was I to do? Again I did not follow my first impulse. My first impulse was to go down and claim the body and see that it had decent burial. Then I saw that would not do at all. In the trail of identification would come explanation, and the secrecy on which Myas-Lade had so strongly insisted would be lost. It seemed to me, right or wrong, that I carried out his wishes best if I did absolutely nothing.

The evening papers had further details of that sensational discovery. The handkerchief and linen of the dead girl bore the initials M. D. The man's clothing which she was wearing was absolutely new. There was a further supply of new clothing found in luggage which almost certainly belonged to her. It bore the same initials, contained clothes which would have fitted her, and had not been otherwise claimed. A later edition said it had been possible to find the stores from which the clothes had been bought, the name being on the buttons, and there was a short interview with the assistant who had actually sold the things. He maintained stoutly that the person to whom he sold them was beyond question a man, and moreover a man who could not have worn those clothes himself. He gave a description of my personal appearance, which was flattering but inaccurate. So far as I was concerned, I felt no nervousness about being drawn into the affair. I have no eccentricities. I dress exactly like other men in the same position as myself. Myas used to chaff me rather bitterly about my passion for resembling other people. I had paid cash for the clothes, given no name or address, and taken the things away myself. Unless they found the cabman who had driven me on that occasion, there was no possibility that the true story would come to light.

The real cabman never came forward. Another cabman did provide a somewhat wild story. He had driven two people, he said, on that afternoon from the stores to a spot on Wimbledon Common. There he had been dismissed and had been paid double his fare. One of the two people answered to the assistant's description of myself, and the other was a girl. His story did not bear examination. It was excessively vague. The only definite thing about him was his desire to make a pound or two out of an evening paper.

I did not attend the inquest, but I was present at the funeral. The body was decently buried at the expense of the railway company, and was followed to the grave by a crowd of people who had never known Myas nor Alice Lade. The effect of a sensational story on an uneducated mind is really very astonishing. Some of these absolute strangers had even sent expensive floral tributes. I wrote to my servants at the cottage that my friend had changed his mind at the last moment and had decided not to go down to the country after all. Old Welsford still quotes this occasionally in his more pious moments on Sunday afternoon, as an instance of what he calls a special providence. I wrote at the same time to Mrs. Lade in America, and gave her a very bad account of her daughter's health. I wanted gradually to prepare her for the news of the death. She wrote back that this was only what she had expected, and that she knew she would never see Alice alive again. It was a comfort to her that I was looking after the girl, and she was sure she could trust me to do all that could be done. She seemed to have grown very fond of her little nephews and nieces, of whom she gave me particulars. She added that she liked America, but that breakfasts there seemed to be a very different thing. It was a simple, kindly letter, and I liked it for its simplicity. Any fool can punctuate, and Mrs. Lade's pages were innocent of all punctuation, but that gift of simplicity is much rarer. It was the one distinguished thing about her.

Thus, in two graves many miles apart, lie the body of a man who loved knowledge and of the woman who loved that man. I do not know whether it is a vain hope that somewhere in the hereafter their souls have met and put old mistakes right again. It is not a thing that one can know, but I confess to the hope. And with that I close all that I can say at present of Daniel Myas and Alice Lade, and turn once more to devote myself to my more important historical work.

Postscript

I

Four years have elapsed since I put down in a rough and ready way my experiences of Dr. Daniel Myas and Alice Lade. It seemed to me at that time that the problem was ended. The body and mind of both of them had suffered what is known as death; their souls were no longer cognizable on this earth.

But since I closed the record, I have been on several occasions tempted to reopen it. There was that extraordinary letter I received from Vulsame, and my strange glimpse of him on the beach at Brighton. There was the long and interesting conversation which I had with Dr. Habaden on the experiment of Myas and the part I had played in connection with it. There was the incident of the telephone message, which is still to me quite inexplicable. I have decided to make a brief note of these things, and there are reasons why it must be done at once. I have been suffering from a revival and extension of the old trouble, which many years ago shut me out from the profession of my choice, and from other things which would have made life more enjoyable. Dr. Habaden and the other doctors whom he has seen in consultation take a serious view of the case and are in practical agreement about it. As I am not a particularly timid or hysterical person, I have persuaded them to speak quite frankly to me. Their verdict is that with care I may last for another six months. Old bachelors like myself are liable to acquire habits of almost absurd punctiliousness and tidiness. I have the feeling that I should like to leave this record finished as far as I can finish it. But I have no exaggerated ideas about it. I do not suppose that the facts with reference to Dr. Myas recorded by me would be of the slightest value to any scientific investigator in his particular field of research. I deprecate research in that field altogether. I would prevent it as I would prevent a child from playing with fire. I have seen the horror of it, and I have grown to hate it. It is not only of the case of Dr. Myas I am thinking, as I say this. I have seen in other instances how that enthusiasm for the sealed and hidden knowledge has led to disaster—to madness and to suicide.

II

About six months after the railway accident, I received a letter signed G. W. Vulsame, which was rather surprising. Perhaps the most surprising point about it was that it contained a cheque to myself signed by him for the sum of forty-eight pounds ten shillings. He told me that he had disposed of his practice, and that he was now acting as assistant to a doctor in Whitechapel. He said that he had to acknowledge with the deepest shame and contrition that he had swindled me. It was to some extent true that the experiments of Myas had caused injurious talk in the neighbourhood, but it was also true that he had already received full compensation from Myas on this account. The decay of his practice was, he said, in reality due to his own drinking habits, which he had now happily overcome. "But," he wrote, "I do not suppose for one moment that you were deceived. You did not pay this money as compensation, you paid it as a bribe to me to hold my tongue. You put temptation in my way and I fell. My conscience commands me to restore this money. I have not the sum of three hundred pounds at present, but I send a first instalment. I will send the rest, as soon as I can save it from the proceeds of my work. It is not for me to judge you for your part in this business, but if your conscience is not atrophied by years of the life of a selfish worldling, you will reproach yourself. Oh, my dear Mr. Compton, I do wish you would let me come and see you. Any appointment you like to make I would keep with gratitude. I am so anxious to bring you to the only true and lasting happiness."

There was another page or two of the same kind of material. I returned him his cheque, and wrote that my conscience did not trouble me in the least with reference to that payment of three hundred pounds, that I declined to receive any part of it back, and that he had better devote the money, if he wished to get rid of it, to some other object. I also said that I did not wish to see him, and that I had given instructions to my servants that he was not to be admitted. There was something about the man, whether drunken and ebullient, or sober and didactic, that annoyed me extremely. It was a positive satisfaction to me to be rude to him. He further infuriated me by a brief and unnecessary reply to my letter, in which he said that I had his full forgiveness.

In the summer of the following year, I had brought my car from Gloucestershire to London, and ran down to Brighton for a week-end. I had a friend of mine with me, a man who was a mighty walker, and on Sunday morning he made me walk over the Downs with him to Lewes. We lunched there and walked back by a different route. The weather was quite perfect, and if my friend had not bored me slightly by his insistence on the good the exercise was doing me, I should have enjoyed it extremely. As we came back along the King's Road to the hotel, I heard the usual cacophony that betokens that a section of the Salvation Army has got to work. They were perverting the beautiful melody of "Drink to me only with thine eyes" to the words of a hymn. As this finished, a voice that I recognized at once rang out in clear and commanding tones. I turned to my friend.

"I know that man who is speaking," I said. "I want to go down and listen to him. He interests me."

"By all means. You will excuse me if he doesn't interest me, won't you? I'll go on to the hotel."

"Right. We'll meet at dinner."

The little group of earnest people on the beach below me were mostly of a low type. They had the crooked faces and stunted frames of degenerates. Still, I want to be quite fair, and I must say that Vulsame, the speaker, seemed to me to have improved immensely. He had lost his bloated look. He had gained something which he had never had before, an air of sincerity. His face was white, his eyes were fanatical. I did not wish him to recognize me, and when I went down on to the beach I took up my position behind him. He was giving, in much detail and with some self-complacency, an account of his own transgressions. This led him to speak of other sinners that he had known. Soon, to my amazement, he was launched on a somewhat fanciful portrait of myself. He considerably overstated my income and my other worldly advantages. He imputed to me a villainy which would require far more of the romantic spirit than my very ordinary nature possesses. His final verdict that I must have led thousands astray was, I think, quite unjust. Every moment I expected to hear him roar out my actual name to the gaping housemaids in his audience. But in this respect he spared me. His moral was that there were many men like myself, not criminals in the eyes of the law, and on the contrary enjoying high positions and the respect of their fellows, who were none the less lost for ever. There was only one supreme satisfaction, and these poor wretches had never found it. He said that he himself had sought that satisfaction in the pursuit of knowledge and in the pursuit of pleasure, and it was not there. He went on to make a fervent appeal to his audience, with no rhetorical skill, but with the most desperate sincerity. Perspiration streamed from his forehead, tears stood in his eyes. Presently, as the band showed signs of renewed activity, I strolled away. I have not since then seen Vulsame again, nor have I heard any further news of him. I have often wondered what became of him—whether, as seems more probable, he had a further relapse, or whether, as is not impossible, there was some further advance and he is now a good Catholic.

But the thing which struck me most—the thought which haunted me at dinner that night—was that here, by some magic touch, had come a change of personality. The Vulsame that I had just seen was not the man that I had seen before. It was a different being. I suppose that to some extent a similar change goes on in all of us. The tissues of the body waste and are renewed. The personality changes with it. What has the child of six in common with the man of sixty that he subsequently becomes? Was the miracle that Myas tried to effect any more wonderful than that normal miracle which is going on every day in all of us? It is strange how we cling to a belief in a permanent personality. Life everlasting means little to most of us, unless it be the life everlasting of the individual.

Can one believe in that? It may occur to my readers that at a later point an answer to this question was given me.

III

One evening in that year it happened that my old friend, Dr. Habaden, was dining with me alone and chanced to speak of Daniel Myas.

"You knew him, I think. What became of him?"

In answer I told him for the first time, very much as I have set it down here, the story of Daniel Myas and Alice Lade. He did not seem greatly surprised. I suppose that these accomplished men of medicine are rarely surprised. His attitude to me was rather one of irritation. He was angry with me.

"Really, Compton," he said, "it seems to me that you've been taking too much upon yourself. Self-confidence is all very well, but it has its limits. You are a layman, and could not be supposed to understand the problem that was before you. But why, knowing yourself to be ignorant, did you not apply to somebody with some knowledge of the subject? Putting it plainly, why on earth, when some appearance of the personality of Myas began to show itself in this Lade girl, did you not consult me?"

"Well, I did not consider it to be some appearance of a personality. I considered it to be the actual thing."

"Nonsense," said Habaden impatiently.

"Then again, it seemed to me to be a thing entirely outside your beat. If I were ill, I should come to you. But how does your special knowledge bear on an exchange of souls? I am an ignorant layman, as you say, but I am quite willing to learn anything that you can teach. What is your view of the case?"

"The only possible view. Myas was a clever man, as I have always admitted to you. And I have no doubt that he was sincere. He probably did believe that by some fantastic method of his own—some weird game with electrical apparatus—this exchange of personalities could under certain conditions be accomplished. Anæsthesis was one of the conditions. His ideas were quite wild and undisciplined, and he was trying to do a thing that is not possible and never has been and never will be. He died in the attempt. Make no mistake about that. Myas died from the effects of the chloride of ethyl. It is dangerous stuff. We use it as a spray to produce local anæsthesis mostly. His soul, if he had a soul, may have gone through various adventures, of which neither I nor anybody else can possibly know anything. But the one thing which is quite certain is that his soul did not enter into possession of the mind and body of Alice Lade."

"Very well. And now, perhaps, you will account for Alice Lade as I saw her in the laboratory that night."

"Certainly I will. What you witnessed was very much less unusual than you think. There are many similar cases of double personality on record, though I admit that the case of Alice Lade has its peculiar and interesting features. There is nothing surprising in the fact that she should have suffered from mental disorder. You know, as well as I do, that every anæsthetic produces a temporary disorder of the mind. This disorder may become in part, and sometimes does become, permanent and persistent. It was not the first time that Myas had given an anæsthetic to that poor girl. On your own showing he had done so frequently. The shock of his death provides another possible cause, especially when one considers the circumstances of it and her devotion to him. The person you saw in the laboratory that night was Alice Lade and nobody else, but it was Alice Lade with a fixed delusion that she was Daniel Myas, and with some very curious but quite unconvincing physical evidence to show for her belief. As I have said, it was a case of double personality."

"You have come across such cases before?"

"They are not in my line. They would not be brought to me. But I have read of them, and I know doctors who have seen them. For instance, a girl who is morose and well educated wakes up one morning as a totally different person. She is now very cheerful, but absolutely ignorant of the things she knew previously. Sometimes the two states alternate. Sometimes in one state the subject has no memory whatever of what has happened in the other. The thing is explained to my mind by the theory of complete somnambulism. Alice Lade was a case for medical treatment. In fostering her delusion, and in allowing her to dress as a man and to go off by herself, you did very wrong."

"Habaden," I said, "the fact that there have been similar cases and that they have been classified, does not impress me very much. Classification is not explanation. You talk about absolute somnambulism. That is, I suppose, the regulation thing, the accepted theory, but I cannot see that it removes the difficulty. When science cannot remove a difficulty, it invents another name for it and is quite satisfied. I almost wish now that I had brought Alice Lade, if it was really Alice Lade, to you. Previous to the death of Myas, Alice Lade knew little or no French. She did not speak it at all. She could not understand it when it was spoken. After the death of Myas, that night when I saw her in the laboratory, she spoke French fluently and perfectly, as Myas himself did. Does somnambulism explain that?"

"No, my dear fellow, but unconscious memory does. There seems to be practically no limit to what the unconscious memory can do. I could give you twenty recorded cases of it, which to you or any other layman would seem almost miraculous. Alice Lade had heard you and Myas talking French together. She had unconsciously remembered the sounds she heard."

"Afraid it won't do, Habaden, unless she also unconsciously understood the meaning and the grammar. The French she spoke to me that night was not a repetition of sounds which she might have heard before. She was expressing her thoughts at the moment correctly. However, I need not labour that point. Do you suppose that Myas and I would ever have spoken French in the presence of that girl, knowing that she did not understand it? Can you suspect us of anything so vulgar and barbarous?"

"Very well. Either you or somebody else must have spoken French in her hearing, because that is the only possible explanation."

"And that," I said, "is about the least logical observation I ever heard from you, and a man of science should be ashamed of it."

"I know what I know," said Habaden dogmatically. "You can give me no other explanation that is as good. For that matter, how do you know that Myas himself did not teach the girl French? He was educating her, you say."

"I am sure that if he had been teaching her French, he would have mentioned it to me. He was educating her only for his own special purpose. And for that special purpose the usual routine of a girl's education would have been quite ineffective."

"Oh, well, it is not only from the medical point of view that you have been wrong, Compton. You have been too sure of yourself. You have taken your own way in a manner that seems to me almost unscrupulous. What right had you got to bribe Vulsame to suppress evidence at the inquest? Why did you lose your temper with him and assault him? What business had you got to allow the body of Alice Lade to go unclaimed and to be buried like the body of a pauper? And what about her money? I suppose you have found some equally high-handed way of dealing with that."

"Well, I think I can give an answer to all your questions. I suppose it was illegal to bribe Vulsame to suppress evidence. All I can say is that I don't care. It was the right thing to do. I knew perfectly well that Alice Lade did not murder Daniel Myas, and I was determined that she should not suffer from the suspicion of it. Nor am I in the least ashamed that I hit the man. If he ever repeated that swinish innuendo to me, I should hit him again. The body of Alice Lade went unclaimed, because I felt certain that it would be in accordance with her wishes and the wishes of Daniel Myas, and I did not see that anybody else was concerned in the matter. It is not true, by the way, to say that she was buried like a pauper. As to her money, I suppose you will think that my way of dealing with that was high-handed. It seems to me to be all right. She left no will, and as sole trustee for her and with a full power of attorney from her, I exercised my discretion. Everything was realized, and the money sent out to Mrs. Lade in New York. I have her receipts and the trust accounts, if you care to look at them."

"Don't be an ass. You know perfectly what I am accusing you of—of taking too much into your own hands, and overriding the law of the land. How did you manage about the Chancellor of the Exchequer? Have you sent conscience-money?"

"I have not, and I intend to send none. If, as I believe, the person who died in that railway accident was Daniel Myas, the duties are already paid."

"But it was not. It was Alice Lade and nobody else."

"There we are back again at our first point of difference. I do not believe it was Alice Lade. It was the body of Alice Lade, if you like. It wrote with the hand of Myas. It spoke with the voice of Myas. Its actions were guided by the soul and personality of Myas. That is what I believe. You, of course, consider it a fairy tale."

"Frankly, I do. But it is no use to discuss it. You have come to a pig-headed conclusion on a subject you have never studied."

"Nor have you ever studied it, my friend—for the simple reason that you have never had the chance to study it. This is something which has not occurred before in the world."

We went on to speak of other subjects, and perhaps it was just as well. Neither of us had made the least impression on the other.

IV

I have the habit of sitting up late at night, and have always had it. It is, I believe, generally supposed to be a bad habit, but I have never found out on what grounds. Probably the supposition is that it is invariably accompanied by dissipation and excess, but in my case that supposition would be incorrect. I do not want to be self-righteous. The simple fact is that dissipation and excess have never amused me at all. I appreciate the good things of life, and know that too much of them spoils the appreciation.

In my library at St. James's Place I have a telephone extension. It can be disconnected or connected at will from the main instrument. After ten at night I have this extension connected up. My servants go to bed, and if the telephone rings I can attend to it myself.

Some months after my conversation with Dr. Habaden I dined one night at the club, played three rubbers afterwards, and walked back to my rooms. I changed my coat and sat down by the reading-lamp with a bundle of documents to examine. They had been sent me by the same man who sent me the Peninsular War Diary, and consisted principally of letters of the same period. Many of these letters were extremely difficult to read. They were written on both sides of the sheet in faded ink. The paper was thin, and the writing was often crossed. When I found any letter which seemed likely to be of some use for my purpose, I made a rough transcript of it in pencil. I had to work with a magnifying-glass, and one may readily believe that my attention was entirely absorbed. I may add that at this time I was in fairly good health, and so far as my memory serves me, no thought of Myas or Alice Lade had entered my mind that day.

As I was working, the telephone bell began to bother me. It did not ring outright. It gave a faint tink-tink at intervals. It had happened before, and I had been told that it was due to wires touching, and that consequently a high wind often caused it. But I personally know nothing whatever about these things. I picked up the receiver, because this continuous tink-tink annoyed and interrupted me. I wanted to complain to the exchange. For twenty seconds, perhaps, I heard nothing whatever, and was irritated by the delay, and then came a gentle sound as of someone sighing.

"Look here," I said. "I want to complain about this telephone. Are you the right person to attend to it?"

The answer came very slowly, with a long wait between the words. It was a voice that I knew perfectly well.

"I am Alice Lade."

"Yes. Go on, please," I said.

She told me that it was only with extreme difficulty she managed to make words and get them heard by me. She thanked me for what I had done. She told me to worry no longer about the difficulties of the case, and that in a very short time I should understand.

"Tell me of Myas," I said.

The voice became so faint that I could hardly hear it. It is my impression that the words were these: "I am Daniel Myas and I am Alice Lade." After that there was no sound at all. I tried to call the attention of the exchange and failed. Suddenly an idea occurred to me. I went out to the telephone in the hall. I saw then that the extension in the library was disconnected. My servant on going to bed had forgotten to switch me on.

I left it disconnected and went back to the library. I put away my papers, mixed myself a brandy-and-soda, lit a pipe and sat down to wait. For nearly an hour everything was quite silent, and then very faintly the bell sounded twice. I lifted the receiver and heard a sound like a woman sobbing. The only word that I could catch was "Cannot" twice repeated. The sound broke off suddenly, and after waiting a few seconds I hung the receiver up again and went back to my easy-chair. There I waited for another hour with no result, and then went to bed.

It is difficult to describe exactly what my sensations were. Certainly they had in them nothing of the horror tinged with disgust that I had experienced that night in the laboratory in the garden. They were not feelings of fear exactly, but rather of awe. Later, as I was undressing, together with that awe came something like a feeling of triumph. What would my friend Dr. Habaden have to say to this? What would be his facile explanation? How would he classify it?

I wanted to be quite certain that I had made no mistake and had observed correctly, so as my man was putting out my clothes next morning, I said, "You forgot to connect the telephone up to me last night."

"Yes, sir," he said. "Almost the first thing I noticed this morning. Sorry, sir. Don't think I ever missed that before."

That morning, as it chanced, I met Dr. Habaden in Albemarle Street and stopped him for a moment. "I want to have a talk with you some time," I said.

"Right," said Habaden. "I've got a couple of doctors dining with me to-night. You had better join us. They will probably talk their own shop a good deal, but you won't mind that. They always leave early, and then we can have our talk."

It was rather a nuisance. I had asked a man to dine with me at the club that night. However, it would be easy enough to telephone that I had given him the wrong date by mistake, and I accepted Habaden's invitation.

It happened very much as he said. When dinner was over, these men, who were keen on their profession, did begin to discuss a medical question. To be precise, they were discussing whether the accepted view as to the normal position of the human stomach was really correct. It always interests me to hear people talking when they know what they are talking about, and I listened with interest. It was while Habaden was speaking that the light suddenly broke in on me.

"Well," he was saying, as he described a case, "we percussed him out, marked with the blue pencil and filled him up with bismuth."

Suddenly I saw the whole uselessness of it. I got his special matter-of-fact way of looking at things. I knew beyond a shadow of doubt what his explanation would be. He would simply say that I was suffering from an auditory delusion, and would make wise recommendations.

When the other two men had gone, he turned to me and said, "Now then, Compton, what was it you wanted to ask me?"

"Nothing really of very great importance, and, as it happens, it no longer matters. It was about a young chap who has been trained as a chauffeur. Some friends of mine are interested in him and asked me if I knew of a berth. He seems to be a first-rate man, and I thought perhaps you or some of your friends in Harley Street might take him on. However, just as I was starting for dinner to-night, I heard on the telephone that he has already got a situation."

"A pity," said Habaden. "I could have placed him. There are not so many really good drivers. By the way, Compton, any further news of the mysterious Myas?"

"No," I said. "I am not going to worry about that any more. My historical work takes up most of my time now. I have got some mighty interesting letters of the Duke of Wellington's that I should like you to see."

It was later that night that I fell ill again.

V

I write these last few pages at my cottage on Consay Hill. I have got rid of my flat in St. James's Place, sold the furniture and even sold by far the greater part of my library. When the doctors say that a man has only a few months to live, property presents very little attraction. It seemed best to turn it into money and leave it on deposit at the bank, and in this way to save my executors some trouble. I saw the collections of many years dispersed in the auction-room in one afternoon, and watched it all without the slightest pang. "Man wants but little here below."

It is quite with the approval of the doctors that I have given up

London and come down into the country. So far as anything can be good for me, I suppose the quiet and the purer air are good for me. But I have come here much more to please myself than to please the doctors. The fact of the case is that the ordinary routine of life—especially when it has been such a worthless and useless routine as in my case—is not endurable in the face of death. I came here by easy stages, taking three days to do it, in a luxurious car with old Habaden to accompany me. I got through it all right, and now that I am here I really suffer very few limitations. I am not confined to my bed. I can walk in the garden, or even take a short stroll across the common land beyond it. Nominally the number of cigarettes that I may smoke per diem is very strictly limited. In practice I do not worry very much about that or any other medical limitation. I smoke when I want to smoke. The time is very short in any case, and one does not want to be grasping about the last moments.

In one respect my illness has been rather a revelation to me. I knew that I had many acquaintances, but I had not the slightest idea that I had so many friends. I am by no means left continuously alone here. Busy men waste their time by coming down from town to see me. Sometimes they bring with them suggestions for a change of treatment. They tell me wonderful stories of unexpected recoveries. They are uniformly and horribly hopeful. Old Habaden has been among the best of them. He has discovered suddenly that it is good for his health to spend the weekend here. He has acquired quite a new manner of talking to me. He treats my opinions with deference. He no longer lectures me. It is really rather pathetic, because, of course, where he disagreed with me before he still disagrees with me. Only he thinks it might annoy me if he said so. Neither that nor anything else will annoy me any more.

The weather has been very good this spring. There have been many warm and sunny days, and I have spent most of them out of doors in the garden. A long terraced walk gives me a fine view of the valley below. Down there among the trees an excellent trout stream runs. I have the fishing rights over some miles of it, and I shall never cast a fly there again. However, it gives my guests from London something to do, and saves them some hours of their self-inflicted boredom. Old Welsford has made this garden very charming. I like his high walls and archways of clipped yew.

"What are you going to do with that bit you've left sticking up there?" I asked him.

"I'm working on that, sir," said Welsford. "It's coming into shape already. In a year or two that will be a peacock."

It really seemed rather absurd that I should not see that peacock. I think if I had my choice I would sooner die out here in the garden than in my bed indoors, and it is quite probable that the end will come as I desire. It will be quick. I shall just throw up my hands and drop. And yet this is not a subject about which I think very much. Far more often I find myself still acting and speaking as if I had a year or more before me. For instance, I find old Welsford working in the garden and give him directions. I watch carefully to see them carried out, and feel glad that the result will be good in the flower or fruit. It will perhaps not be till some minutes afterwards that I will suddenly burst out laughing at my own silliness. Of course, whatever the result is I shall not see it. I often wish now that I had spent more of my time in this garden. During the greater part of the week I am alone, but I never find myself bored here at all. I have more books than I shall have time to read, and I have this writing to finish. It even pleases me to sit on the terrace in the sun and to do absolutely nothing—except to watch the cloud-shadows chasing one another over the pale bracken, or the sparkle of light on the water below in the valley.

Dying men are made much of. They get the idea that they matter. Perhaps that is the reason why I have been so egotistical. Yet it is not my own story that I wish to tell here.

It is an old idea that at the approach of death one may become endowed with spiritual powers of perception, of which one was previously unconscious. It may be—and I suppose it is more likely—that when the body is ill, the mind is no longer to be trusted, and that one has illusions. I write down quite simply that I have seen within the last few days Daniel Myas and Alice Lade, but I have not said a word to anyone about it. I can see old Habaden stroking his pointed grey beard and saying humbly that my experience is really very extraordinary. And I can imagine tactful questions which would follow, in order to find out if I had suffered from any other form of illusion. I cannot say myself what I actually believe about it. My opinion changes. At times I seem to know definitely that I did see them, and at other times I can put the thing aside and call it, as Habaden would probably call it in private, merely symptomatical.

It was early in the morning between five and six o'clock. Unable to sleep any longer, I had got up and dressed and gone out into the garden. A great deal of mist hung over the hill, not in one unbroken mass, but in flying patches. Sometimes they melted and joined together. Sometimes they seemed to open out like a flower and then vanish in the sunlight. I stood watching the scene for some time, and then I made my way slowly up to the top end of the garden. There is a door here in the high wall, which leads out on to the common. It is kept locked at night, of course, but I had my keys with me. I opened the door, and immediately, within five yards of me and standing with their faces towards me, I saw Myas and Alice Lade.

I saw them for a few seconds only. They had not the appearance of ghosts—filmy things. They looked solid and natural. Afterwards, when I tried to recall everything that I had seen, I noted one point particularly. They were exactly as they had been when I first saw them. Myas was bare-headed, but he wore that flowing necktie which I persuaded him to abandon when he came to London, and looked as young as on the day when I saw him at the Hamiltons'. Alice Lade was in a poor sort of grey dress. It was the dress she had worn when I saw her in the little room behind the shop in Knox Street. The sunlight shone on the red-gold of her hair in a way that lent realism to the picture. The expression on the faces of both of them was similar, and was moreover rather curious. It was the expression of someone who welcomes a person with a smile. The effect upon myself was rather curious also. I had not the slightest feeling of fear. I walked rapidly towards them with my hand outstretched. It was only when they vanished that I began to be afraid. Close to me a couple of sheep moved among the bracken, hidden from sight by it, and their movement startled me. I went back into the garden to my seat on the terrace.

It was impossible for me at first to believe that I had suffered from any delusion, or that my imagination had shaped the flying mists on the hill-side into human forms. I told myself that it was delusion, but I could not make myself believe it. Her hair had caught the sunlight just as it would have done if she had been actually there. Their bodies had not been transparent and had shut out what was actually behind them. That expression of welcome was to me consolatory. I liked it. It seemed to approve of all that I had done. After I had rested for a few moments, I once more went out on to the common, in the hope that I might see them again. I even called to them, not loudly, by name. But that morning nothing further occurred.

Since then I have twice thought that I saw them, but never with the same clearness or with the same feeling of certainty as on that early morning. I have seen them as figures at a distance in the dusk of the evening. I have seen them amid the trees of a wood on the hill-side. In both these cases I could readily believe it to be a mistake of my senses. But on that early morning it still seems to me at times that there was no mistake, and that I did in reality see them.

This view is strengthened by a conviction for which I can give no reason. It has been born in me and it grows stronger every day. I believe in it, as I believe in my own existence. It is a conviction that the story of Myas and Alice Lade is not yet finished, and that at some future time I shall take part in that story.

I suppose no man goes through life without at some time trying to picture what happens after death. Because we do not know, we take an analogy and make a guess. For a long time it satisfied me to think that just as all the rivers run into the sea, so all the personalities are hereafter merged into that of a supreme being. I find myself unable any longer to hold that theory. It had its philosophical consolations for me. I had missed most of the best things that life holds. My own personality had been baulked and insignificant. I believed that death ended it, partly, perhaps, because I wished death to end it.

As I have said, I can no longer hold that belief, though I can give little plausible reason for the change in me. The fact remains that I face death with some of that feeling of pleasurable excitement with which one starts out on a journey that promises new sights and new adventures.

What awaits me on that journey must necessarily be beyond my power to imagine. The souls of the dead are cognizable, not by body nor by mind, but in some way beyond human experience or thought. It was, I think, with great difficulty that these two people, whom I shall shortly rejoin, sent me any message from the life beyond. The message came in a form that science would call illusion. It may be. It does not necessarily seem to me to condemn it. It does not lessen in the least the hold it has upon me, and my conviction that I shall now begin rather than end my story.

Thus, then, I start out with pretty good hopes—*per iter tenebricosum unde negant redire quemquam.*

Breinigsville, PA USA
24 December 2009

229731BV00001B/2/A

LAZARUS

LAZARUS

HENRI BÉRAUD
Translated by Eric Sutton

With an Introduction by S. T. Joshi

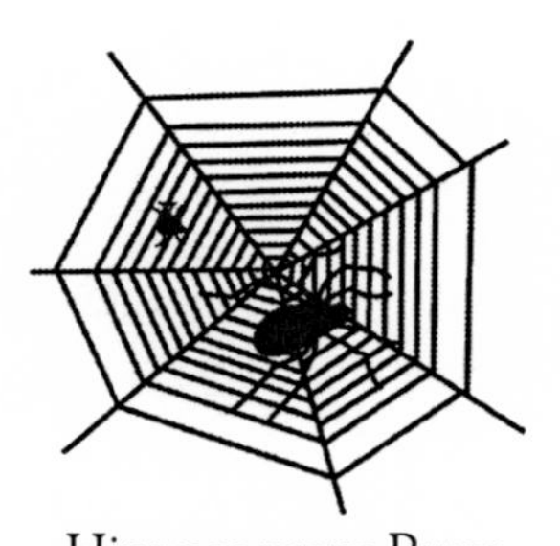

Hippocampus Press

New York

Published by Hippocampus Press
P.O. Box 641, New York, NY 10156.
http://www.hippocampuspress.com

"The Raising of Lazarus" by Ralph Fabri is used by permission of Phyl Newbeck and the Georgetown University Library, Special Collections Division. Cover design and Lovecraft series logo by Barbara Briggs Silbert.

Hippocampus Press logo designed by Anastasia Damianakos.

First Edition
1 3 5 7 9 8 6 4 2

ISBN: 0-9771734-4-5
ISBN-13: 978-0-9771734-4-0

Introduction

In Henri Béraud's *Lazarus* (1925) we have a case where both the author and his work are now virtually forgotten. Béraud (1885–1958) himself proves to be of some interest in his own right, not so much for his prolific writing (even though he won the prestigious Prix Goncourt in 1922), but because in the 1930s he joined the French fascist movement and later collaborated with the Nazis. He was condemned to death for treason in 1944, but his sentence was commuted; he was placed in prison and finally released in 1950.

Béraud wrote voluminously—chiefly historical novels, travel books, and political tracts. The novel *Lazare* (1924) was one of the earliest of his writings, but the author's momentary celebrity caused it to be among the first of his works to be translated into English. It appears to be Béraud's sole excursion into weird fiction.

This novel presents a man, Jean Mourin, who remains in a hospital for sixteen years (for the period 1906–22) while suffering a long amnesia; during this time he develops a personality (named Gervais by the hospital staff) very different from that of his usual self. Every now and then this alternate personality returns; once Jean thinks he sees Gervais when he looks in the mirror, and later he thinks Gervais is stalking him. This simple outline ought to make it obvious to any well-informed reader that the novel bears a striking resemblance to Lovecraft's great late tale "The Shadow out of Time" (1934–35); indeed, the amnesia of Nathaniel Wingate Peaslee in that story occurs at approximately the same time as Mourin's (1908–13), although perhaps these dates have an autobiographical significance, as they correspond exactly to the period when Lovecraft himself, having had to withdraw from high school, descended into hermitry. Perhaps he had himself come to believe that another personality had taken over during this time.

Certainly it is not surprising that Lovecraft, when he read the novel in early 1928, wrote that it was "a remarkable study of a vivid phase of madness."[1] He had long been fascinated with the idea of mind-

---

[1] H. P. Lovecraft, Letter to August Derleth (c. February 1928), ms., State Historical Society of Wisconsin.

exchange, and "The Thing on the Doorstep" (1933) was manifestly influenced by a somewhat similar novel that Lovecraft had read, H. B. Drake's *The Shadowy Thing* (1928; first published as *The Remedy*, 1925). In that story, of course, the exchange of minds had occurred only between two human beings; in "The Shadow out of Time" he breathtakingly postulated exchange of personalities between a human being and an alien entity from the depths of space—and time. Could *Lazarus*, with its fascinating premise that what passes for amnesia is in fact the result of one personality ousting another, have given Lovecraft a plausible plot device to convey the essence of his own conception? Certainly, Jean Mourin's behaviour upon recovering his memory bears striking similarities to that of Peaslee; at one point Mourin, like Peaslee, even begins an historical study of past cases of split personalities in an attempt to account for his plight.

But *Lazarus* need not justify its continued existence merely as an adjunct to a more celebrated work. It is a gripping, intense novel in its own right, and some of the scenes and tableaux are as riveting as anything in Lovecraft. By focusing so intensely on Mourin's dazed and harried confusion, the novel develops an existential terror that even Lovecraft cannot match. One of the high points of the novel is when Mourin looks in a mirror and thinks he sees Gervais there:

> Jean who hoped he was mistaken managed to gather strength to look again. Might it not be a distortion of his own face produced by some effect of cross reflection? No: there are two faces: one pale and haggard, that of Jean Mourin, the other masculine and healthy, belonging to Gervais . . . He had to come back: and he had come. . . .
>
> But such things aren't possible! Gervais had no longer any real existence, Jean knew that perfectly well. If Gervais was to erturn Mourin would have to fall back into the abyss of madness.

The mingling of horror, pathos, confusion, and dramatic tension renders *Lazarus* a quiet triumph of the weird, even if nothing supernatural can be said to have occurred in it.

—S. T. JOSHI

LAZARUS

PART I

I

On the 13th of December, 1922, as night was falling, Jean Mourin awoke. As he shook off his torpor he felt as though he were climbing up the steps of an interminable staircase towards the daylight. For a long time a monotonous tapping sound had been breaking into his sleep: at last he recognised the noise of the rain against the window panes. Then a pinkish light seemed to penetrate his eyes: he opened them: everything round him was white and bare. He sat up with an effort. He recognised the place perfectly well though he had never seen it: it was the hospital.

Jean Mourin was waking up in a room in a hospital. He felt his shoulders, his stomach, the top of his head. Hurriedly he stretched and bent his limbs, like a swimmer. Nothing. He felt no discomfort, no fever.

He began to think. To wake up without knowing how or why in a room in a hospital, was this all? A feeling of rest, the softness of a sick bed, nothing more. He accepted his adventure calmly: what surprised and frightened him was rather, by a singular inversion, the fact that he was neither surprised nor frightened.

Jean was certain, absolutely certain, that he knew neither the brass and iron bedstead, the painted furniture, nor the high wall with its elongated crucifix, nor the number 67 pinned onto his linen curtains.

He could not remember ever having worn the coat and trousers of grey frieze thrown in disorder on to a chair, nor the heavy socks nor the slippers, nor carried that stick with its handle polished by use. And yet . . . All this seemed new and yet familiar. He passed his hand over his forehead, and tired of looking for an answer, lay down again.

He was alone, enveloped in a heavy silence save for the incessant and invisible patter of the rain against the windows as it fell from the dim sky. Darkness entered. On the table beside his bed Jean observed a reflector lamp which shed a crude light on to his pillow. There was no smell of drugs in the room, but there was an odour of tobacco. In a corner half hidden by the darkness was the shape of a door of which the upper part was of ground glass: doubtless it opened on to a badly lit passage, carpeted and rather narrow. Jean assumed this from the pass-

ing shadows which were outlined on the milky screen of the glass.

People came and went beside him; but he did not speak. He lay back motionless under the bed-clothes. The failing light affected his will. He felt swallowed up although he was strong, healthy, and rested. Then on his left, on the side opposite to the door, he heard something going on. People were talking behind the partition. The words were indistinct and the man in bed could not hear them; but he distinguished a woman's voice and several men's voices: probably the doctor on his rounds. Suddenly a short cry, some remonstrances, then orders in a tone of authority, a cough, footsteps, the sound of a latch, and silence once more.

Jean Mourin could bear it no longer. He called out with all his strength. As he did so the door opened and a Sister's cap appeared.

"Well! what is it?" she said. "You must keep quiet."

With one hand she tried to make the sick man lie down, and with the other she put the bed straight.

"Come, come now."

"Where am I?" said Jean Mourin. "What has happened?"

The Sister started, changed colour and dropped the bed-clothes.

"What!" she said: "you want to know . . .? He's coming back! He's speaking! Doctor, doctor!"

She ran to the door and disappeared down the corridor.

The man trembled as he lay on the bed.

A group of people entered the room.

"I want to know," he said, "tell me the truth . . ."

They came quickly up to the bed, and the doctor, whose name was Hugues, put his hands on Jean Mourin's head, turned it to the circle of light and looked deeply into his eyes. The group of students gathered closely round his white coat. The doctor frowned and shook his head gravely.

"Don't be impatient," he said quietly. "You will be told all. Is there anything you want?"

"I want to go away," said Jean Mourin. "Someone must tell my wife at home: at once! I don't know what has happened or why I am here. I feel quite well, perfectly well. Do let me go, doctor: I must go . . ."

He stopped. No one answered him. He noticed a sort of embarrassment in the silence. The doctor and the students seemed astonished to see him cured and to hear his voice: they avoided his question. But he wanted to know the truth: he insisted on it. An accident? What acci-

dent? An illness? What kind of illness?

"Don't excite yourself," said Dr. Hugues. "I promise you shall be told when the time comes."

And without a change of voice he turned to the students and added:

"Here we have what no one could have foretold. The older you get the more you will realise that you must reckon with this. Sister Céline, give him everything he wants. But—" and here he spoke with emphasis—"nothing that may excite him. Don't leave anything about, Sister—no newspapers. And—above all—quiet!"

They all went out except the Sister. She gently urged the sick man backward and made him lie down, lowered the lamp for the night and slipped noiselessly out of the room.

Outside the voices disappeared in the distance. Jean Mourin put his hands to his head and began to search for recollections in the obscure corners of his memory. He could not find the shock of any accident, or the feeling of discomfort that goes before an illness. Perhaps a sudden disaster—a fire, a fall, or an attack of madness—had destroyed the past. But apart from the fact that he was lying in a hospital bed he remembered a thousand perfectly connected events that had happened quite recently. Why yesterday, only yesterday, he had been having lunch as usual with his wife. He remembered even their conversation, their everyday conversation about music.

It was after this that there was a gap. A sort of sleep, a sudden dizzy collapse, blackness.

Jean Mourin sat up and turned up the light. He could bear it no longer. His veins were throbbing. He must get up and walk up and down. Anything rather than this immobility, this solitary struggle against the unknown.

He put on the blueish woollen clothes. Mechanically he felt in the pockets. They contained various things that belonged to him: a pencil-holder, a pocket book, a tuning fork, a briar pipe, a bunch of keys, a pair of smoked glasses, a pouch full of tobacco.

Standing up beside the bed he looked at the things which he placed one by one on the quilt: all these possessions seemed old, out of date. They must belong to someone happy and in good health, no longer to him. He shrugged his shoulders, put them all back in his pocket and raising his head looked in front of him.

Opposite, on the wall of the room, by the window against which

the rain was ceaselessly beating, was a dressing table and a looking glass. No. 67 went up to the looking glass and suddenly his whole body quivered.

What Jean Mourin saw clearly in the mirror *was the face of an unknown man.*

• • • • • • •

Staring into his own face he bent forward till his forehead nearly touched the glass. There were his own eyes, large, brown and a little troubled, and under them livid shadows stretched down towards his cheek. He went over his features one by one, feverishly scrutinising the mask before him, looking for the man that he had been. His beard had grown: short, hard, and grey, his face was framed in it. How white his hair had become—from some shock he supposed. As he carefully examined the face before him he gradually began to recognise his own features: the lines of his forehead, the corners of his lips and the join of the nose were more marked and the face as a whole had grown thinner. His complexion had lost its brightness: it was now a pale yellow fading into nearly white round the temples. His entire forehead seemed to have grown broader and higher, the arch of his eyebrows was harder and more definite while his mouth betrayed an indifference which was in the strangest contrast with the thoughtful and sad expression of his face as a whole.

Nevertheless he remembered clearly the exact appearance of his features. His face was clean shaven and of a rather rustic cast, relieved by his hair, which he wore long in the Liszt manner, as young musicians often will. His hair had been cut short by the same rough hand no doubt that had trimmed his stiff beard almost level with his face, like a thatch. Who would recognise the composer Jean Mourin under this semblance? Even his wife might find a difficulty.

This reflection suggested another. How did he come to be in a place like this without friend or family by his bedside? Perhaps they did not know he was ill. He would give his address and those of his friends. That would be soon done: he had so few. Lescot, old Lescot, would come at once: he would quickly leave on his table those orchestral scores of his that no player in theatre or concert hall would ever be troubled to make out: he would take up his hat and stick . . .

Though perhaps it might be better to send for Desnoyers the lawyer: he would know how to break the news to Jeanne and prepare her for the sight of a husband so prematurely aged; he would tell her the

truth tactfully and without unnecessary abruptness.

The truth! Jean Mourin stood beside his bed and searched for it in vain among the shadows of his recollection. He thought and thought until the effort grew painful.

The mind of the sick man was full of his wife Jeanne, her beloved name, her features, her tenderness. It seemed a long time since he had seen her: and yet it could only be yesterday. He searched his memory again: he struggled in a black chaos. But when he tried to penetrate the past, always at the same point he came upon this invisible impalpable wall, behind which was hidden what he had to find out, cost him what it might.

Yes, some appalling disaster must have happened to him. But why hide from him what he must sooner or later discover? Was he not well again? Here he was standing up firmly on his legs, nothing the matter with him. Of course. Then why were his wife and friends kept away from him?

But Jean Mourin, his back turned to the windows, could no longer hear the slightest noise outside his room. He stared in vain at the ground glass pane of the door. No shadows passed. He opened it.

Outside was a long corridor and on each side of it to left and right a line of white doors, all numbered. It was like a row of cabins in some great steamer. Some feeble lights faintly illuminated a long strip of carpet. The blinds shook as a sharp wind whistled through them. Just beside Room 67 another corridor turned off at right angles giving on to a deserted stairway a few steps further on. It must be the dinner hour in this white establishment.

The patient found the bell-button, but he thought:

"I will ring later on."

By this time he had reached the table and opened the drawer. In it were books, cotton, buttons, and one of those little linen bags used for drugs and medicaments. Jean Mourin picked it up. It contained some metal objects. Two women's rings, a wedding ring, a pendant, a brooch, a watch-bracelet, a little gold net purse.

Why did Jean feel a blow at his heart? Everything grew dark and yet in the depths of his consciousness there appeared a faint light. In the silence and solitude he stood there awaiting the revelation of some extraordinary event. These jewels, which he balanced in his hands, seemed as though they were in possession of a secret.

Sister Céline and the hospital orderly who came in on their rounds

a moment later found Jean Mourin standing up, motionless, like a statue in the darkness. He was holding a handful of jewels in his right hand: he would not answer any question: but he allowed himself to be undressed and put to bed like a child.

• • • • • • •

Later on when these hours of anguish had become a mere recollection, Jean Mourin found a note book in one of his pockets. The pages were covered with irregular writing, part of which was indecipherable. Here he had written down his impressions following his awakening at the hospital. A diary without times or dates, of which even the author had lost the thread.

"Where am I?" he wrote. "What hospital is this? *Is* it simply a hospital? The people around me seem to have an appearance of curiosity and also of apprehension which suggests a mad-house. I don't know. How should I?"

Here followed some lines crossed out and written over which he could not read. Then:—

"I feel surrounded with lies. They tell me lies everyone tells lies here, people and things. I feel surrounded by lies as a tree that does not thrive is packed in straw at the end of winter. I have questioned all of them; no use and I have given it up. Even things deceive me. Who put my pipe, my note book, my keys, my tuning fork in the pockets of this hospital uniform? How is it that these are things that belong to me, while I have never seen that stick and pipe and thimble? And when did Jeanne leave her jewels in the room? And why? We aren't rich but we are not poor. The hospital expenses would not trouble us. How is it?

"No answer to my questions, or only evasions."

Three pages savagely scratched out: then:—

"If this is to go on, I shall really go mad. I am well and cured, yet I am not allowed what is never refused to anyone who is ill. I am in complete control of myself. They admit it, but they forbid me the right to communicate with my own people. I cannot write to them. The injunctions of that ruffian Dr. Hugues are savagely obeyed. And, except the Sisters, everybody in this devilish place is strange to me. The doctor I have never seen again. The student who looks after me looks like a strolling player with that smooth face of his: insolent too!

"What can I do? Escape? I don't know the building and I should certainly be caught before I reached the gate.

"Besides I don't know what is going on outside. Even the date they

hide from me. The date! What sort of existence is this? I am a prisoner.

"And always these lies, that I feel everywhere, that stifle my life, and prevent me hearing the voices outside.

"It must stop."

The last pages of the note book were covered with figures and a strange drawing, the sort of thing that the fingers trace unconsciously when the mind is burdened by some gloomy preoccupation.

• • • • • • •

When Jean Mourin opened his eyes, on the morning of December 17th, he saw by the side of the student in his hospital jacket an attentive looking young man who seemed to be watching for him to awake. This individual was dressed in country clothes and was sitting down near the window. Jean Mourin looked him over but did not recognise him, and turned to the student. He had grown so nervous that he said abruptly:

"As you will not leave me alone even when I am asleep you ought to know why I am kept here against my will. Are they going to let me out or not?"

"Perhaps. It is nothing to do with me."

"I don't know why I am treated like this. All these lies, this silence . . ."

"Patience. The doctor will be here in a moment. He wants to talk to you himself."

"Words, nothing but words!"

The young man shook his head without replying. The room was full of a hostile silence. A motor horn sounded outside. A faint cold sunlight spread over the bare whiteness of the wall on the left hand side of the room above the head of the young visitor as he sat there motionless with his bag on his knees.

The sick man lay back again. His head with its greying hair pressed deeply into the pillow: his left hand with unconscious automatic movements twisted and untwisted the point of his beard.

The student, doubtless under orders, did not renew the conversation. But, as the sound of a step was heard he whispered:

"Here he is."

Dr. Hugues came in, followed by Sister Céline, whose cap fluttered like a sail against the sky.

Jean Mourin raised himself up and got a closer view of the doctor. He was a tall man, bald, vigorous, and of a rather forbidding appearance. He spoke in a military tone. Before addressing the sick man, he turned to his student.

"Nothing special?"

"Nothing."

He went up to the bed and seemed to hesitate.

"M. Mourin," he said after a silence, "do you feel strong enough to bear what we have to tell you?"

"I insist on the truth."

"You shall have it. But first I must ask you one question. Do you know how to make clothes? Could you make a garment like this?" He pointed to the hospital overall lying on a chair. "You think the question absurd?"

"Yes, absurd and out of place. You may not know it but I am a musician, quite well off enough to be able to go in for music and nothing else. My wife and I . . ."

"I know. You live at Meilles, near Paris. Yes. I am obliged to go on like this with questions. I am not asking you useless ones. Where do you think you are at this moment—I mean where do you think this house is? . . . Don't try and think. Do you know the Bourg d'Oisans road at Briancon?"

"Certainly."

The doctor stopped, as if to allow the man he was questioning time to recover his memory. Jean Mourin, with a troubled expression, his eyes fixed, was striving to read his own mind. He was now afraid of what might be said. He felt the secret within him surrounded by menace and horror. If he could only disentangle it himself, without help, and without the pain of being told. But he searched his memory in vain and after a silence he could only say, in a trembling voice:

"Yes, I know the Lantaret road. Well?"

You have been over it?"

"Yes, several times and quite recently."

"In a charabanc?"

"Certainly: what then?"

"You were with your wife?"

"Tell me, tell me, what is it?" cried the sick man.

The voice of the doctor did not change. He pressed his questions with quiet firmness.

"Now listen carefully. The last time, *the other day,* you left your house at Meilles for the Alps. Do you remember what you took with you?"

"Yes, of course. A small trunk and a knapsack."

"And then?"

"We took the nine-o'clock train and then crossed Paris in a cab. At the restaurant at the Lyons Station . . ."

The doctor interrupted.

"I wish you would tell me how you started off in the charabanc. It was . . .?"

"At Grenoble, in the Place des Alpes, as usual: just like every year when we started for Queyras."

"For Queyras?"

"Yes, of course."

"And . . ." the doctor said slowly, "do you know where you stopped this time?"

Jean Mourin trembled. He felt something like a shock go through him. His staring eyes gazed anxiously and fixedly into those of Dr. Hugues. But the effort soon became intolerable. He still wanted, in a feeble fury, to find and push aside the dark presences that kept the secret of his suffering. But his courage and strength failed him. He fell back gasping: but almost at once he sat up again.

Then something seemed to crack inside his head. It seemed as though a curtain had been suddenly drawn back *behind* his eyes: and Jean Mourin, bent and haggard, saw something that was known to him alone. He hid his head between his crossed arms that he might not suffer that vision again.

In a flash he saw it all once more. The departure of the charabanc at dawn in the square at Grenoble with all the lively tumult of the start of the *diligences* in old days. Seated at the side of Jeanne, Jean Mourin went through the streets of the still sleeping town, and past the military barracks whence came the sound of bugle calls. Then through the gates with their pyramids of cannon balls and on to the road that stretched out before the gaily moving car full of tourists that would never reach their journey's end.

Everything came back to him. The images projected on the screen of his memory grew clear and appeared in a definite succession. The moving landscape, the smoke rising from the hamlets down in the hollow of the valleys, the waterfalls breaking into floury dust over the rocks, the blue vapours and the scent of lavender rising from the Romanche.

The engine roars and hums. The car climbs like a giant insect up the capricious curves of the road, slips through tunnels, and dashes

hooting around the bends and over the bridges: the birds begin to twitter. Beyond Les Alberges the road narrows and skirts a precipice along the edge of which is a parapet reaching about knee-high. The *Infernet* it is called. This is the place. Here the journey will end.

While they were all looking at the snowy crests, far away, of the Barre-des-Ecrins, while they were singing and laughing, suddenly the landscape seemed to turn over. The car tipped up, and with a single movement of its huge vertebrae it leapt the parapet, and for the space of a breath, hung as it were suspended in space.

What followed seemed a mere dizzy confusion. The landscape turns over in the air and changes places with the sky, while the clouds and the blue heaven descend in a whirlwind to take the place of the red and blue carpet of the fields. Immediately the heavy car seems to be rushing up to a ceiling of trees, torrents, and houses while the sky falls away below with fearful, incredible speed. . . . A roof of dark green comes down swiftly on to the car. Bodies fall out, twist and turn round the hurtling mass. The vision cracks and goes blind. The speed of this endless fall increases as it meets a wind that blows from nowhere. Then a blow—a blow of unutterable violence striking the whole body at once.

After that, nothing.

Night.

• • • • • • •

Dr. Hugues had put his strong hand on to Jean's shoulder. Silent and grave he waited until Jean had ceased to gasp for breath.

His body was shaken by sobs like a succession of hiccoughs. He wept in paroxysms until he could not breathe, as children do. He called for his wife with confused and agonised words. Suddenly his cries stopped and he lay as if exhausted.

"Is she dead?"

The doctor bent his head. "Did she suffer?"

"Killed on the spot. You were the only one who escaped, Mourin: you fell first on a stack of straw. You were picked up by some peasants, your head split open, your legs broken and your reason gone. . . . And now try and pull yourself together."

"Yes," he said dully, "I can rely on my courage. I want to go home, doctor."

"Later on, later on. You can't go alone. One of your relatives, your only relation has come to see you."

"Relations," said Jean. "I did not know I had any since . . . My poor wife and I were orphans, without a family. There was only a child . . ."

"As soon as you were cured, the Superintendent had this young fellow here informed. He lives abroad and was in France by accident. Do you recognise him? Come nearer, sir."

The unknown came up to the bed.

"No," said Jean Mourin, "I don't know the young man."

"He is your brother-in-law."

"Who? I don't understand you. My brother-in-law, the brother of my wife?"

"Precisely."

"There is some mistake. Louis Thévenet, of whom you are speaking, was lodging this summer, at the time of the accident, with a country woman just outside Valence. He must be three and a half years old."

The young man stood in the light, with an awkward air and a questioning look at the doctor. The latter seemed to hesitate, then made up his mind.

"Do you remember," he said, "the exact date of the accident?"

"Wait a moment . . . it must have been June 14th."

"In what year?"

"This year, of course."

"And this year is . . ."

"1906."

"Mourin, you will need all your will-power. The time has come to tell you the whole truth. What I am going to say places all of us here outside the common laws of life. That man you see by your bed is really Louis Thévenet, your brother-in-law. Look at him, recognise him. He is going back to Canada tomorrow. Make an effort, as great an effort as you can. It is very important: do you recognise him?"

"I can only say that he is a stranger to me. My wife had a brother. I have told you his age."

Yet he felt uncomfortable. He recognised in the young man's face the glimmer of another look. Though he spoke with vehemence a doubt began to rise in his mind. He looked again at the so-called Thévenet and then at the doctor. What was this cruel game? Why were they putting him off, ill as he was, with this fresh deception? It was all pretence and concealment in this hospital. At each step Jean came up against invisible barriers, lies, always lies: or, if they were not lies . . .

"Am I losing my reason?" he murmured. "Is my mind so bound up

with memories of so long ago that I have forgotten what happened recently? Is that possible, doctor? Isn't it a fact that Louis Thévenet was only a child this summer? Have I been dreaming? Am I still dreaming? Once and for all I want to know everything."

"Well," said the doctor, "here is the truth. You remember the accident, in which you were nearly killed, happened on *June 14, 1906.* You are sure?"

"Yes."

"Read this."

The doctor held out a paper, his finger pointing to a corner of it on which Jean Mourin read *Dec. 17, 1922.*

He made no sign; he lay motionless, unseeing. But he felt as though his heart were going to burst within his breast.

He understood. As the doctor approached him he demanded silence with a gesture. Explanation was useless, it would only make *the* mystery more formidable. Jean Mourin would have nothing to do with the pathological scaffolding of his case.

He knew the kind of words that learned men throw like melancholy rockets into the darkness of human ignorance. What was the use? Alas, what was the use, since nothing could ever console him for a bereavement over which he had not wept and a life that he had lost. Perhaps he would forget his trouble if, instead of defining it in tortuous phrases, they left him the last resource of uncertainty. Perhaps in the future he might find the tranquility that follows an evil dream when without remembering the moment of his return to reality, the dreamer knows that his agony has passed with the shadows of the night.

"It is my duty . . ." began Dr. Hugues.

"No," cried Jean Mourin. "No, leave me alone."

"This is childish: listen to me. Even if your case seems to you extraordinary, there is nothing to frighten you. . . . I must tell you. . . . It is essential that you should know . . ."

The doctor spoke at length. Jean, stretched on his back, his head lying motionless among the pillows, saw nothing but the pale square of ground glass in the recess straight in front of him. During the whole explanation he lay thus, prostrate, showing no sign that he heard anything.

The student and Sister Céline listened vaguely to the explanation which had so often been repeated in their presence, in that same Room 67, while the doctor was on his rounds. Young Thévenet recog-

nised here and there words from the report which had been sent to him.

"Local transference, a case of dual consciousness, which we at first took for some hysterical impersonation and then for a passing condition of mania. . . . You will find the details of the accident in these papers. Your case, which is fairly common, you know, is one of dual personality supervening on a violent traumatism. Briefly, you have been someone else, until the morning of the 13th December.

"Now you have found yourself again. You remember nothing of the other man. That is an invariable rule. You kept your automatic activities, but nothing else. To be exact, your original self, the one before the accident, left to your intermediate self completely organised processes: walking, manual labour, reading, speech, the use of tobacco. Try and understand me, Mourin. I mean that your double smoked, worked, talked, read the papers, yet a certain number of automatic acquirements did not reach the new self. It was ascertained that you were a talented musician and an excellent pianist as well. But from that day you did not know your notes and you could not strike a chord. You learnt a trade here—tailoring: it is certain, scientifically certain, that now you would not know how to hold a needle. On the other hand you will find yourself once more able to read music at sight and play the piano as if you had never ceased to do so. The other man, the first self, the real Jean Mourin, has come back."

"Sixteen years," murmured Jean Mourin.

The doctor went on patiently. "If I have made myself clear, you have had two selves. Between your real and present self which you recovered four days ago and the identical self of before June 14, 1906, a strange personality intervened, whom you do not know, who did not know you and whom your cure has destroyed. This personality was morally in no way like you. But there is no need to describe it. You will find all that in the report which will be given you on your discharge. But you are not listening to me, Mourin. You are cured, I tell you, cured."

"Sixteen years," he said, in a voice which sounded to him toneless, far off, a voice coming from some alien throat. "Sixteen years."

He said nothing more. Nothing could be got out of him except these two words. He repeated them mournfully, whether he was alone in Room 67, or in the bustle of the corridors, among the medical students, the orderlies, the Sisters and the visitors, as he wandered past them like a man walking in his sleep.

Three days went by in this way. The doctor watched his former patient in silence. Jean answered his questions stupidly, shewed ill-temper and a strange susceptibility if any mention was made of the man he had been during his long stay in the place. He seemed to be afraid that he would be regarded as responsible for the actions of this "double." It was no use reassuring him.

"Gervais," said the doctor one day, "was docile, modest, of a very equable temperament, but common and rather furtive."

Jean Mourin started.

"Gervais?" he asked.

"Ah—of course. We had not told you that. As often happens in cases in which the personality is affected, you would not answer to your name. So we had to give you one: we took it from the calendar, the day of your admission to hospital."

"Just like a foundling?"

"Yes. You were brought here, it seems, on the day of St. Gervais. So the name was given to you. You took to it very quickly. For sixteen years, you have been called Gervais."

Jean seemed to be thinking. After this conversation, he said nothing to anybody. He allowed his brother-in-law to continue his journey to Quebec with a surprising indifference.

A week passed. Jean Mourin spent it in his room, tortured with impatience, irritated by everything that surrounded him, reading and re-reading the diary which, by Dr. Hugues' orders, had been left in his room.

At last, on December 23rd his personal belongings were given back to him, a country suit with a leather belt: he put it on without a word. As he left the room the Sister kissed him with tears in her eyes.

An orderly in felt slippers led him along the corridors to the Superintendent's office. First of all his papers were given back to him, a pocket book with his identity papers.

"And now your letters," said the steward, opening a little package tied with a string and sealed, which disclosed a little bundle of envelopes of faded yellow.

They had been opened, two hundred months before, "by direction of the authorities": about twenty letters. The correspondents had soon grown tired: a man disappears, life goes on, friendship grows weary, the recollection is but a word, even sorrow itself betrays the affections—thus had oblivion woven her veil between his neighbours and himself.

"There are still some more," added the official.

And he handed to Jean a short report by the Superintendent which was in fact his permit of discharge; a kind of diary of his illness, a copy of a communication signed 'Hugues'; and lastly a burial certificate signed by the Mayor of Bourg d'Oisans, where by the arrangement of Maître Desnoyers, notary at Mielles, administrator of his estate, Jeanne Thévenet, wife of Mourin, had been buried, with a concession for thirty years.

To Jean, awake and cured, these were like the events of a dream. He felt as if he had seen it all before. All these gestures and voices seemed far off, slow and deliberate, bathed in that veiled light that envelops the unreal and the mechanical.

Jean put everything they gave him into his pockets, one after the other, and then buttoned up his waterproof overcoat. Without turning back he crossed the courtyard and reached the open door of the hospital.

The porter, in his lodge, had his back to the window and was reading a paper. Jean slipped out as if he were escaping.

He carried away with him the vision of patients perambulating the galleries, and invalid chairs in which were stretched out somnolent beings covered with shawls.

Jean found himself in an avenue. A cold hard wind like the edge of a spade rasped along the pavement. In front of him was a wall, and in the middle a gate with a pediment bearing the legend "Arsenal" in tarnished gilt letters. Above it the figured dial of a clock stared down. Some hurrying passers-by and a few dogs came and went along some palings.

A bleak prospect—this sordid suburb, which called to mind pauper funerals and discharges from prison. But Jean Mourin put his bag on the ground. Then raising his head to the sky, he took off his hat, wiped his forehead, and breathed deeply.

II

He walked a few steps along the pavement. On the right the clear and icy waters of the Isère slipped by. A boulevard crossed the avenue. In the distance, straight in front of him, Jean noticed the station. He had only one desire: to escape from the place as soon as possible, get back to his own corner of the Paris suburb and try and take up his life again. He felt trapped. Nothing could have kept him at Grenoble. He began to walk very quickly, driven by a fear of missing by a few minutes the first train to Paris.

Indifferent to his surroundings, he went on, though his clothes made him feel awkward. In spite of his haste he hesitated, feeling the asphalt with his feet, like a man who has lost his sense of space. Yet he passed unnoticed. All along the station avenue people were hurrying to their lunch.

Jean avoided them with a kind of aversion. All that he could imagine about the life that was before him, its excitement, its variety and its difficulties, left him indifferent. What more had he to learn? The diary of his illness which he had read twenty times over in the solitude of his room at the hospital had exhausted his powers of astonishment.

The war? Ah, yes, the war; and then?

He could only find room in his heart for an immense weariness and the egotism of the convalescent. Should he try and reconstruct for himself, retrospectively, the emotions of that time, imagine its splendours and its horrors, grasp its place in human affairs, he, Jean Mourin, the only living being who had never for one moment felt its reality? What was the use? He accepted it as a whole. He believed that he had, in a few days, learnt all that he had to learn. And now he cleared his mind of everything which did not help his wild desire to live and to forget. No suffering could exceed his own. After all, what was the metamorphosis of the world compared with the miracle of his own resurrection?

The station hall was nearly deserted and the ticket office was shut. Jean Mourin looked at the time table on the wall. The Paris Express left at twelve minutes past four. Twelve o'clock had just struck.

In spite of his nervousness Jean made up his mind to sit down

alone in the waiting room. He knew very well that nothing could defeat his impatience, yet in a confused sort of way, he was afraid of everything that might distract him from his thoughts.

The variegated pile of newspapers did not tempt him. He sat on the green velvet bench and waited, his chin on the knob of his stick.

Outside a couple came across the square. The woman, tall and graceful, was leaning on the arm of her companion, a thoughtful looking young man of about thirty.

"My age," thought Mourin.

He had to make an effort to grasp the certainty of the time that had gone by: he was a widower of forty-four.

He owed his departed wife sixteen years of pious recollection.

• • • • • • •

Beloved Jeanne, Jeanne, his tender and innocent companion, his chosen sister, his fellow-orphan. A common love of music had brought them together, and then thrown them breathless into each other's arms. Their married years had been a long wandering together outside the reality of life, a sad and mournful holiday, a sort of melodious autumn of which they had been the affected and entranced spectators. He burst into tears.

However, the station began to show signs of life. People came out of the refreshment room. Cabs and motor cars came up with travellers and luggage. From the end of the square soldiers going on leave approached in groups. On the line a train moved backwards and forwards with an obstinate slowness under its clouds of smoke. The prolonged whistles from the engine composed a rhythm with the warning bells of the luggage-cars. Very soon the waiting room was full and Mourin was almost astonished to hear the travellers talking about their vulgar troubles, quarrelling loudly and, in the French way, full of accusations against important personages who were not present. A thin individual with his tie undone was disputing with some official. No one answered him and he went on to the platform. Jean Mourin left the waiting room to join the queue which was lining up outside a ticket office. His turn came.

"One first for Paris," he said.

"Single?"

"Yes, single."

A corpulent gentleman and an army captain entered his compartment after him. The train moved off. Jean looked through the window at the bare and snowy country which he had seen only the day before—

as it seemed—sparkling with sun and foliage. The light was falling. With a long whistle the train entered the Voirans Tunnel, by the end of which the heavy darkness of a December evening had come. Jean put his alpine hat on the seat and fell asleep at once.

At Lyons the carriage was attached to the Paris Express without his noticing it. He did not wake up till after Laroche, about three in the morning. He felt very cold. The train was running through the night. One passenger, rolled up in his rug, was snoring with his mouth open. The officer was smoking a pipe in the corridor with an impatient air.

It was five o'clock and pitch dark when Jean found himself on the platform of the Lyons Station. A creaking taxi took him across to the Est Station. He had some breakfast at the buffet. It was his first meal for twenty-four hours.

• • • • • • •

When he got out at Meilles, dawn was breaking, a reddish ill-looking dawn, threatening snow. The station was some distance outside the village and overlooked it. The road lay along the wall of a park and up a slope leading to the steps of the church.

Jean Mourin, who had not long—before his accident—settled in the village, knew only two people; the school master Segard, of the same age as himself, twenty-seven, and the lawyer Desnoyers, an old gentleman of much learning and friend of his late uncle Claude Mourin; it was he who had advised his nephew to buy the villa in which he had been living for a few months in 1906.

Among the papers which the steward of the hospital had handed to Jean when he left was a form of release for his property signed by the magistrate at Grenoble and stating that the key of the villa was in the hands of the administrator of his estate, the notary of Meilles.

The office was at the far end of a garden court behind an iron gate. Jean Mourin rang. A young clerk ran up.

"Is Maître Desnoyers up yet?"

The young clerk looked with surprise at this early visitor who was so ill-informed.

"Maître Desnoyers," he answered after some hesitation, "died in 1910. His family has left the neighbourhood. Maître Brondin has succeeded him. Would you like to see him?"

"Yes."

He followed the lad across the court and was ushered into a room in which a log fire was crackling. Nothing was changed: the roll-top

desk, the files of papers, the gay display of notices—all were there.

"Whom shall I say?"

"M. Jean Mourin, owner of 'The Willows.'"

The lad looked at him and went. In a moment a door opened and the lawyer came in. His face betrayed an anxiety which, with a self-control proper to men of his condition, he attempted, as an official of the State, to disguise. Clearly he was amazed at the reappearance of this client. In 1910, when he had bought the practice, "The Willows" was already called "the madman's" house. And here was the madman himself, a man growing grey, of composed appearance but with an expression of indescribable desolation.

In response to an awkward gesture from the lawyer, the visitor sat down. A silence fell. Jean waited motionless with his hands spread on his knees.

"Monsieur," said the lawyer at last, "I congratulate you on your recovery. I am glad to see you, to see you again, I should rather say, because I paid you a visit at Grenoble, of which you have no doubt no recollection. In 1911: let me see, was it in 1911?

Jean looked at his pale face traversed by a pepper-coloured moustache. The face was quite unknown to him and yet there was a vague something . . .

Maître Brondin went on

"My late predecessor was, if I am rightly informed, a friend of your family. It was on those grounds that he was appointed administrator of your estate by a family council of your friends at the time of your—your accident. I have been notified of the release of your property and I have myself notified the Superintendent of the hospital. All that I have to do now is to give an account of my administration. This formality can be disposed of as soon as you like—say on Thursday."

"Very well, Thursday," said Jean, with the air of a man half asleep, and following a business conversation with difficulty.

"I can tell you here and now that your securities are deposited with the Discount Bank in Paris. Your property, although uninhabited and damaged by wear and tear, has about trebled in value. Propositions for the purchase of 'The Willows' have often been made to me. It is a pleasant property for which you would find many buyers, especially now. But the law, as you no doubt know . . ."

"No," interrupted Jean, "and I do not want to know. I want to keep the place."

"Very good," acquiesced the lawyer.

He went to the safe. He produced the key of the house which was tied on to the tape surrounding a bundle of redeemed mortgages on certain properties in the neighbourhood.

"I have no doubt of your identity, Monsieur," Maître Brondin went on, "but . . .

"Here are the papers."

The lawyer took them, looked at them carefully and composedly.

"The law does not permit the accounts of the administration being closed until an interval of ten days has elapsed. As regards the mortgages which have been redeemed in your absence, I have the money at your disposal. You would like, I expect, to go to your house at once. Here is your key."

"Thank you," said Jean Mourin in a softened tone. "I am delighted to make your acquaintance" (and he held out his hand which the other took) "but I would sooner have received these matters from Maître Desnoyers, who was one of my few friends and had known me as a child!"

"I quite understand."

After a silence the lawyer got up and said:

"I will send someone with you."

"No, thank you. I wish to be alone."

• • • • • • •

One of the witnesses of his old life had gone. The news of the old man's death, already far off and forgotten, was a fresh blow to Jean Mourin. He had so few connections.

At Meilles he only knew Maître Desnoyers and Segard the schoolmaster, whose taste for music brought him nearly every evening to the villa.

Little groups of children were going along to school. Jean questioned them. Segard had been killed in the first days of the war. They knew by heart the story of his death which the new master had made them learn like a lesson.

Desnoyers, dead of old age in his office: Segard killed on the field of battle. Mourin felt as if a little of his own self had vanished, like smoke, into the past. And there would be no longer a face that he knew at Meilles. He had lived so much in the happy dream of his love, that he had hardly noticed the faces of the inhabitants, and since then they had grown worn and faded, marred and pale, and would not arouse in

him a single recollection. He would as easily have recognised the farm carts and machines which still stood in the same places under the sheds, with their tapering shafts pointing up to the beams.

Everything seemed to centre round the house that he remembered. What connections had he outside the place? Ten or twelve at the outside. This was all his acquaintance after an orphaned youth spent in the parish of his uncle Mourin, a wealthy priest in La Vendée who had died in 1905 and whose money he had inherited. Now that the lawyer was dead and the school master killed, he had only these few scattered friends, nearly all musicians or interested in music.

There was old Lescot, an old bachelor in Paris, friend of Desnoyers and Uncle Claude, who composed operas and symphonies in the leisure allowed him by his profession of accountant: a relation of Jeanne, Madame Pagès, a lady of independent means living at Rouen: an obscure organist, named Baborier, living in the Latin Quarter: three clerks, Philiponneau, Marge, and Bourbon, his neighbours at the Hotel du Jura in the rue Monsieur Le Prince, when he first came to Paris: a priest, the Abbé Dufour, precentor at St. Philippe du Roule: the manager of a bank in the rue St. Lazare: this was the entire catalogue of his friends.

Nearly all of them had written to him soon after his accident. Theirs were the faded letters that had been handed to him when he left the hospital. None of them was dated later than 1907.

"What has become of them all?" thought Jean.

The children stopped by the wall of the school and watched this unknown traveller. And Mourin reflected that at the time of his departure, which for him was so recent, these young people were not born. With these thoughts in his mind, he reached the black and rusty gate of his house. It creaked as he opened it. He went in.

• • • • • • •

It was like an abandoned cemetery. Tall grasses shivered in the wind. Along the walls of the front garden the outstretched arms of the fruit trees looked like great bats. It was a garden without an owner. The brambles had grown so high that in the middle of winter, when the frost was on them, they formed a solid mass. Moss had grown over the seats and corroded the paths. Stones fallen from the borders of the beds lay like fragments of pavement under the wilderness of plants. Flights of starlings swept with a soft flutter across the sky.

To get into the house Jean Mourin pushed aside the network of shoots and thorns. The paint on the door and the shutters had all come

off long ago, and everything had a mouldy tint: over every aperture, and on the rusty pump-handle, were spiders' webs, blackened and frayed by time.

The key turned with difficulty in the lock and when the door opened the house gave out a sort of fetid sigh.

Jean entered as if he were going into a tomb.

A leaden-coloured covering carpet of dust lay over the floor of the hall on which the tracks of mice had left symmetrical patterns. In the room which he entered, a thin light covering without a fold seemed to envelop everything. As the shutters were thrown back Jean felt a shock. Everywhere were the signs of a hurried departure. In this room, as in his own heart, the timepiece of his life had suddenly stopped. And at the same time it was the only place in the world that could give Jean this feeling: and he felt it with all the force with which an anxious mind sees a truth which no one understands.

Through the half open doors of a cupboard he saw a heap of collars and ties. A half smoked cigarette lay in an ash-tray on the mantelpiece. The floor was strewn with pieces of paper, and an umbrella which it had been finally decided not to take was leaning against the wall. A newspaper was still lying open on the table. Jean picked it up and, blowing off the dust which covered it, he read, "June 11, 1906 . . . Grand Prix day: Spearmint wins. M. Ephrussi summoned to M. Fallières. Suicide of the poet Charles Frémine. Earthquake in Calabria. King Sisowath lands at Marseilles. Mobilisation test on the line Nérac to Mont-de-Marsan. Exhumation of the ashes of Waldeck Rousseau." Also a record of a debate in the Chamber and an account of a fight between two cabmen.

Mourin read with eagerness. He knew that for him *alone* these forgotten events represented living and present reality. Who remembered Sisowath, the ashes of Waldeck Rousseau, the victory of Spearmint? All this had no existence. What was left of it? Neither more nor less than the drops of rain which had fallen on the race course as M. Fallières arrived, on the coffin of the dead minister, on the cloak of the Cambodian king.

But he, Jean, was familiar with every detail of these events, which he had discussed *yesterday* with Desnoyers and Segard, who had been dead for several years. But were they dead? Was not this newspaper, these commonplace items, the truth of the visible world reconstituted once more? As he read the paper Jean saw again the succession of persons

and events which the unexpected revelation of his injury had severed without altogether destroying. Why, all this was quite recent! Six thousand days and six thousand nights, fallen into the abysm of his sleep, had lasted but the interval between his departure from that room and the moment when the charabanc fell over the parapet on the *Infernet.*

Since then Jean, *the true Jean, had lived for three days and the paper that he held in his hand was three days old.*

The other, the false Mourin, "Gervais the tailor," did not belong at all to this past. He was merely a dream, without body and without persistence. Could a doctor's science, even the changes of the world, prevail over truths of which Jean was as certain as of the beating of his heart? All that he had learnt of a new life since his awakening was no more than a pale light obscured by a vast illumination. These were awful thoughts. Was he to be overwhelmed "in further madness by these frightful perplexities?"

Where did dreams end and reality begin? What meaning for a living mortal man has an invisible succession of days that he has not lived, that another, in his own body, has lived in his stead? What is such time? Nothing. Not even the duration of a second. A heavy dreamless sleep, the thick night of death—nothing.

Jean drew back before these mysteries. He was filled with dizzy secrets. As he stood in the extraordinary silence of his house where the sound of his steps, deadened by the dust, had as yet awakened no echoes, he felt himself the prisoner of invisible prisoners. He was surrounded by his contemporaries who had died, while he himself was outside humanity, as dead as a dead man, wandering in the shadowy country of madness whence the traveller, if he returns, brings back no more recollections than a departed soul arising from the clay would bring back from the blind and deaf world to which the sexton had consigned him.

The piano was at the end of the room, ponderous and tarnished, standing on its four feet like some grey beast in a museum. Jean opened it, trembling. The keyboard shone, new and bright, in the heavy light of this dusty tomb. Why not play, shake off the obsession of this silence, and—who knows?—by the help of the emotions of music, live once more his real life, the far off and yet recent past which he carried in his soul, that was no longer one but two.

Jean sat down. He laid his fingers on the ivory keys, and the vibrations of a chord that sounded false and sickly broke into the silence.

The chord died away: and the echo that came back sounded padded and heavy, as if weighed down by sleep. Jean struck the keys again, and then began to play mechanically. He played to the shadows that floated round him that song of Rollinat that Jeanne had been so fond of, full of a sensual bitterness and laden with a mortal sorrow. The air could hardly be distinguished. It seemed like a forest of sounds cut into by the heavy strokes of the bass.

Jean, dazed by sorrow and by recollection, dared not look behind him. He felt as though the magnetism of the sounds had drawn her back again: her beloved and sorrowful presence was surely moving in that shadowy corner behind a ray of dusty light. He managed to control himself at last, and turned. Nothing, nothing but solitude. He covered his forehead with his hands and walked quickly up and down the room, feverish and distraught. The baffling truth of his recovery and the deception of his madness lay before and behind him like two abysses. He felt himself grow pale, and staggered. A tarnished mirror hung over a sideboard: he could see nothing but the shadow of a man wearing a hat and with so wild an expression that he looked as if he had been caught intruding in his own house.

On either side of the oval mirror were two portraits: his mother whom he had never known, and his uncle Claude with his clerical bands under his chin. Both their faces looked down at him with a gaze of penetrating but revealing melancholy. Little by little Jean began to grasp the secret which, in his illness and his recovery, lay behind the infinite and cruel impossibility of his destiny. Fifteen years of his life had passed, fruitless as the rain that falls on rivers. Outside and far away humanity with its even tread had gone forward a few steps on the road of time.

And Jean, alone among the millions of the living, had stayed behind, forsaken, forgotten, betrayed, like a dead man.

• • • • • • •

He went towards the window and lifted the curtain. It looked out on a street corner. Passers-by came and went. Some of them, who knew what had happened, looked up at the "House of the Madman," and met Jean's eyes. Not a face that he knew.

For the first time Jean realised that he had not met a soul that he knew from the time he left the bed at the hospital until he had reached the gate of "The Willows."

"I must speak to somebody: I must have some friendly voice to

celebrate my return. Tomorrow without fail I shall go to Paris."

He had spoken out loud and the sound of his voice dispelled the kind of trance that had seized him. At the same moment there came over him a loneliness so awful that no living man had ever known the like. And he felt something cold fall upon his shoulders, something inert that rustled like a shroud.

PART II

I

Monsieur Lescot, accountant to the Marble-Cutters' Company, lived in two small rooms in the Rue de Fontarabie, in that part of it that juts out like a promontory between the Rue de Bagnolet and the Rue des Orteaux. Jean Mourin knew his lodging well. The dining room of an old artist, with its decoration of presentation wreaths, discoloured photographs and a mask of Beethoven: out of this opened a melancholy looking recess with a bed in it, a narrow kitchen, and a little sitting room, smelling of wood fires and pipe-smoke.

Here M. Lescot would discourse at length of his disappointments. Everyone in the neighbourhood knew him. All the year round he walked home from his office in the Boulevard de Charonne, and took his napkin from its pigeon-hole in a little restaurant in the Rue des Orteaux. He ate his dinner, climbed up six flights of stairs and shut himself up till the following day. He composed music. Some dozen of his friends considered he had genius but they could not get him known. No conductor would ever undertake his works. Obscure, industrious, and without vices, M. Lescot opened the door to the friends of his art, whom he called his pilgrims, and, without waiting to be asked, played to them arrangements for the piano of his symphonies and lyrical dramas.

Jean Mourin and his wife formed part of the little circle which, every Saturday, gathered round the piano of this unrecognised composer. Jeanne sang. Her warm, pure contralto emphasised the flow of the melody, breathing a mysterious spell over the little group. Lescot and his guests used to be quite overcome by it.

What had become of all these odd visitors? Jean wondered as he walked along. He tried to get used to the reality of time. According to his recollection his last visit to Lescot had taken place the week before, but his reason, in deference to the evidence of the facts, assured him that it was sixteen years ago. And in future he would have to carry out this troublesome readjustment in every action of his life.

Thus reflecting, he approached the Rue de Bagnolet living once again more vividly the past that everyone had forgotten but which was for him so near and so alive.

Two days before their departure on the fatal journey Jean and his wife had been to visit the old man. In their honour he had played to them the second movement of a sonata. This was on June 9th, 1906. Yet Jean Mourin, though he had hardly reached his old friend's house, could smell already the odour of tobacco and wood smoke: he could see, as if it were yesterday, the panorama of roofs and chimneys stretching away below the windows, and, far off, the paths and borders and vaults of Père Lachaise like a draughtboard with squares of white and pink and green.

He felt deeply moved. Among his few old friends Lescot was the one who had written most frequently to the hospital. He urged Jean to get well and as soon as he had done so to come along to the Rue de Fontarabie. Then he had grown tired. The last letter was dated 1907.

Jean knocked at the porter's door. The concierge did not know of any Lescot. An Armenian soldier's family was living in the apartment that the visitor described on the fifth floor.

"Since when?" said Jean.

"Since about the armistice."

"And before that?"

The concierge thought for a moment.

"Before that," she said, "there was a Monsieur Husson who was arrested."

"Had he been there long?"

"How should I know?" said the concierge impatiently. "I haven't always been looking after this house. But since I've been here I've never heard the name of Lescot, and that is all I can tell you. Is it a long time since you came to see him last?"

"Sixteen years."

The concierge thought he was laughing at her and was going to shut the door, but she was touched by Jean's sad expression.

"You should ask the bootmaker on the third floor. He has lived in the building a long time and he could tell you . . ."

The bootmaker looked at Jean over his spectacles.

"Lescot," said he, "old Lescot? He died in 1910, on the evening of All Saints Day. He was found on the ground, half paralysed, just in front of the door of the cellar. It didn't last long: in two days he was done for."

Jean Mourin went away. Although the circumstances of the old man's death distressed and upset him, the news itself hardly surprised

him. Of course it would be so. Something warned him, a kind of presentiment that had troubled him ever since he had left Meilles: all his attempts would end in similar disappointments.

Thus everywhere that Jeanne and he had been, others had come whose footprints had effaced theirs: and others had gone who, in a forgetful world, had left no trace behind them. Death gave him the measure of time. It seemed to him natural and even encouraging that during Mourin's sleep others should have grown up, changed and grown old: at any rate it strengthened his will to live and go among his fellows. But these deaths that came upon him one after another shook him like the bereavements that await a traveller after a long absence: it pained him to think that he had not done all his duty towards these people who were dead and who had been buried before his return. And the thought of it, while he made further enquiries in other places, made him realise most vividly his strange position.

Paris was moving at top-speed, and in every part of the city Jean Mourin thought he was in the centre of a whirlwind. All round him were hooting motorcars. As he crossed from the pavement to a refuge he felt hemmed in by noise and movement.

In the Place de la République he took a motorbus. He hated the jostling people on the footboard but his mind was full of a kind of expectation. A heavy sky brooded over the city: rusty looking clouds seemed to be overhanging the roofs of the houses. He looked at the crowd and watched the streams of people passing in the street. A dry cold enlivened everyone and kept the loiterers moving. Jean got off near the Opera and took his place in the stream of passers-by. One thing astonished him: his shrunken suit, his flowing necktie, and his cloak with its narrow braid round the edge, did not attract any attention. Doubtless he was taken for some foreign dealer.

He soon grew tired of walking and hailed a cab. What would be his next discovery?

A surprise awaited him. Madame Pagés, the lady of independent means, was not dead. At least no one knew that she was. Some years back the old lady had left to join a relation in the country, like herself old and widowed. But where? The concierge did not know, as her predecessor had lost the book which contained the addresses of previous lodgers.

Jean Mourin pressed her.

"But supposing it were a matter of importance"—The concierge

could offer no help. What was he to do? The house was at the end of Saint Ange alley. It was no use asking the tradesmen of the neighbourhood. Yet Jean Mourin could not make up his mind to go away.

"We have never heard the lady's name since we have been in the lodge," the concierge went on, "though, wait a minute: until the end of last quarter there was a lodger who had lived here for more than twenty years. He left last year after the death of his daughter, and I believe he is living in a boarding house. One moment . . . here it is. Rouaix, Pension Célestine, Rue du Ranelagh. I should go and see him."

"I know him," said Jean.

He thanked her and went away. M. Rouaix was concluding his existence in an armchair, staring at the fire.

"Madame Pagés," he said. "Yes, I knew her well; she was very religious and only priests went to see her. A dear good lady, a little older than I am. Where does she live now? Why, at St. Brieuc. No, not St. Brieuc: I'm wrong. St. Omer or St. Nazaire, I think. St. Brieuc, what made me think of that? . . ."

Jean left the old man mumbling to himself. In spite of everything he still kept a vague hope of finding one or other of the people he was looking for. After a hasty lunch in a dairy in the Rue de Boulainvilliers, he called at the addresses of his remaining friends. Their houses, which Jean remembered, were in various parts of Paris.

From Passy he went to the Quinze-Vingts, and from the Quinze-Vingts to the Goutte d'Or. At each turning and at every crossing there was something unfamiliar. The whole day was a long voyage of discovery. He was greatly astonished, though less so than he had previously thought he would be. His breathless expeditions soon accustomed him to the rhythm of this unknown city. His obsession did the rest. If, in all this noise, only a few cabmen reminded him of the Paris he had known, the change struck him chiefly because of the freshness of his recollections. That was the secret. He had been there too lately and the absence of perspective diminished, in his eyes, the changes. He did not feel that he was in a strange town: it seemed rather as if he had suddenly come upon everything in the midst of one of those preparations for a fête which change in a few hours the appearance and movement of a city.

Besides he was soon deep in his search once more. His motives were gradually changing. A kind of pride not unmixed with anger was now driving him forward. Was it really possible in so few years to disappear without anyone keeping even the recollection of one's shadow?

Was the distance between Paris of 1906 to Paris of 1922 so great as that? Hardly the age of a youth.

A fresh disappointment shewed him the uselessness of his present attempts, and it occurred to him to consult the directory. He was discouraged by the fact that he could not find the name of any of his friends. They were, in general, little people who would not appear in such publications.

He went on again.

Everywhere the same surprise and the same replies. It seemed almost ridiculous to do so, but he went to the Hotel du Jura in the Rue Monsieur-le-Prince where at the time of his accident, two clerks were living whom he had met at old Lescot's. The hotel had disappeared. Jean met his disappointment without emotion: he was incapable of feeling any further blow.

The only person of whom he found any fairly recent traces was M. Baborier, the organist. Jean discovered that he had nearly died of cold in 1917 in his small lodging in the Rue de Buci. He recovered by a miracle and almost as soon as he was out of hospital he was seen trotting backwards and forwards between the parish where he played the organ and the library of the Conservatoire. He coughed and grew thin, until he almost floated in air in his beggarly old overcoat. For four years he carried on. No one knew what kept him alive. In October 1921 he took to a publisher, who accepted it, his completed manuscript of a History of the Gregorian Chant. Then he died.

An old man, a friend of the organist, told Jean the story in the hall of his lodging.

"Are you a relation?" he asked.

"No," Jean replied.

He stammered his thanks and excuses. He began to understand that the life and death of M. Baborier did not interest him. What he was looking for all over Paris was a face that he knew, a voice that he had heard. He now realised that he would not find them. To discharge his conscience he went to see the Curé of St. Philippe du Roule. The Abbé Dufour had gone to Rome to attend to his duties as Vicar of S. Louis-des-Français.

• • • • • • •

Night was falling, rainy and menacing. Jean, moving with the crowds in the Rue Royale, felt a weariness that he could not overcome. The cold, which whipped up the passers-by and hurried them along,

did not touch him. On the contrary he was conscious of a clammy and disagreeable warmth under his clothes. He sat down at the Café Weber which he used to frequent in old days.

People came in and went out: the revolving door turned ceaselessly. All who entered went straight to a group of friends or to a woman who was powdering her cheeks while she waited.

Not a face that he knew. Jean looked in vain at all these people—not one of whom knew of his existence. They were business men and people connected with the theatre. And there were others, countless others, in Paris and all the world, who were keeping appointments, shaking hands, and mingling their lives with those of their fellowmen.

The waiters slipped dexterously between the groups, the café was full of the clatter of saucers and spoons. The noise of the street penetrated in bursts as fresh people passed through the door. Some were called to the telephone. To Jean it seemed like some fête and to be present at it in this way, alone, lost, and silent, increased his melancholy.

He began to look at his neighbours with more attention, observing particularly those who seemed to be about his own age at the time of the accident. But he soon grew tired. All their faces seemed like masks without features, like coins with their effigies effaced, like the vacant faces on old playing-cards. And there were millions of others like that in the world. Millions of faces who would look at him without changing their expression. Wherever he went, whatever he did, not a living soul henceforward would ever greet him by his name. As far as society was concerned, Jean Mourin, after sixteen years of absence, was wiped out, as if he had been buried for a thousand years.

He tried to find some pleasure in his bitterness, but to his surprise, all he felt was a dreamy dejection. Yet he was fond of solitude. He had grown up alone, in the company of a priest, who had been misanthropic almost to madness, and he had never wanted companions in his games or young friends. His wife, an orphan like himself, avoided company. From the day of their marriage they had lived fiercely alone. When, after the death of Uncle Claude, they bought the villa at Meilles, it was to shut themselves more closely in the silence of their love. They had lived for their affection and for music.

• • • • • • •

Jean began to dream. Their love, their evenings together . . . The confused movement of the cafe seemed enveloped in a mist, and Jean, with his elbows on the table, his chin in his hands, found himself back

at Meilles one evening at the end of the dim room where the lamp shed a deep reflection of motionless light on to the ebony of the piano. Jeanne was singing. Her form seemed surrounded by a sort of halo, and Jean could see once more the beautiful, weary, pale face, moved a little by the passion of the music. One evening she was singing . . .: in all the clatter of the Café Weber he reconstructed this evening of long ago, so near and yet so far away—: she was singing. The room, softly lighted, enclosed its tiny illumination and the sound of her ardent voice, in the midst of the dark enveloping silence of the country. Jeanne was standing by the piano and Jean was playing:

> The foliage is fading, the hum of the insects grows hoarse
> The swallow sobs
> And disappears on the pale horizon.

It was a song of Rollinat, haunting and sad. An arpeggio of notes followed the melody, hurrying down on it as though to stifle the woman's voice repeating the despairing lover's call—she who will not die without having loved once more.

> Come let us gather one more lovely day
> In despite of time that is breaking us,
> And let us mingle the farewell to our love
> With the last perfumes of the breeze.

It was her singing of the song on that evening that he chose to remember, the sweet cadences of her voice that he could still hear in his heart: with a sort of presentiment she had loved this song better than more distinguished pieces which did not bear the signs of fate.

It was only yesterday: . . . they had left the room silently as their lips met, locked in a deep embrace: without a word they reached the bed in the alcove and sank down on it, clothed as they were, still trembling, his mouth on hers. And the morning found them still lying on the bed which they had not disturbed.

On other days, other nights, Jean abandoned all control and plunged with the ardour of despair into the memories which made his grief more living and more cruel. He felt too, once more, that need of solitude that had united him and Jeanne outside the world and outside life. The few friends whom they had in Paris were a burden on them. They reproached themselves often for their neglectfulness and paid a

few visits. But they always agreed not to make new acquaintances.

Jean Mourin sank into gloomy meditation. The crowd became so dense that newcomers could not find a place. Some common fellow came and sat down opposite him, addressed the waiter with familiarity, and made it clear that his friends would soon be joining him. Jean Mourin paid and got up. The other, overcome by his own rudeness, stammered some excuses. But Jean was anxious to get out.

At the Madeleine crossing a clock that was lighted up reminded him of the time of his train. Should he go back to Meilles?

His mind full of thoughts of Jeanne, he pictured to himself the dark and hostile station, the roads, and the house. At that time the village was hidden beneath the rain driving in gusts through the night. To hurry through the darkness, a shadow crossing the feeble light from the shop-windows and arrive alone, chilled and desolate, in those rooms where beloved memories were burning out and mingling their ashes with the dust of years . . . Jean shivered. The utter loneliness appalled him because in his mind it was peopled with images.

In any case, he thought, I shall have to go back tomorrow, there is no use going for one night.

He decided to dine somewhere near the Exchange and to sleep at a hotel. Anything was welcome that rescued him from the evil power of his recollections.

The restaurant that he chose at a venture had only a few customers in the evening: bachelors who were eating alone, for the most part, with a newspaper propped against their bottle of wine.

Some young couples were climbing up a circular staircase to the room above. The proprietor, with a napkin under his arm, moved from table to table, offering advice to the diners. The food was mediocre. But there was something warm and familiar about the atmosphere that Jean liked. Nobody seemed to notice his old-fashioned clothes nor the distracted appearance of the unknown customer. And Jean, finding satisfaction in an incognito, registered at the hotel under a borrowed name.

He took an immediate liking to the "Pheasant" Hotel, a clean and quiet house in the Rue Notre-Dame-des-Victoires. The floor was like that of a country inn and his heels clattered as he moved about. Pale gleams of light were reflected from the furniture. Curtains hung down in thick folds from the canopy over the bed. Jean Mourin undressed and lay down. Sleep began to steal over him and, in the last glimmer of consciousness, only the last hours of that harassing day were present to his mind.

• • • • • • •

On the following day about eight o'clock he took the train for Meilles. The lawyer Brondin was awaiting him in the study, and his colleague Deschavannes was also present, a cadaverous old gentleman, afflicted by a nervous twitching, who occupied himself by warming his hands at the iron stove during the entire interview.

M. Brondin put on a serious expression. A file of papers lay open on his desk. He drew a chair forward and began his explanations.

"When the magistrates at Grenoble placed you and your effects under restraint on September 14th, 1906, your estate was worth about three hundred and twenty thousand francs, in personal and real property, as follows:

"Your house 'The Willows' valued at thirty-five thousand francs: some land at Bourneau-Mervent in the Vendée, rather more than six acres in extent, valued at twelve thousand francs: various sums lent to certain landowners in Meilles, through the agency of my predecessor, and covered by mortgages, amounting to ten thousand francs in all."

"Quite right:" Jean Mourin interrupted.

"Your holdings of stocks and shares, of which I have the statement here, was as follows: five shares in the Bank of France, ten bonds on the Bank of Portugal, twenty shares in the Suez Company, four hundred Russian Government bonds of 1867, three hundred of 1906, three hundred Paris Municipals 1878, and sixty Northern Railway bonds. On September 15th, 1906, these holdings amounted to two hundred and sixty-two thousand one hundred and twenty-five francs. Now I must inform you that stocks belonging to persons under restraint must be inscribed and not bearer bonds. M. Desnoyers dealt with the matter. In short the Russian holdings had to be replaced by bonds of the Bank of Agriculture and Government stock. To sum up, your personal property has diminished in value by about thirty-two per cent. You will be able to judge by the abstract of accounts which I have here. I hasten to add that the sum total of your property has increased, in the first place by the amount of interest accruing, after subtracting the cost of your treatment in hospital, taxes, and various outlays, and secondly by the increase in the value of your real property, especially of your house 'The Willows.' I should judge that the value of this property has almost quadrupled since the time when you purchased it under the advice of M. Desnoyers."

The lawyer detailed with complacency the operations carried out by

his predecessor, and, his eyeglasses in his hand, he emphasised the happy results of so able an administration. M. Deschavannes here observed:

"M. Mourin's financial affairs could not have been better managed."

"I quite agree," answered Jean Mourin.

He seemed to have heard these words somewhere else. But where? M. Brondin had admitted that he had paid a visit to Grenoble a long while back. Jean thought he could recognise his short-sighted blinking eyes, his gestures and the sound of his voice. Absurd yet consuming uncertainties. Jean made an effort and shook them off.

Henceforward there was an alertness in his expression which surprised M. Brondin. Could this be the client, who, three days before, had been incapable of giving his attention to an official statement of his case. Here he was, turning over the documents relating to the administration of his affairs. He asked for further information on various points. The lawyer explained, not without a certain professional pride, the law affecting persons under restraint and how in this case, which was in this respect peculiar, the family council, held after the pronouncement of the Tribunal at Grenoble, had consisted only of friends of Jean Mourin.

"May I ask their names?"

M. Brondin put on his glasses and picked up a document with an official stamp on it.

"Here they are in order:

"'In the presence of M. David Lardière, Mayor of the Commune, and of M. Desnoyers, notary, the following being present, the Abbé Dufour, MM. Lescot, Philipponeau, Marge, Segard, Baborier, Bourbon . . .'"

"You tell me that the securities are at the Discount Bank?"

"Yes. I ought to remind you that, as the law stands, the accounts of the administration cannot be cleared for ten days. But if you are in need of money in the meantime I can advance you whatever is necessary out of the money in hand from the paid off mortgages, about which I told you at our first interview."

"I am much obliged to you. Can you let me have six thousand francs now?"

"Certainly," said the lawyer.

He went to the safe at the end of the room and while he was opening the lock, he added:

"While you were away, I have had the rooms in your house cleaned and put in order. I would have had this done before your first visit, but I had expected you some days later. I suppose you are still in the same mind about the property? Because if your views have changed I have an offer . . ."

Jean said nothing. He put the money in his pocket and departed. M. Deschavannes shook hands with him with a sympathetic air and M. Brondin went with him to the gate.

• • • • • • •

He could see from the road the wall of the villa and above it the leafless branches and slate roofs. It was about ten o'clock. On the market place a steam roller was emitting puffs of black smoke. A horseman went by at a trot. He noticed the servants standing on the window-sills and polishing the window panes. The butcher's horn sounded in the cold air. Jean walked with slow steps in the direction of "The Willows."

He had a feeling of some apprehension. The lawyer's final words seemed to indicate that he had had the villa put into its usual condition. Jean was afraid that deprived of their enshrouding dust the house and its contents would seem nearer to him and alive once more. They would awaken his sorrows again and with them that mirage of the past which carried him back into a time that had gone forever.

He opened the gate and crossed the garden with a quicker step. As he stood on the threshold the house looked as though its wounds had been dressed. Jean pushed the door open (the knocker was clean and bright). The moment he entered the hall he saw that his presentiment was realised. In the clear cold light of the morning he could see how everything had been put in its place once more. In the larger room in which Jeanne and he had mostly lived, it seemed as though some vivifying air had entered—furniture, curtains, chairs, books looked as they had always done. Everything seemed alive once more. The tick of the clock was like the beat of a heart. No more dust. Order and cleanliness reflected in the mirrors and the polished floors.

Jean had feared the shock of the past: he felt it so acutely that the tears came into his eyes.

The place was full of urgent memories of Jeanne, the beloved companion who had gone. The warm touch of her hand seemed to lie on everything. Her delicate shadow would surely pass the windows. The creaking of the floor betrayed her footsteps and her well remembered voice would break the clear silence.

Jean opened a cupboard. Sad discoveries. A hat, a wrap of black lace, a feathered boa. Each one a recollection of his loss. They were certainly alive, these witnesses of a broken happiness. He felt them too terribly near as he stood and wiped the tears from his eyes. The walls themselves distilled the subtle poison of his evil dreams.

No, he would not give way to the bitter embraces of the past. He must live. He would be faithful, with all the force of his being, to the memory of Jeanne. But he must not live with these lying relics which would always torment him with the dream of an impossible return. The beloved image of his wife lived within him, clear and ineffaceable. His own sorrow and affection could evoke the melancholy charm of her presence: he needed no lifeless witnesses such as these to help him.

In the dark corners of his being Jean was conscious of a fear which he dared not admit. He was afraid of passing the gloomy evenings of winter alone in this house, so long abandoned, and haunted by the presence of his wife. His mind was still weakened and full of fears. Do the dead know the reasons for our absences and, when they seem too like forgetfulness, do they forgive us?

Jean imagined to himself night time at "The Willows," the house besieged by the surging darkness, the north wind howling in the chimneys, the rusty creaking of the weather-vanes. Recollection and regret would be too frequent visitors. Far better the sullen isolation of evenings in Paris where those pursued by great sorrows may at least lose themselves in the mazes of the city.

His mind was made up: he would sell "The Willows," he would stay in Paris and escape the fatal influences of a place so loaded with the miasma of recollection. Perhaps he had some presentiment of the horrors which his strange destiny was preparing for him.

Before leaving the villa he carefully put aside in one room, which had been used to store odd belongings, everything he wanted to keep. Then, after a long look at the scene of his broken youth which he would never see again, he went off at once to M. Brondin.

"The Willows" was put up for sale the next day, and was bought, with the furniture, by a M. Chancramy, a Swiss broker, for one hundred and five thousand francs, and paid for by two cheques drawn on the Bank of Holland.

When Jean got back to Paris he bought some mourning clothes. He blamed himself for not having thought of it before. Full of the miracle of his cure he had found as yet no place in himself for the more truly

human sentiments. It was through the medium of sorrow that reality came back to him once more. What was he at the present time? A husband dressed in black, plunged in grief, and more alone in the crowd than a lost child.

His life was meagre and awkward: he hated to think he was carrying about Paris the secret of his "cure." Sometimes Jean doubted whether he had really become Jean Mourin again, free, and confronted with the task of reconstructing his existence. From time to time he acted as though he were outside himself, a stranger. Was he alive? Was he a guest at the spectacle of his own life? Present and past impressions crowded one upon another and the idea that he had seen something before was constantly with him.

Fortunately his affairs kept him occupied. In spite of the energy of M. Brondin, matters proceeded but slowly. He had to pay several visits to Meilles. His constant fear that some indiscretion might reveal that which at all costs he wished to keep hidden suggested many difficulties in connection with the re-establishment of his civil status. Here also M. Brondin's help proved invaluable. At last on January 20th, a month after his return from Grenoble, he resumed possession of his property and his fortune. After the sale of "The Willows," and the payment of the expenses of his treatment at the hospital, he had a little more than three hundred thousand francs, of which one hundred and thirteen thousand were in cash and the remainder in inscribed bonds, which, as a result of the cancellation of his restraining order, he had to get transferred without delay.

As soon as the deed of sale in respect of "The Willows" had been drawn up and signed he went back to the Pheasant Hotel. A certain superstition not unmixed with gratitude attracted him to the hotel and restaurant which he had come upon by chance. He booked his room for a month and paid for it in advance.

II

One evening, Jean Mourin, who had, as usual, dined alone, sat late in the restaurant. Outside was a windy, soaking evening, the sort of weather that envelops one like a garment of wet India-rubber. The diners were in no hurry to leave, nor the waiters to take off their aprons. The conversation began to take an almost familiar turn. Jean, who never read at table nor talked to his neighbours, sat dreaming, with his hand against his head. The rain stopped, and Jean went out: it cost him an effort to leave the warm and intimate atmosphere for the streets where the passers-by were being hurried along by the sudden gusts of wind.

Once outside he hesitated. Should he go back to the Pheasant Hotel, to his room with its heavy curtains and melancholy candelabra, whose sombre neatness re-awakened his sorrows?

For Jean was suffering deeply. He was one of those for whom to think was to suffer. Most bitterly he loved his dead wife, and if he snatched a little rest it seemed to him like a betrayal. He saw before him the image of Jeanne, melancholy and proud, and her look accused him of ingratitude and forgetfulness.

Forgetfulness, no. He was not trying to escape from the memory of his dead wife. He was piously faithful to her and it pained him to grow accustomed to his grief. For time had already begun its work of gloomy consolation: the image of Jeanne was already growing fainter. Her portrait, the oval pastel which he had kept, was a poor rendering of her beauty whose sorrowful and dreamy expression softened a little the too firm, almost masculine, features. Her clear forehead and her shining hair, the sombre brilliance of her eyes, of those there was but a feeble reflection under the glass of the pastel.

But solitude had, for Jean, even more formidable effects than this. He felt a menace hanging over him. He knew his fears were absurd, yet he could not get rid of them. He felt surrounded by something, some impalpable essence from beyond the grave. He only felt safe in the noise and conversation of the streets.

By the clock of the Exchange it was half past twelve. Where should he go? His room, the room of a bachelor traveller, ceased for the first

time tonight to offer him a refuge against the phantasms of solitude. The rain had stopped. He walked down the Rue Richelieu to the boulevards where, in spite of the showers, there were still some people.

It was Saturday. Couples came and went along the gleaming ebony of the pavements. The wind had fallen, the air grew soft, full of the light movement and premonitions of the spring.

In the dark corners, near the Gymnase theatre, women stood, loosening their cloaks, and seemed to bend towards him like flowers in the night. Jean Mourin retraced his steps. Everything seemed to drive him back to his room in the hotel, where no one was waiting for him, to the cafés where under the shifting clouds of smoke sat hundreds of people who looked at him and would always look at him, with vacant eyes. He went back with an empty heart.

In the vestibule of the hotel was a traveller dozing between two suit-cases. The night porter sat reading a novel in his glass compartment. Jean took his key and went noiselessly upstairs.

He thought he had never felt so full of despair. Thick heavy shadows fell from the ceiling, shrouding in mystery the canopy of the bed and the dim furniture. A wood fire was dying down on the hearth, and he could hear the ticking of a marble clock which was drowned from time to time by the rumble of the last motor-buses. Jean Mourin went to bed.

Then it was that for the first time he called up an image that he thought had disappeared: his double, the man that he had been, *Gervais the tailor.*

Jean, who was not asleep, saw once more his other self as he had appeared in the hospital, on the night of December the 13th, in the mirror in his room. How well Jean remembered the shock and terror of that sight.

But this odd creature Gervais, the other Mourin, had not been destroyed on the night of December 13th; he had become part of Jean's own being. Nothing dies. Gervais could not entirely disappear. And Jean saw clearly, so clearly that it hurt him, his dual personality. He had lived, he had died, and now he lived again. But from the moment he began to move, the dead man who lived once more felt that he was being followed by a tenacious ghost, a pale reflection of his soul from which he could never escape.

He heard two o'clock strike. Almost immediately he felt overcome by sleep. In the morning the noise of the servants woke him up. He

rang the bell, ate his breakfast quickly, and dressed to go out. The morning was clear, bright, and dry. Jean felt more cheerful and laughed at his fears of the night.

His own affairs occupied the day time. He lived for a week in an alternation of days that were almost happy and nights that were haunted by the figments of his weakened brain. This period of his life was strange and uncertain. Sometimes he sought company, at other times he avoided it. But everywhere he maintained the silence of the solitary traveller.

• • • • • • •

Perhaps it was the first effects of his solitude which, working on a mind inclined to melancholy and foreboding, encouraged the aberrations of his imagination. Or perhaps the dismal aspect of the room produced a kind of temporary delirium. At any rate, in the days that followed, a singular uncertainty began to disturb his meditations.

Up till then, Jean had thought of his second self with a kind of uneasiness. This other Mourin (which had been substituted by his terrible disease for that collection of thoughts, recollections, habits, knowledge and affections that formed his personality), Jean could not think about him without a certain mortification. But it never occurred to him to think about the other as a being foreign to himself. Mourin-Gervais and Jean Mourin were one. They were no more separate than a man who is asleep and dreaming is detached from his conscious and waking self.

But Jean began to give way to certain dim ideas which threatened to obscure his judgment.

"Gervais," he thought, "no longer exists, at least, he does not exist in me, Jean Mourin. But this personage had his own existence. Dr. Hugues' remarks, when he first really explained my case to me, surely made quite clear the particular existence of Gervais the tailor.

"He smoked, he read the papers, he had learnt to sew. And, on the other hand, his knowledge of music had been destroyed. Moreover his speech was ordinary, almost common, while his character was docile, modest and equable.

"Therefore," pursued Mourin, "this is clearly another entity. Perhaps a double. But that very word contains the idea of a distinction."

Yet these enigmas were in contradiction to the ideas that Jean Mourin held, in common with most men, regarding physical reality and appearance. Even his imagination rejected them. It was possible, certainly, to believe in astral bodies and spirits outside the material world.

But every distinction that can be maintained between knowledge and hallucination must make impossible the existence of a living entity that can duplicate itself in space, or the existence of two beings possessing contradictory qualities and amalgamating under the form of one individual.

These were the singular speculations induced by the solitude of Mourin's lodging at the Pheasant Hotel. He began to forget the original cause of his trouble. An unimportant incident which occurred a few days afterward recalled it to him and restored for a while the balance of his mind.

• • • • • • •

One afternoon he was walking slowly up the Rue Soufflot. Along the gleaming asphalt of the pavement a priest was coming towards him. An ecclesiastic with the face of a scholar, in a cassock without bands, in the Roman fashion, and wearing a cloak of thick cloth with the lining edged with red ribbon. Jean Mourin stopped, his heart beating quickly: it was the Abbé Dufour, Vicar of St. Louis-des-Français, much older indeed, but the friend of his uncle, someone who would share with him some memories of his real and veritable existence. He approached him quickly. It was not the Abbé Dufour. Jean tried to excuse himself. But his explanations were so odd and incoherent that the old priest went off rather alarmed thinking he had been talking to a lunatic.

This encounter left within Jean not only the sense of grievous disappointment; it made clear to him the necessity of keeping his secret. This was indeed almost as burdensome as living without friends and without a past. We need witnesses even of our most intimate anguish. Jean began to understand by a sort of analogy what the obsession of a remorse must be like. As yet he felt no hatred for all these creatures, men and women, who passed carelessly on, engrossed in their business, their lives and their calculations, without realising that, at the corner of the street, on the stairs of the underground, they were passing close to someone who was severed from the human tree like a rotten fruit, condemned to live and die without any natural contact with the world which he heard around him. Jean felt no hatred but a dark envy began to grow within him.

Often, after his walks abroad, his existence in his melancholy room gave him a kind of pleasure. It even frightened him for he realised he was beginning to be afraid of everything: he no longer dared to analyse himself or to reflect. How could anyone understand the double effect

of the passage of time on his duplicated life, since with all his exhausting efforts he could not distinguish Jean Mourin from the patient in Room 67?

As to the monstrous happenings of the war of which people round him were continually talking, and which he was incapable of realising, he reminded himself that his double had followed them day by day, since according to Dr. Hugues' report, the other Jean Mourin read the newspaper and joined in the conversation in the hospital.

Thus he plunged into the strangest contradictions and as the days went on he began to think that himself and the *Other* were two successive aspects of the same individual, two persons in one human being.

After a great deal of hesitation he suddenly decided to take up the study of his case. Libraries had been written by specialists on the variation of personality. Jean began to frequent with assiduity philosophical and medical book-shops. He kept, with a sort of uneasy shame, at the bottom of a trunk which was always locked, books by Ribot, Bourru, Hesnard, Edward Angel, Betchterew, Sloeving, Decourtis, Esquivol. He lived in a sort of nightmare while he was reading these authors. At last he began to feel his reason giving way, and he locked them up, together with certain novels in which troubles like his were used as the foundation for surprising and shocking adventures.

But all the characters in the novels and the cases described by the learned authors came back to his memory. He began to imagine their presence in his room in the hotel. In the evening he seemed to be surrounded by plaintive grotesque creatures, searching for their own selves under the furniture and behind the curtains. He began to think that sooner or later this melancholy troupe of idiot phantoms would seize on him and drag him to Room 67 where Dr. Hugues was waiting for him, standing up in his white overall.

He swore he would never again open the box of books. For two days, three days, he kept his word. But the struggle was too great, he went back to his studies. The desire for knowledge drew him on as a man is drawn to the edge of an abyss.

For whole nights and days he buried himself in those mysteries of neuro-psychiatry which come so perilously near to us in our daily lives. He discovered how his ego can become enfeebled under the influence of a morbid condition, and how its contact with the exterior world may be broken. In the light of all this information he was better able to understand the copy of the long statement which Dr. Hugues had handed

to him on the day following his cure. With intentness and horror he studied the character of his second self, the man of Room 67, "Gervais the tailor," and he tried to discover any characteristics in himself that might connect him with the other. It was in this way that the image of which he had tried to get rid began to implant itself in his mind and even to haunt his waking hours. Gervais gradually became his inseparable companion.

This was the origin of the crisis which attacked him in the early part of February. It began on Friday evening, January 30th.

• • • • • • •

Jean had just got into bed. A lamp was burning on the table beside him. For a long time he lay awake with his eyes closed. A brilliant pink light penetrated his eyelids. He recognised the sensation: he had felt it recently. But where? He remembered: it was at Grenoble on the evening when the soul of the *Other* had disappeared into infinity.

The *Other*, always that *Other*. Jean wondered if he was really dead. Gervais would surely return mysteriously one evening and claim and reoccupy the place of which he had been dispossessed, annihilating once more the personality of Jean Mourin. It would probably be an evening like this, cold and sinister, peopled with the phantasms of solitude. . . . Horrible doubts! Everything seemed to exaggerate the fears of a soul lost among his kind, and especially the silence of the winter night which in the midst of Paris isolated him from his fellows.

Jean put the lamp out. Immediately he felt a presence in the room. He could not bear it. The *Other* was there, in the darkness, watching the sleeper like an enemy. And at the same time he felt himself, *his present self,* outside his own entity, and in an access of delirium, he imagined his two personalities, at the foot of the bed on which he was lying, locked in a dark and silent struggle for the possession of his body. Covered with sweat, and shaking from head to foot, he lit the lamp. He was alone in the room. The light faded away *in* the oval reflection of a mirror and all he could hear were the gusts of wind howling down the Rue Notre-Dame-des-Victoires. Jean trembled and felt himself growing pale. He could not move: an absurd fear kept him from getting up and going into his dressing room, for he would have to pass in front of his mirror: and he was afraid he would be caught and shut up for ever with his own reflection behind the silvered glass.

His fears increased as his mind grew more disordered. His thoughts seemed to be moving in a dream, outside his experiences, like a man

walking in his sleep: then he seemed to fall heavily and re-enter himself, and his consciousness was enclosed once more in his own person. And afterwards the *Other* came back as if he had the power of going through the walls of the hotel, and it was in vain that Jean tried to eject him.

All night he lay there shivering, sleepless, on the verge of madness. And the nights that followed did not bring him back the calm that he longed for. It was in vain that he burned the doctor's report and sold his books. At last he began to think that the silence of his lodging enveloped the walls in a sort of isolating medium, enclosing him in the most utter and silent solitude, cutting him off from his neighbours. The very idea suggested a remedy. The bustle of some noisier habitation would dispel these fears, these terrible illusions. Undoubtedly the best thing he could do would be to live in some cosmopolitan hotel and distract his mind with the din of the orchestras, the coming and going of the visitors, and the incessant movement of the lifts. But he could not think of it for want of money. The alternative was to take some furnished rooms where the noise and wholesome vulgarity of the life around him would force him out of his imaginings. He went to look at some on the following day. But the appearance of the landlords and the coarse looking rooms repelled him. Yet he did not give up his idea of leaving the sombre and silent Pheasant Hotel.

Chance came to his assistance. A regular customer of the restaurant, employed in the postal service, had applied for and obtained a post in Sénégal. He was looking for someone who would take over his lease and give him a good price for his furniture. It was a bachelor's apartment: three rooms on the fifth floor of a house in the Rue St. Sauveur. Two of the rooms contained all that was necessary for a man living by himself: the third was a little drawing room with a sofa in it and just space enough for a piano. The three windows of the little room opened on to two streets. A grey carpet covered the floors and on all sides was a good deal of reassuring noise.

The owner wanted six thousand francs for the lease and the furniture: Jean paid him the same day. The rental was twelve hundred francs. Jean had his trunks and clothes taken round to the Rue St. Sauveur and what was left of his music from the villa at Meilles, together with a miniature grand piano that was the wonder of the neighbourhood. He believed he had saved himself.

• • • • • • •

Having paid his bill at the hotel, and made sure that his belongings

were on their way to his new lodging, Jean took his departure by the Rue de Réaumur and, full of satisfaction at walking abroad on this warm March afternoon, he turned down the Rue du Sentier.

The passers-by followed each other along the narrow pavement. Near the corner of the boulevard Jean stopped to look at a jeweller's shop window. On one side was a display of large silver objects, laid out on crimson velvet, and endlessly re-duplicated in an arrangement of mirrors. Jean was amusing himself by watching how the reflections were continually effaced by the traffic and the passers-by, when a kind of sudden fascination kept him standing stiffly against the shop window. He wanted to move: he realised that he ought to move. But a sensation of awful emptiness held him rooted to the ground and he looked in front of him.

In the open street, in the midst of all the movement of a Paris morning, there came upon him the same shudder that had seized him away in Grenoble, in room No. 67, when he had observed in his toilet mirror that mask of the *Other*, the stranger, Gervais the tailor, that aspect of himself, that bearded personage so well known to the doctors and the nurses but of whose existence he himself had been ignorant for sixteen years.

He had seen him every day, morning and evening, at his dressing and undressing: how was it he had never noticed him? And now for the second time he felt the same disquiet.

This face belonging to another, to the *Other*, with its beard of greying hair and linen cap, the impersonal countenance of a working man in hospital, there it was still on his shoulders. He felt painfully uneasy. He meant indeed to remain unknown in a world unknown to him: but at least he wished to be himself and a single individual.

But the face that he had caught sight of among the kaleidoscopic reflections of the street recalled Mourin to the reality of his double life. He was in possession of his senses, cured, a reasonable being, yet he carried with him the appearance of a mysterious madman whose words, actions, and interests had been unknown outside the room of a hospital in Grenoble: he, the living man, was the husband of a dead woman whose ashes had been years ago so cruelly scattered, and whom, to the hour of her death, the man that he, Jean Mourin, had been for sixteen years, had never known.

He understood suddenly that his life was like a film cut off and joined at random. An episode that he believed destroyed might sud-

denly emerge from nowhere, upset the order of events, and introduce for the second time the gestures and expression of a personage who had disappeared. Fearful mysteries indeed. Jean thought he had found an immediate remedy for these uncertainties: he would destroy once and for all the appearance of the false Jean Mourin, the face of Gervais which by a disquieting anomaly had survived its owner and covered like a mask the face of the musician who was now restored to health. Just as Jean had left his intermediate self in the room of the hospital at Grenoble he ought to have destroyed, on his return to the society of the living, the very appearance of the man that he no longer was. He would discover his real face again, get rid of his beard, and alter the cut of his hair: why had it not occurred to him before?

He found himself by the Chateaudun crossing. There was a barber's shop at the bottom of the Rue des Martyrs. Jean pushed open the door quickly as if someone were pursuing him. There was no one in the shop but an assistant idly turning over some illustrated papers. While he was unfolding the towels he looked at the customer who was in such a hurry to alter his appearance. But Jean did not notice him: he had no eyes but for his own grey-bearded visage which he was going to destroy, and which neither he nor anyone else would ever see again. And he reflected with a certain sombre pleasure that what remained of the occupant of room No. 67 would now be removed from the world and that Jean Mourin, unrecognisable and completely reconstructed, would make an attempt at a new life. The personage who was to make the acquaintance of the good people in the Rue St. Sauveur would be the Mourin of old days, recovering from life such measure of his youth as had been left to him.

Meanwhile the hairdresser was busily stropping the razors and washing the scissors. The firm round mask of the new Jean Mourin gradually detached itself from the soap that covered it. With the aid of the brush his hair recovered its romantic waves. Jean felt that he was escaping, that with his everyday face he was recovering his name, his inner life, the baulked youth of a man who has grown old without living: the loving faithful heart of a man of twenty-eight, though he was a widower of forty-five abandoned by everyone, whose only companions were the forgotten dead.

• • • • • • •

He was delighted with the house in the Rue St. Sauveur. In other days it would have filled him with disgust. In the lodge which opened

on to the vestibule the porter with a cap on and sleeves rolled up was playing cards with one of the tenants. Jean reached his apartment by a staircase which, from floor to floor, passed through four distinct layers of smells. At the top of the stairway draughts from three windows blew down the corridor. A passage led to the right through three rows of numbered doors. A little further on an iron sink absorbed and ejected the contents of slop-pails. Jean, who began to become acquainted with his neighbours, called them to mind as he passed their doors.

Near the beginning of the passage lived two taxi-drivers. Opposite them lived an Italian, a traveller in soap, wearied by his visits to the wash-houses of La Villette and Ménilmontant. Further on was a certain Gade, a retired clock-maker, a hunchback, with a spine curved like a fish-bone. In No. 38 lived a sort of broken-down military man, always to be found in shirtsleeves and elastic sided boots, one Brielle de Chuinaz, a retired officer of dragoons, whose interests were mainly erotic. His habits and his conflicts with the police were well known. On Sundays from time to time at the beginning of the month he came back to the hotel after a stormy night so broken and ravaged, that his jaw had dropped like the hinged front of a box-file. The adjoining room belonged to a working man who, when inflamed by alcohol, created a violent disturbance in the corridor in the middle of the night. Next to him was old Mother Petiot, a kindly good old lady who mended umbrellas and lived with her mother, a paralytic endowed with immortality. Last but one, next to Jean Mourin's little apartment lived the potman of a bar in the Rue de Mont Orgueil, an invisible Savoyard, who came home late at night and every morning on awaking poured out blasts on his accordion.

• • • • • • •

In the little drawing room Jean found a wood fire nearly out which he re-lit: he took off his overcoat and sat down on the sofa. What a relief! To add to his enjoyment, he went over step by step his movements since his awakening at the hospital. And his pleasure was increased by his having no part in the cares and struggles which surrounded his island like a storm. With a cold bourgeois egotism he took refuge in the past: his solitude seemed to prolong its duration and he was able to enjoy it alone like a forbidden drug.

Sometimes in the course of his wanderings he came upon old fashion papers, old theatrical and sporting magazines, where he discovered the appearance of a society of which he was the sole surviving contem-

porary: groups of elegant ladies photographed at the races or the skating-rink in wide skirts and ribboned hats seemed to him to recall the friends of her whose loss he was so recently mourning. He could only breathe comfortably in a world that had disappeared. One day as he was crossing the Passage Brady, he was touched to notice an antiquated vestige of a smart lady of years ago who was gazing with dim eyes at a milliner's window display.

Everything that was connected with the past brought his youth back to him and all his will was absorbed in the effort to live again.

In this way he came back to music. Before leaving "The Willows" he had put aside, together with certain family portraits, Jeanne's dresses, and the contents of a desk, his piano and his music, the works of the Masters and his own compositions. For a long time he hesitated. He did not dare to open the piano. He could not dissociate music from the recollection of his dead wife. All his admirations had been hers also. To play once more would perhaps only bring back echoes of the joys that they had shared. An attempt to re-awaken these ardours and delights would be too like those gloomy and sacrilegious pilgrimages that are made alone to the scenes of ancient affections. Surely it would disturb her shade, she who had never heard his steps approach her grave, and was there not a risk that the spell of his music would evoke another phantom? All manner of fears tormented him and he was torn between the horror of the silence and solitude, to which Gervais would certainly one day return, and the magic of music which would call up the living image of his wife among the moving waves of sound.

One day—it was a Sunday afternoon—he ventured to open the piano. His love of music overcame his apprehensions. He began to play. It was like a feast to a starving man. He played greedily with the blissful energy of all his being. There was no more thought of sorrow or of exile in that poor room which was filled with the rhythms composed by the Masters long ago. He played from memory, and the flood of music seemed to flow from his brain along his outstretched arms and fall in rapid drops upon the keys.

The music was like a strong and simple consolation; it enveloped his whole being. He bent forward over his hands on the keyboard and the sad festival of harmonies continued. The instrument obeyed his will and created, in that little room, dreams and forgetfulness. The light began to fail but he did not notice it. The dusk began to cover everything with the faint hue of a spider's web: only the soft whiteness of his

hands could be seen moving over the ivory keyboard which a last ray of light reflected in the dead blackness of the piano.

Jean got up unsteadily. The hooting of the taxi-cabs could be heard from below. The street began to light up, while the upper stories gradually melted away into the violet dusk. Jean stood by the window and watched the masses of the buildings disappear into the surging mist: the eddies of smoke and the electric sky signs flashing their alternate red and white lights.

Should he go out, and scatter these delicious terrors? No, he had some bachelor supplies in a cupboard: from those and the remains of his breakfast he made his dinner. Then he carried the lamp into the drawing room and with a kind of savage obstinacy sat down to the piano again. How long did he go on? No matter. That evening he absorbed music like opium. He thought he had found a cure for his obsessions: a festival of dreams that he could enjoy at will, above the hostile noises of the city upon which the rains of February still beat down.

The time that followed was like an awakening. Midnight had just struck and the familiar noises of the fifth floor began. The cinemas had closed and the lodgers were coming home. All over the house were heard bursts of laughter and of talking and then a sharp clatter of footsteps down the corridors. From behind his glass door Jean watched all the neighbours of his story as they passed.

M. Brielle de Chuinaz came home singing, one of the earliest: after him the taxi-cab driver. The retired clock-maker brought home the elderly spinster: they talked for a long time between their two doors and finally made up their minds to retire to their respective attics of which the portals slammed simultaneously behind them.

Jean listened carefully to all these noises. They marked the time as exactly as a public clock. As soon as these folks had got into bed the fifth story fell into its first sleep. It was awakened for a moment by the arrival of the Savoyard potman, and again later on, about the time the markets opened, by the return of a certain ancient cabman whose life and times were disappearing in the neighbourhood of stations and certain dubious haunts.

Jean spied on all these comings and goings and found a relief in it. He knew that when the noises had subsided the bitter burden of silence would descend on him with all its force. The nightly noises of the street—the endless succession of lorries and market gardeners' carts—

could not dispel the fear that he felt that night of seeing the dark and silent witnesses of his former madness appear in his room.

In a few days, perhaps, he would overcome once and for all these evil presences that were the offspring of his mind and battened on his solitude like blind and monstrous fishes in the unlighted depths. He had found light and a companion. What a relief never to be alone again, to triumph for ever over fear and silence.

The *Other* had no more terrors for him. In his intoxication Jean thought that his deliverance was merely an affair of the will, and he saw himself strong and resolute, crushing his horrible visitor of the night boldly and suddenly, as if he had rushed at him and strangled him.

A door opened. A fantastic and lugubrious song filled the corridor, accompanied by a kind of drumming noise. It was the drunken occupant of No. 59 arousing the neighbourhood. This happened from time to time about the middle of the night, more especially when the rain was beating on the sloping lid of his garret. Jean got up from his chair and went out. The man was wandering about in the darkness dressed in a shirt and pants. He was marking time to his songs with the key of his room, with which he was beating on the cover of a slop-pail.

Some other doors opened and half dressed people emerged. The drunken man went on singing and paid no attention to their protests. Suddenly a light appeared at the bottom of the staircase, as the outer door of the house shut. A heavy step creaked up the stairway. The old coachman of the Urbaine Cab Company was coming back to his garret. His white hat appeared, looking like a dirty paper bag, and then, behind a cloud of blue smoke from his pipe, a muffler surmounted by a strawberry coloured countenance.

"Come along, old boy, time to go to bed," he said, as he noticed his friend, who without a protest allowed himself to be pushed into his room.

"Good-night, everybody," grunted the cabman with hoarse good nature. The clatter of his sabots could be heard as he moved among his belongings and on the bare floor of his habitation. Soon the voices grew silent. The far-off whistle of a locomotive was borne over the roofs on the gusts of rain. Jean stirred the fire and went to sleep by the hearth, sitting in his mahogany and velvet arm-chair.

III

The spring arrived. Jean lived in silence, outside the passage of time. His neighbours, whom he met at the common sink in the corridor and whom he greeted with the most careful politeness, had given up trying to account for him. They all called him "the gentleman" with that touch of slightly contemptuous respect which the lower classes show to the broken bourgeois. They knew that the musician did not earn his living by his talents, that he lived alone, and quietly, without mistress or friends: his habits were known and there was no information to be had from old Mother Petiot who looked after him. At last they decided that the new lodger was a man who had no need to work, a little eccentric, without vices, who had suffered misfortunes.

Several months passed in this way, while Jean, among the harassed and agitated lives of his neighbours, lived like an artist of days gone by. Food, rent, personal expenses and new music, of which he grew quickly tired, this was the sum-total of his expenditure.

He thought with sadness of the joys of past days, the simple ardent delights of the musician. Those Sundays at the Châtelet concerts! They lived again in his mind, images grown somewhat blurred. Jean knew very well that he would never go to a concert again. He would find too many regrets and too much bitterness under the low ceiling of the gallery. What sort of audience had taken the place of those bearded and mystical bohemians bending in the darkness over the sounding cauldron of the auditorium whence surged up the genius of Beethoven or Wagner, while the romantic Ride, launched with loose reins, shook the walls of the old theatre. That was nothing but a haunt of sorrow and of the past. He made up his mind and finally shut himself in like an aged recluse. A lending library provided him with novels which he read at a sitting but without enthusiasm. He wrote a few sonatas which he destroyed almost at once. He rarely opened a newspaper, but he was an enthusiastic reader of the *Illustration.*

About the middle of April he felt a sort of physical disturbance. His seclusion began to be burdensome: he felt once more the desire of seeing the faces of old times. Perhaps the lawyer Brondin could

find some traces of them in his records. He wrote to him. The lawyer came and regretted that his researches had been in vain. But his client seemed ill, uneasy, in an almost enfeebled condition, and he expressed his anxiety.

"You live too much alone. Don't you go to a café at all?"

"I never go now."

"You must amuse yourself."

Jean promised and kept his word. From that date he began to take long walks. A pale sunshine played over the posters on the walls and the young foliage on the trees. Quick showers sent the taxis hurrying along, then a fresh breeze blew down the streets and everything seemed suddenly to look cheerful.

In the open daylight Jean saw himself more clearly. He had grown thin and pale. His head seemed laden with his thoughts. He walked slowly, aimlessly, always led by a sort of instinct which brought him back to the places to which he had been most attached. Sometimes he avoided the passers-by with a sort of shrinking movement which made them turn round: some of them would stop and watch the disappearing figure whose gait, expression and pallor displayed so profound a melancholy. As he walked about in this way a singular idea came to him. "How," he asked himself, "would this Gervais that was I, have looked at all this, what impressions would he have felt at this new Paris that has become so feverish and diversified?" This notion, which at first seemed purposeless, came back to him frequently and finally became an obsession. He could only get rid of it by hurrying on, or by speaking to a passer-by under some futile pretext.

One day he thought he would consult a doctor and only changed his mind when he was at the door and about to ring the bell. He felt, indeed, troubled and uneasy, and he began to be afraid of experiencing once more in the Rue St. Sauveur, the nights at the Pheasant Hotel. But he had an even more lively fear of doctors, of their scrutinising looks and their questions.

If, when tired of walking, he sat down outside some café, the idea came back to him, even more powerful and compelling. He conceived himself then under the twin aspect of a duplicated individual, his two entities seated side by side, or opposite each other, and consuming identical drinks. But as the days went on the image of Gervais began to reconstruct itself in Jean's mind with more and more precision. He did not see the *Other:* he felt rather as though he himself were being in-

spected by him, and experienced that sort of annoyance that is produced by the too attentive regard of a stranger. This soon became intolerable: he called the waiter and went away quickly without turning his head.

This went on until the beginning of June. Jean had taken up smoking again. At first the use of tobacco, which he smoked freely, as man without occupation does, relieved him to an extraordinary degree. His hallucinations grew less frequent and finally disappeared. Jean recovered his peace of mind, until he began to be troubled by faintness and had to give up his pipes. Once more he shut himself up. He watched the traffic gloomily from his window as it crossed in two streams like the movement of shuttles, and wove along the base of the buildings a living stuff coloured with purple shadows and yellow sunlight.

• • • • • • •

In the following week Jean began to go out again. His normal expression had come back and he seemed quite sane once more. But it was merely seeming. He was inspired by a morbid instinct which made him simulate normality. Moreover it was noteworthy that the opinion of his neighbours worried him.

At the same time his obsession that he had seen things and persons before increased upon him: he was continually looking into people's faces searching for and finding resemblances. Where had he seen this M. Brielle de Chuinaz, and the Savoyard with his plaintive accordion, the hunch-backed clock-maker, and the red-faced cab-driver, living side by side in lodgings like this, in the ancient top story that with its rows of numbered doors seemed to move over Paris like the deck of a ship.

Also the crisis that Jean Mourin had just gone through left certain abnormal obsessions behind it, notably the necessity of keeping the door of his lodging bolted.

It was a glass fronted door with an overhanging lintel and crossbars such as can still be seen in the top floors of certain buildings in Paris. A coarse curtain, sewn in tucks, and stretched on two rods, concealed the entrance from the view of the passer-by in the passage. As soon as he got up Jean was constantly pulling this curtain over the corners of the glass panes. He never lit the lamps without hanging some thick stuff over the door. And he so arranged the furniture that the door of the drawing room was no longer behind him while he was playing the piano—as he did for hours together.

He was continually listening to the sound of steps which could be

heard tapping down the passage outside the partition wall: and he listened eagerly as though he were waiting for or dreading the arrival of someone.

• • • • • • •

Summer came quickly and promised to be hot. Jean, who got up early, spent the morning wandering about the squares and gardens. He lay down in the middle of the day and at dusk got up again to play the piano. Then he went off for a walk always alone down the quays of the Seine. He avoided company more and more, realising that in everything he was a stranger to his fellow-creatures. Did he not differ from all his fellows who were accustomed to consider life as a continuous phenomenon, while for him, Jean Mourin, any conception of the universe must include the idea of intermittence.

Existence seemed to him like a series of three rooms, of which the second, the middle one, was dark and moreover geometrically impossible since it had no outlets and no walls. He had passed through these rooms alternately feeling his way and dazzled with light. Thus his intelligence gradually accepted the idea of resurrection. He had sojourned for a time in a tomb and he was now approaching the confines of a second death so that in his mind the relations of succession appeared at once destroyed and inverted.

These fearful fancies haunted his mind and music completed its ruin. He used music with despair as a sick man who knows that he is lost uses a poisonous remedy. Sometimes he spent the whole day at the piano, no longer turning the pages of the volume he had picked up and opened at random. He played from memory and gradually deserting the text plunged into passionate improvisation. His hands moved heavily as they struck chords full of a savage majesty. Thus he went on at the mercy of his delirium, absorbed in his talent, but paying no more attention to the empty sounds he was creating than a man pursued would notice the charms of the landscape.

Night invaded the little room and it became enveloped in shadow. Jean continued to evoke his mirages.

The echo of the notes seemed suspended in the night like an aroma. The arpeggios unrolled themselves like invisible creeping growths. The hazard of inspiration and the recollection of his hands reconstructed in the darkness once familiar melodies and forgotten rhythms. A confusion of sound broke up gradually into intimate harmonies. The player found a momentary salvation and dedicated to

Jeanne, to the recollection of their dead youth, the dark intoxication of his senses.

The power of music freed him from the laws of time as it broke the spell of his affliction. The Rue St. Sauveur, the hostile city, the muddy evenings when the enigmatical Gervais was concealed among the anxious crowds returning from their work-shops or their offices—all this had disappeared.

In his thoughts he went back to "The Willows"—to the time of shaded gardens, love and youth. The wild concert took on an enchantment. The shadow of his beloved moved again about him. The subdued light of the lamps, under their lace shades, lit up the depths of the mirrors and the portraits of their forebears. Or again it was the time of his betrothal at the house of Uncle Claude in a country priest's garden scented with jasmine and melon-flower.

Again he would feel suddenly surrounded by flames. He was forging his harmonies in the awakened fires of his passion. He wept, he called upon her name even as he hammered on the keys. His head thrown back and his face wet with tears he gave way to his intoxication until weariness overcame him. And weariness came before satiety. Jean collapsed at last on to his bed and slept the heavy sleep of a man exhausted by excess.

He awoke in the morning fully dressed, his face lined and creased like a silk handkerchief. He acquired a new strength from his walks abroad. He could be seen coming back with hurried steps and taking his breakfast at some pastrycook's along the street. There was something edged and sensitive about his appearance at this time which was quite appalling. His body, wasted with fever, seemed continually in need of support. His whole being quivered. The breaking point was near. They talked about him in the evening in the seven lodgings on his floor, so full of misery and despair, and they all thought that his condition was the fantastic caprice of an idle bachelor, extremely irritating to his neighbours.

• • • • • • •

About the middle of June the city lay prostrated by the heat. A wind from the south blew through the streets, fetid, burning, and loaded with invisible dust. The neighbours disappeared from view. At intervals the clock-maker could be heard cursing. The retired soldier appeared in the passage half naked and waving a fan. In the heaviest heats the house seemed abandoned.

Very early on the morning of the 13th, Jean Mourin rushed out of his lodging. He carried a valise in his hand and greeted his neighbours as he hurried towards the stairs. He looked like a man who had awakened too late and was afraid of missing his train.

Without slackening his pace, he ran down the stairway. At the corner of the Rue Montorgueil he hailed a cab.

"To the Lyons Station."

He recovered his breath as he sank back on the cushions and took out his watch. He thought he would get there in time to catch the express for Grenoble. His whole being was possessed and intent upon this hope. If he caught this train he would arrive on the morning of the 14th, at the platform of a small station buried among chestnut trees under a blue cliff seamed by torrents: Bourg d'Oisans. There lay Jeanne Mourin and the 14th June was—for him—the first anniversary of her death.

The train was just moving out of the station. Jean managed to clamber into a carriage. As far as Dijon he looked through the window at the passing fields and roads. And when his eyes grew tired of the chequered landscape whirling past he fell to watching the antics of the smoke that seemed rushing at full speed to meet the train. It mounted up into the sunshine, projecting on the fields fantastic shadows which gradually disappeared among the shivering grasses as the flakes of smoke faded into the blue heaven.

Opposite, an obese gentleman was wiping his brow. In the other corner a priest was dreaming over his breviary. Both of them had tried to engage Jean in their banal conversation. Finally, giving up their taciturn fellow traveller, they had taken to conversing with each other and for hours without ceasing they had been lamenting together the evils of the time. Jean had to change at Lyon. Night had fallen when he reached Grenoble. A night without sleep. In the early morning he took the Vizille tramway and from thence a winding path which brought him about midday to the bottom of the road, at the entrance to the Bourg. A moment later Jean went in to the little mountain cemetery which was more full of white graves than a Mussulman necropolis. For some time he searched among the tombs. Jeanne's grave was at the far end near the wall between two family vaults. An iron railing confined the wild growth that slipped between the bars like strands of hair. Two crowns of immortelles and blackened ornaments hung with their torn ribbons on each side of the melancholy enclosure. But there were, too, flowers whose scattered

blossoms lay among the dark grasses like the remains of a shattered garland. In the middle of all this disorder was a stone cross

Here lies
Jeanne Mourin
died June 14th igo6
aged 26 years

The inscription was becoming effaced: a patch of moss had blurred the beloved name, and the date had become almost a matter of conjecture, so weathered had the stone become with the rains of sixteen years.

When he reached the grave Jean felt all the pain of weary hearts at the sight of the resting place of their beloved. For the first time tears burst from his eyes. He leaned against the railing and his tears fell upon the little deserted mound. Jeanne was there. In this place her mortal remains were dissolving, and yet he who was bending over the earth in which this frightful process was being accomplished felt more acutely there than anywhere else the presence of his departed wife. He managed to restrain himself from calling her name aloud in the sunny silence of the cemetery.

"Jeanne, it is I, it is your husband who has come to look for you."

His legs trembled and gave way, and he fell upon his knees. Then with a sudden effort he got up and walked quickly towards the town. He is looking for a gardener. Someone points to a door. Flowers, flowers! He buys an armful, holding them against his body, unbound and without leaves. Flowers alone, flowers.

He runs to the cemetery, and pushes back the gate. The sun which had gone in for a moment has appeared again. Jean moves quickly among the graves and flings his perfumed burden with open arms into the melancholy enclosure. Then he takes off his hat and with expressionless face and dry eyes departs without looking behind him.

• • • • • • •

He spent the morning idly in Grenoble. He felt stronger and more at ease and took a physical pleasure in breathing the keen air of the Alps. He realised suddenly that this pilgrimage, whose urgency had come upon him in the unquiet moments of an awakening, might be the means of rescuing him from the fatal slavery of his dreams.

He walked in the shade of the Victor Hugo Square like a man relieved of a long anxiety, who goes upon a journey and comes again upon familiar scenes not without a certain satisfaction. He turned to the

left along a few short streets through which were passing officers and soldiers. Just as he was entering the Avenue Lesdiguières, he felt that someone was walking behind him and at the same moment heard a voice addressing him in a strong local accent:

"Why it's Monsieur Mourin! Good morning, Monsieur Mourin!"

He turned round as if someone had struck him. Was there someone in the world, a living being who knew his name! Someone was calling him by name, putting a name to that face of his that had arisen from the dead—a human voice was breaking the bonds of his solitude. His first movement was one of fear. The gesture that escaped him must have been like that of a guilty soul who after years of hidden life hears his name suddenly called out by a policeman. But a foolish hope filled Jean's heart.

"Sir?"

He saw before him a man of fifty of reddish countenance with a moustache and of a common appearance. He was wearing a suit of drill and carrying a stick with an awkward air. Jean's attitude did not appear to surprise him. Raising his hat he came nearer and observed affably in a jovial voice:

"Ah, I recognised you although you have had your beard shaved. Of course I knew you first just as you are now, only a little less gray and a little fatter. Lord, that wasn't yesterday. . . ."

"Sir, I have not the honour . . ."

"You don't recognise me, of course. I understand. But it gives one a funny feeling after being together for so long. You were an extra special case, you were. They can't deprive you of that."

And he added politely as if he were paying a choice compliment:

"I've seen some cases of madness, the finest of them: but I've never seen one like yours."

Already a few idlers had stopped at the edge of the pavement.

"Sir," said Jean, much annoyed, "I beg you not to speak so loud. First will you tell me who you are."

"Certainly," said the other in a lower voice but with the same playful air, "chance is a wonderful thing. I'm Auguste Francoz who looked after you in hospital. I saw you admitted: so you can imagine I know you pretty well! But this is the best of it. Only yesterday we were talking about you in Dr. Hugues' wards, just as he was passing your room. No. 67, wasn't it? He turned to Sister Céline and me who were going round with him as usual. 'And Mourin,' he said, 'don't we get any news of

him? Odd, I should have thought he would have written.' Then as he was going downstairs Dr. Hugues said, 'It's annoying not to keep up with one's patients. Besides I have got something to give him.'"

"To give me?" said Jean.

"Yes."

"And what did he say about it?"

"Nothing. You know he doesn't say very much. . . . Well, Monsieur Mourin, I won't give you any advice, but as you are here, if I were you I should look in at the hospital."

A sudden light flashed in Jean's eyes. At the word hospital he felt a sharp shock. Then he appeared to reflect and make up his mind.

"Well anyhow I'm glad to have seen you," said the man . . .

"Thank you, Auguste, I will go and see the doctor."

"I forgot to ask you whether you were living in these parts. No? I'm sorry. And go and see Sister Céline. She was there too when you came. She will be as pleased as I am."

"Good-bye, I will go and see them."

"Good-bye," said the man, moving off.

• • • • • • •

"This is a surprise. Sit down," said Dr. Hugues.

Jean recognised him at once. Tall, solid, moving easily in his loose coat tied in at the waist with a linen belt. And in his military eyes the same direct look that seemed to come from far off and fasten like two arrows on the face of his visitor.

"I was talking about you a little while ago."

"I know, doctor."

He did not seem to hear the answer. Mechanically, with the powerful detachment of the scientific mind, he took possession of his patient. Jean made no protest, and allowed his head to be bent backwards. Dr. Hugues placed his hands like blinkers over Jean's temples and looked carefully into his eyes.

"Everything going all right?"

"Yes, doctor."

"No headaches, no giddiness, no nightmares? You ought to keep in touch with us, Mourin. Don't you trust us?" He took hold of his wrist and went on talking while feeling his pulse.

"Do you sleep well? I think you have got thinner."

"Doctor," said Jean Mourin, "I met someone just now."

He related his interview with Francoz. But he had the impression

as he spoke that his voice was becoming thin and weak and far off. He felt as though he were going to sleep and the sounds that reached him seemed dim like those that are heard in the brief moment that precedes sleep. Dr. Hugues watched him steadily with that cold pale look that was so apt at discovering passing symptoms and penetrating the secrets of his patients.

"Come," said the doctor, without moving his eyes, "I see that you have entirely forgotten Gervais."

Jean tried to answer. Should he confess his fears and recount his dreams, relate to this man, who might be able to rescue him, the hallucinations of the Pheasant Hotel? Perhaps Dr. Hugues would be able to show him some remedy. Should he speak? No. Suddenly, something held him back. They might keep him here, shut him up once more. What was this force that controlled his actions so that he no longer recognised the agency of his will? He felt now as if he had been betrayed into entering this white room, into the presence of this stern man of science, between these walls that were smoother than porcelain. The real fear of a child shut up in fun who believes he will never get out again. The friendly reproaches of the doctor seemed to reach him through a partition. It seemed as though night were falling and that the gate was about to be shut when the refectory bell rang. Then he would never be able to get away.

"No," he replied, "I don't see him any more."

The doctor looked at him with even greater intensity. Under his regard Jean felt himself diminished, giving way.

"You no longer see whom?" asked the pitiless voice.

"Why, Gervais."

He heard a burst of laughter which seemed to come from far off. But the cheerful countenance of the doctor seemed to threaten him. Everything was moving: the white walls with their framed diagrams, the lacquered chest on which stood a chemist's jar painted with pink carnations, the book-case with its dull glass windows and melancholy volumes of formulae, the table covered with brass mechanisms and microscopes, the glass case of nickelled instruments, the light with its uncovered reflectors. . . . Jean, caught in this seizure, did not dare to move or to breathe. But the doctor ceased to look at him and suddenly everything in the room seemed in its place again. Sounds became once more clear, and it seemed as if the doctor was talking very loud and saying . . .

"Well, good-bye, good-bye. I am very glad to have seen you to-

day."

At last Jean was able to answer.

"I won't keep you any longer, doctor. Anyhow, I must think about catching my train . . . Yes, for Paris, Rue St. Sauveur, a little bachelor lodging. But what was it you wanted to tell me?"

"To tell you?" said Doctor Hugues. "Ah, yes, of course I had something to give you. Nothing special." (He opened a drawer.) "Here you are: two photographs that were taken of you last year, in front of the laundry. It is exactly as you were with your beard, at least. . . . Gervais, you understand?"

"Yes," said Mourin.

He held out a hand that trembled slightly and took the photographs.

"Ah, here he is," said Sister Céline gaily, as she came in.

She wanted to embrace Jean, and she looked with a certain maternal pride at this man with the greying temples whom she had so long looked after.

The affection with which everyone in the place seemed to regard him Jean felt only indirectly. These manifestations were surely addressed to the other, the false Mourin, to Gervais the tailor who was the only one these people had known, and whose portraits he now held in his shaking hand.

"You are not looking at your photographs," said Dr. Hugues.

"Yes, I am."

Jean saw himself as he had been on that evening of rain when his cure had taken place. The snapshot showed him standing with his legs apart in front of a door with heavy locks, bareheaded with woollen socks on his feet, dressed plainly in a regulation shirt and a pair of coarse trousers tightened at the waist. Near him a hospital orderly sat on a garden chair meditatively smoking a pipe.

The doctor took down the telephone receiver: he gave orders in a calm firm voice. The Sister went off on tiptoe. And Jean, far away from his surroundings, was looking eagerly at the photographs.

Even in the shirt he was wearing and in the full light of the hospital yard, he recognised the man who was pursuing him, the haunting appearance which had taken the place of his own. Yet who had stood for this photograph? Undoubtedly himself. And in the face of this piece of evidence he felt more than ever the fearful reality of his double personality.

A voice cut short the thread of his recollections.

"You are staying long?"

"I am leaving to-night."

Voices came up through the open window from the garden. Jean thought he recognised them and shivered. Then the thin melancholy drone of a harmonium could be heard, followed by oaths and bursts of laughter.

Jean pulled himself together.

"Good-bye," he said.

"Well, well," said Dr. Hugues, "good-bye. Have you taken to music again?"

"It is my only occupation."

"Don't overdo it. By the way, leave your address. Bon voyage, then, and this time let us hear from you. Good-bye."

• • • • • • •

On the following day about twelve o'clock Jean was walking down the slope in front of the Gare de Lyon. With his small suit-case in his hand he made his way quickly towards the entrance to the Underground. The weather was grey and heavy and exhausted without warming him. He felt chilled to the bone.

Having fled from the hospital like a man who still doubted his freedom, he had sat in the night express counting the hours till daylight, and he only recovered complete confidence when the train was running through the stations and the gardens of the southern suburbs. He would soon reach Paris, where he could proceed to lose himself, and defy the implacable vigilance of this Dr. Hugues, whose power against him was unlimited.

Give him his address indeed! He congratulated himself on having evaded the question. And now—

They were getting near Paris. Darker and more populous suburbs revealed on either side of the line the approach of the city. Jean felt as if he were coming back into harbour. He forgot his fears, the menace of that crouching, furtive, watchful shadow that he thought so often he had recognised against the walls behind the endless procession of the passers-by. At the moment he could only see in Paris that power of absorption, the quality of a social melting-pot in which he who wishes to disappear soon becomes nothing but smoke and recollection. The high walls of a labyrinth, all the mighty quarters of the city rising up to the clouds, the earth rumbling in its countless subterranean galleries, hordes of adventurers, Yankees, half-castes, cocaine-fiends, and busy scoun-

drels, all the caravanserai of Babel moving in the lights of Montmartre, the ruffian hangers-on of dancers and prize-fighters, a debased orgy, thefts in open daylight, all this detail, which Jean in his excitement composed into a tumultuous panorama, promised him a fresh confidence in his destiny. Henceforward he would be free.

But when he reached the Rue St. Sauveur, disillusionment began. The concierges, who hated the mysterious tenant (M. Mourin had not received one letter or one visitor during his six months' residence), had just summoned the police. Pretending to believe that the tenant had decamped, or had met with an accident, they requested that the door of his apartment might be forced by a locksmith. The unexpected return of Jean put an end to their plans. But the police authorities were anxious to clear up an investigation for which they had detailed two constables and made enquiries in the neighbourhood. Jean was overcome with terror. He had never thought of the secret of his life being discovered, of his "case" being served up in the newspapers as food for vulgar curiosity. He hurried round to the police court.

There he found, in an enclosure of which the wooden barriers had been worn smooth by the elbows of the public and the police, an official with a paternal aspect and a surly voice, who raised his head and asked:

"What is it?"

Jean gave his name.

"Ah, yes," said the official, "your papers?"

"Here is my identity book."

Taking out a handful of memoranda out of a pigeonhole, the other began to write, dictating aloud to himself.

"Mourin, Jean-Albert, born at Fontenay-le-Comte (Vendée) March 5th, 1879, son of Pierre-August and Marie Berard, independent, husband of the late Jeanne Blanche, née Thévenet, born August 12th, 1881, at Saintes, daughter of Louis and Anaïs Violet . . ." Then, turning to Jean he observed:

"It appears that you live a great deal alone and in rather an unusual manner. That is your own affair. Only when you go away it would be better to let the concierge know."

"But why? I receive no letters."

"I know. Anyhow, that is your own concern. I am giving you some good advice. Take it or not as you like." Jean took back his identity book which the other handed to him still open. *Widower:* He noticed the

word: it had been entered in 1906 a few months after his admission to the hospital. Thus his life, his legal life, had gone on while he himself was worse than dead: deprived of his soul. He thought over all this while walking slowly back to the Rue St. Sauveur, and suddenly he remembered that he still had in his waistcoat pocket the two photographs of Gervais.

His doubts fell upon him once more. The movement of the streets surrounded him like a hot whirlwind. Passers-by in a hurry jostled him. He went on, his only sensation being a feeling of emptiness and unreality. He reached the Rue St. Sauveur: he felt that he was being observed. The shopkeepers, who are resting at that hour in the afternoon, seemed to be awaiting his return. They were talking about him. Jean, in a confused sort of way, realised that he was intruding in a world in which idleness is not distinguished from vagabondage. He felt himself that he was out of place. He went past the porter's lodge timidly and climbed furtively up to the fifth floor.

All seemed asleep. Jean slipped into his apartment. Everything was in its usual place. A ray of sunlight fell upon a portrait on the wall, a pastel done of him long ago by Uncle Claude, who had been a clever draughtsman. The piano was open. Everything seemed at rest with that egotistically intimate air that distinguishes bachelor dwellings. Jean felt almost happy, and sitting down in his arm chair found no difficulty in dispelling his load of troubles. Why could not he always be like this? Would not oblivion come with the quiet resolve to live like a man among men? And he who had thus been restored to life thought for a long while about the little cemetery in Dauphiné where for one sunny hour he had felt the exquisite shock of a really human sorrow.

• • • • • • •

This it was, this sudden flash of recollection that finally destroyed his control. He realised it the following day when he tried to settle down to music again. Over the surge of his passionate hallucinations hung the image of the railings and the flowers of that grave.

The ideal sepulchre of Jeanne which he had constructed with his fingers, in the madness of his solitary ecstasies, would never rise again under the dark cedars of the forest of dreams peopled with happy shades. O beloved wife! She would never again lend her wandering form to that magnificent interment, the myriad folds of that shroud and the delicate grave clothes of those encircling harmonies. She lay beneath the earth now, nothing more than a frozen skeleton, at the foot

of the cruel mountains that had killed her, under the muddy tears of the snow and rain.

Jean knew it. It was an aspect of reality that defeated his most cherished means of consolation. Should he close his piano as if it were a coffin from which music would never again arise?

And how was he to live? Everything failed him. He realised now that before his journey to Grenoble and his meeting with the hospital orderly the thought of Dr. Hugues was like a far off lighthouse through the fog. But what was his experience when they had met? A bitter deception, a sharper doubt, fears renewed. He had even lost the refuge of his melancholy isolation and he felt hostile forces bearing down upon his existence from every side.

PART III

I

An aimless walk and, as it would seem, chance alone had led Jean Mourin to this street in which was the entrance to a large music-hall: a square of vivid light, a display of posters and under the electric globes, dark groups of people standing about during the interval.

Jean came up. He did not in the least want to finish the evening at a show. But he stopped in mere idleness, read the programme, and was just moving off when it began to rain. He found shelter in the vestibule. From all sides people came in running. The rain went on: taxis moved off slowly through the puddles in which glimmered the reflection of the street lamps. Many of those who had taken refuge near Jean decided to go in to the promenade. Jean followed them. It was the evening of September 20th.

After a moment he was glad he had decided to go in. What he saw amazed him. The usual women and people smoking elbowed him in the corridor. He could hear around him every sort of language. No one listened to the singers: from time to time when the din of the orchestra suddenly ceased the audience watched the perilous antics of the acrobats. Then the promenade began to move once more. Passions, perfumes and lights matched their forces once again. All this took Jean's mind off his thoughts and he felt a little bewildered and almost happy.

In one of the intervals he followed some of the audience out into a kind of semi-circular foyer, hung with photographs of singers and gymnasts famous long ago, whose style, like their moustaches and their costumes, seemed to everyone but Jean extraordinarily out of date.

A bell rang. The corridor gradually emptied. A few of the people from the promenade still lingered. Jean feeling a little tired walked around the foyer once again. He wondered whether he should wait till the end of the programme. The noise of the bell ceased and an attendant came and turned down the lights. Still Jean did not go back into the theatre. Later on he wondered why he had strayed in this deserted passage, he who had always been nervous of solitude. But are not the most significant events in life always brought about by some involuntary action? For the space of one second a man steps outside himself and obeying some secret impulse which later on he will mistake for

chance, acts in the face of his own desires. A second is enough; in that second an entire existence is overthrown.

Jean Mourin stopped idly in front of a mirror. Tarnished and badly lighted, it shed a pale glimmer round the fringes of its red curtains. It was one of those ancient mirrors in places of public entertainment which seem to have lost their powers of refraction. Their surface is like that of dead water and the light grows dim and fades away into leaden reflections. In one corner of the foyer there remained a haze of tobacco smoke which obscured the outlines of the shabby purple upholstery of the furniture and gave a look of unreality to the collection of theatre notices, frames, and flowers, as if they were seen through a veil of gauze.

Jean, wandering alone in solitude, absent-mindedly hitherto, stopped for a moment and looked at a programme nailed to the wall and listened to the murmur of the orchestra from far off. At that moment without knowing why he turned his gaze to the mirror. And he nearly fell backwards.

Beside him, a little behind, in the blueish mist reflected in the mirror a figure stood motionless. In a flash Jean recognised him.

It was Gervais.

Jean who hoped he was mistaken managed to gather strength to look again. Might it not be a distortion of his own face produced by some effect of cross reflection? No: there are two faces: one pale and haggard, that of Jean Mourin, the other masculine and healthy, belonging to Gervais—the face that Jean had seen on the evening of December 13th, in the looking glass of the hospital at Grenoble, the face of the photographs—the face of Gervais the tailor. He had to come back: and he had come.

He was looking quietly at his reflection, with a wooden pipe in his mouth, his hands deep in his trouser pockets. He was dressed like a working man on a Sunday, with a certain nonchalant air, a quizzical careless look that suggested the secretary of a Trades Union. The face was unmistakable: there it was, in every feature, the face of the inmate of Grenoble hospital, encircled by the coarse and greying beard, rings round the eyes, yellow complexion and that indifferent mouth which seemed so ill assorted to the rest of his countenance. No, Jean could not and did not question it.

And yet he could not take his eyes off that face, which in the badly lit mirror seemed to lurk like a second figure in the background of a portrait.

But such things aren't possible! Gervais had no longer any real existence, Jean knew that perfectly well. If Gervais was to return Mourin would have to fall back into the abyss of madness. But Mourin is here, in a Paris theatre, he knew himself to be in possession of his reason, wholly alive, and in control of his actions. Come, he will turn round, with a sudden movement, and he will laugh to find that he has been at the mercy of an hallucination. He will look behind him. He is quite certain he will see nobody. He turns round.

The man is there, really there, a man of his own height—the man whom he would recognise among a thousand as having seen three times in three different mirrors and whom now he could touch with his hand.

They exchanged looks. Gervais stays where he is looking good-naturedly at his nervous neighbour and calmly removes his pipe from his mouth to release a puff of smoke. And then he smiles.

In the theatre a singer was warbling a Tyrolese song. The shrill roulades reached the foyer and were lost among the noises of the streets. Jean and Gervais are alone, face to face. A little way away a cloakroom-woman sat dozing in a chair. An attendant walked quickly through, turned and disappeared into the staircase leading to the boxes. A noise of applause and then silence.

"What do you want?" said Jean trembling and stammering as he faced the other.

"Nothing at all. I am merely walking about," said he, "I came to amuse myself, and the singer, you see . . ."

He stopped. Jean was standing against the wall and in his eyes was something so wild, such an expression of terror that the unknown added:

"I am very sorry, believe me. I took you by surprise. You can't hear yourself move on this carpet—but I didn't mean to."

Jean tried to pull himself together. His salvation depended on what was going to happen now. He realised this and summoned all his powers of will. In vain. He had not the strength to enter on an explanation which he knew to be necessary. He only wanted one thing now: never again to see this terrible personage.

"Go away," he shouted, "go away!"

"Go away?"

Jean was beside himself.

"Yes, go away at once."

The man was not easy to move. He shrugged his shoulders without answering. The scene seemed to him incomprehensible and, no doubt, a little ridiculous. Why should he be told to go away? He would like to understand. Honest people try and explain themselves, don't they? He moved slightly in Jean's direction. He did not look in the least quarrelsome or evilly disposed. But Jean shivered with terror at his approach.

"Don't touch me, I tell you, I forbid you to touch me."

"But what's the meaning of all this?" said the other, by this time thoroughly annoyed. "What is all this? After all I'm quite ready to admit I'm in the wrong. I took you by surprise, I know. I should have coughed as I came up to you from behind. But you needn't make such a fuss as all this. There now—he's going to faint. Come, come, Sir!"

The attendant woke up, shook her apron, put her bonnet straight and ran to ask for help.

A policeman and the doctor attached to the theatre were summoned. The check-takers ran up from the auditorium. No one understood a word of the explanation of the man with the pipe. The policeman took a note book out of his pocket. Jean was lifted on to the armchair and remained speechless, paler than if he had been drowned. Everyone stood round him talking: the doctor loosened his necktie.

In the meantime the only witness of the incident gave his account of the affair to the policeman who looked at him silently and with suspicion, his note book open in his hand. But what astonished the doctor was that at every word uttered by the gentleman with the pipe, Jean trembled as if he had been galvanised by an electric shock.

Fright, a nervous collapse, thought the doctor, as he began to dip a towel in water.

But Jean got up. His trembling stopped and he began to listen. In order to hear better he staggered towards the little circle that stood round the policeman and the witness. The latter was talking in louder tones, and Jean whose expression showed his passionate attention, looked at him fixedly. He paid no attention to what the man was saying: what he was listening for and what he heard was what no man assuredly had ever heard before: his own voice coming from outside himself, the sound and intonation of his speech, obeying a will other than his own and reaching his ears with the awful precision of an echo, but an echo without an original.

"Anyhow," said the policeman, turning towards him, "you have no charge to bring. This gentleman did not strike you?"

Jean shook his head.

"Still I must make a report, and you must give me the usual particulars. You, Sir, you say you are a tailor. Workman or employer?"

"Workman, at present out of employment; times are bad just now."

"Your name?"

"Gervais."

Jean started up. He collected his strength and leapt at the man with his fingers bent like talons. They all rushed forward: the man made as if to defend himself. But Jean moved but one step: his arms felt vacantly for support, his mouth gasped for air, and he collapsed and fell unconscious.

• • • • • • •

When he opened his eyes, Jean saw a number of faces round the bed on which he was lying fully dressed. He recognised his neighbours. A confused murmur filled the room: he could hear other voices in the sitting room. Jean breathed deeply. A doctor was bending over him: not the previous one, but an old gentleman who lived in the house and wore a beard like tangled grass descending over an impoverished student's necktie. His colleague of the theatre had handed over the patient, after his address had been ascertained.

This prolonged fainting fit—which had lasted for more than an hour—alarmed the doctor. He had done everything he could to rouse Jean from what he took to be an attack of syncope, and he was wondering whether he had not better try caffeine. But Jean's sigh relieved him from his perplexity. He quickly removed his glasses from the end of his nose and said, in a cheerful voice:

"Good! Now we're feeling better."

The doctor's firm tones put an end to the conversations that were going on. The neighbours who were standing round came in closer. They all watched for an expression on the musician's face that should satisfy the curiosity of his fellow lodgers. Jean turned his head slowly on the pillow and looked at them absently.

"He does not want to talk," said a voice.

"Now then," said the doctor, "we must not tire him. But he can't be left alone. Will anyone undertake to spend the night here?"

The neighbours consulted each other forthwith and, having provided their excuses one by one, they began to move off home. M. Brielle de Chuinaz, the retired dragoon, went out first, with his military step: after him went the clock-maker, the cab-drivers, and the traveller in soap.

It was old Mother Petiot, the umbrella mender, who offered to stay.

"I've got my mother to look after," she said, "but I can go backwards and forwards . . . Shall I make some *tisane?*"

"No, let him rest. You must try and sleep, M. Mourin. I will come back and see you tomorrow."

Without opening his eyes Jean expressed his understanding by a movement of the head.

The doctor went to take his hat off the stand and was just going out when a voice was heard from the next room.

"And what about me? Who is going to pay my fare?"

"I will," answered another voice.

And with these words Gervais appeared in the doorway.

Jean sat up as if some powerful grip had seized him by the shoulder and pushed him forward.

The doctor put his hat down again, turned to Gervais and asked:

"Are you a friend of M. Mourin?"

"No, I don't know him. But I am in a way responsible for the accident . . . So I thought I ought to come back with him and pay the cab."

"Very proper," said the doctor. "Your feelings do you credit."

Jean was sitting up, his face convulsed.

"Take him away," he cried, "I won't see him. He follows me about. In my own house! O God, in my own house!"

The people who were on the point of going stopped abruptly, and a silence followed. Gervais stood in the doorway, looking alternately at the sick man and the doctor who said:

"But you have just told us that you did not know M. Mourin. What does this mean?"

"How do I know?" said Gervais, shrugging his shoulders.

In a composed manner he related what had happened just as he had done to the policeman in the entrance to the music-hall. He did not leave out a single detail, with the useless exactitude of people who pay more attention to facts than causes. His good faith and kindliness were perfectly clear.

"I can't think what he had got against me," he said by way of conclusion.

"Don't listen to him," said Jean Mourin. "It is he, the *Other one.* I thought he was dead when I left Room 67. He follows me about. Dr. Hugues lied All the books lied. I beg you all, deliver me from this man,

inform the police. O God, what will become of me?"

He flung himself to the end of the room, behind Mother Petiot, and stood trembling in childish horror.

"Nervous fever," said the doctor.

"As you see," added Gervais.

But Mother Petiot who was used to illness managed to lead Jean towards the bed.

"Go away, all of you. He will go to bed quietly."

Gervais crossed the room and went out without turning round. The doctor added as he went through the door:

"If he gets too excited, send for me."

"I will put on some cooling compresses," said the good woman, "and make him some lime-water tea."

• • • • • • •

Mother Petiot spent a whole week with Jean Mourin. From time to time she got up, put his bed-clothes straight, and with a gentle gesture that meant, "You must behave yourself," she went off on tiptoe to her own room. She looked like Sister Céline, and Jean, without thinking much about it, noticed the resemblance at once.

He felt comfortable. The companionship of the old woman reassured him. A heavy dreamless sleep overcame him every evening as soon as darkness fell, and the only illumination in the room came from the alternating lights of an electric sky sign.

In the morning Mother Petiot was at his side mending, or preparing some brew. This went on for a week and then Jean began to get up.

When the doctor paid his last visit Jean expressed his regret for an incident which he no longer seemed to understand at all and the good doctor took himself off ingenuously pleased with his diagnosis.

His old neighbour asked no questions. She had seen other and worse cases. She had known Mother Pommier in the Rue des Amandiers, whose husband had gone mad from alcohol and died of the fear of wildcats. She thought solitude and too much music had deranged the mind of the poor gentleman, so amiable and so polite.

"You ought to marry and sell that thing," she said, pointing to the piano.

Jean smiled, and as she persisted—

"I won't play so much." he answered.

"You haven't been the same since you went away last month, you can take it from me. I don't usually pay any attention to my neighbours:

but here we all live on top of each other, don't we?"

"Yes," said Jean Mourin dully, "I dare say that journey was the cause of everything—and the photographs . . ." He stopped. Mother Petiot raised her eyes and looked at him over her spectacles. Then she shook her head and went on sewing, muttering . . .

"What photographs? Some more ideas of yours?"

"Did I talk in my sleep, I mean at first?"

"You certainly did."

"And what—what did I say?"

"O how should I remember? Just nonsense. Keep calm, Monsieur Mourin. You talked about Dr. Hugues, who frightened you very much, about a cemetery, and also about these photographs. Come now, you're not sensible: you're keeping too much to yourself and doing yourself harm. You're using your brain too much."

"Yes," said Jean: and after a silence he repeated, "Yes."

They said no more. Mother Petiot shook her head and started work again. Jean walked up and down. He hesitated about going into the drawing room, but after looking at the peaceful old woman he decided he would. Everything was arranged with almost monastic precision. The portraits glowed gently in their frames. A delicate light was streaming through the soft net curtains. It was the beginning of October.

He heard Mother Petiot's voice from the next room.

"I'll make you a fire tomorrow."

"Thank you," Jean answered.

The next day he was awakened by the crackling of the logs. He felt happy and grown younger. He noticed under a table the old magazines of 1906, which he had not looked at for weeks. He picked them up and read and re-read them with the idle patience of illness.

Then he took up a novel which was lying by the fireplace. He opened it and something fell out: the photographs. Jean bent down quickly, picked them up and put them away secretly.

Mother Petiot, sitting sleeping in a chair, was darning his socks. From time to time she looked at her patient without raising her head or ceasing the movement of her needle. Two days later she put her spectacles in her pocket, collected her sewing and the various objects she had brought with her. She considered her neighbour entirely recovered and informed him that she did not intend to return. She would accept nothing for her services.

Jean found himself alone once more. His first care was to get the

photographs which he had hidden away in the drawer with the precaution of a miser. He acted like an automaton: his gestures, his very intentions, gave him the sensation of something made up in advance, decided by a will external to himself. He expected to be deeply shaken as he took up the photographs. He was surprised by his calmness and by the doubts that began to rise in his mind. He began really to believe what he had said to the doctor and he wondered whether the incident of the looking glass had been anything but a figment of his dreams. Had Gervais really come into the room? Had he uttered words in which Jean could hear nothing but the sound of his own voice? Or had Jean been merely the victim of some vision in his sleep? Was he an abnormal case?

Who knows?

Have not all men their Gervais, impassive and obstinate, who follows them step by step, slips into their bed beside them, and watches them ceaselessly, ready to ravish their soul from them, live on their body, and share horribly in their death? Perhaps these doubles, who are always present, are only visible to some of us who are thus cruelly privileged. But he who listens to the beating of his heart, and watches his thoughts moving over the great abyss of the world, knows that at his most intimate confessions a witness is present, a witness with penetrating eyes who probes him and judges him and promises again and again the complicity of silence. Who has not felt in his joys and celebrations the obscure presence of this silent messenger? Who has not sometimes suddenly cut short his laughter without knowing why, because within his breast he felt the blow of a melancholy warning? Who can say that he walks alone, moves alone towards his end, and can stretch out his arms without touching the mysterious unknown—Gervais?

• • • • • • •

On the following day, which was the 10th October, Jean decided to resume his old habits. He went about Paris again. He wore out of doors a cloak and hat which he thought made him unrecognisable. He was full of feverish explanations to anybody who expressed surprise at his appearance. In a few days he had entered on the usual round of his existence, which was divided between meals, music and walks. He came in and went out with furtive steps after observing the stairway with extreme care. Having done this he passed his hand over his forehead and made a dash for it, keeping very close to the wall.

These actions betrayed a certain consistency of mind. In his own

lodging he thought he had nothing to fear from Gervais, the avoidance of whom was his continual aim, this presence who stood like a calm contemptuous sentinel on the threshold of those mysteries in which his imagination was lost. But out of doors he thought there was every risk of running against him. Yet in spite of this Jean could not resist the temptation of that danger which drew him like the edge of an abyss.

Jean, after many mental peregrinations, came back again and again to the same point. He felt the presence of his "double," and yet he was doubtful of his existence.

Gervais was like those creatures of the films who, transparent at first, assume bodily form and move over the scene and then fade away again into no more than a shadow with a human form, shed by the light on the moving surface of the screen.

Jean thought about this in the street. If he had expressed aloud his views on the successive materialisation and impalpability of Gervais, the people round him, who were going rationally about their affairs, would have taken him off to the hospital of the district. And yet every evening these same people, so proud of their good sense, accepted similar possibilities, rendered under their own eyes by the artifice of the cinema. The fact was that they could not distinguish external reality from their own experience.

• • • • • • •

While Jean Mourin was thus contending with shadows, a sort of conspiracy was being formed against him in the Rue St. Sauveur. The porter and his wife were in it. The neighbours of this "gentleman of means" had taken their part when the police, before disposing of the affair of his journey to Grenoble, came to reprimand them for their excess of zeal and the undue promptitude of the action they had taken. Still these grievances would have been forgotten if, after the incident of September 21st, Jean, on recovery, had not persisted in his contemptuous attitude towards the people of the house.

Who was he, after all, this personage without employment, so proud and so reserved? Did anyone know of his means of subsistence? Where did he come from? And who was that workman individual who had come on one evening only and had been the cause of the scandal which the house still talked about? Except Mother Petiot, so patient and so like Sister Céline, all his neighbours on that floor showed the musician that aversion which sooner or later condemns a fellow lodger who is too discreet. If after ten o'clock he touched the notes of his piano there would

be shouts and banging of fists on the partitions. Coarse jokes were chalked up on the panels of his door. When he crossed the passage he would hear on his way allusions to the mystery of his existence. They roused the drunkard of No. 40 against him. The only letter that he ever received was an anonymous one. Thus only looks of hatred reached the abyss of his appalling solitude. Had he come back among his kind after so many years merely to suffer, and like the man summoned from his tomb by the voice of Jesus, was he to invoke death with his lamentations and beg that this miracle might have an end?

These were cruel days. Harassed and hunted down, Jean resumed his wanderings through Paris as the only remedy for his depression.

Thinking to avoid an encounter, the very thought of which froze the blood in his veins, he only went out in the day time. At the first sign of fading light he hurried back to the Rue St. Sauveur. And he was to find this terror of the night was not unjustified, though it may have been but the figment of his imagination.

One evening, when he was later than usual, as he was walking rapidly towards the Carrousel, he noticed under the gates of the Louvre a shadow waiting, which he thought he recognised at once. He tried to alter his course and go down the quays. But the force which always defeated his designs drew him under the dark passage. He walked through very fast but he could not help looking at the motionless figure.

It was *He*.

He seemed to be waiting for someone and was looking far off towards the Pont Royal. Jean kept on his way. He did not dare to look back until he reached the arcades of the Théatre Français.

Gervais had not followed him. Nevertheless Jean jumped into a moving auto-bus from which he got down shortly to lose himself in the crowds on the boulevards. When he got home he was almost glad to hear again the hostile hammerings on his partition walls that had now become almost continuous. He shut himself in and pushed the heaviest piece of furniture against the door.

• • • • • • •

Gervais! Paris was surely large and populous enough for one man to avoid meeting another. Where could he hide himself? Was there nowhere in this vast city, in its thousand stony furrows, a refuge for those pursued by the phantoms of fear? Or would she reveal her millions of inhabitants like those in the Valley of Jehoshaphat whom nothing shall conceal when the heavy marble jaws of the tombs begin to gape and

the dead are vomited forth and the earth re-peopled with those who have come to life?

Terror changed his appearance to such an extent that his neighbours were struck with it and forgot their bitterness against him. M. Brielle de Chuinaz, the retired officer, tried to make a polite demonstration in the name of them all. Jean opened his door an inch or two and shut it again, without a word, in the face of the emissary, who withdrew holding his greasy hat ceremoniously against his chest.

Jean had no more need of his fellow men. He plunged into a savage isolation, no longer opened his windows, and left the dust on his furniture and his papers. He spent his nights and days on the watch, lifting up the curtain over his door, and as soon as the noise of a step shook the partitions, he withdrew hurriedly into his lodging.

His gait grew hesitating and like that of a blind man. People in the street stopped and looked at him, thinking he was walking in his sleep. When he went to the restaurant he followed a complicated course, retracing his steps and confusing his tracks: and, full of his obsession, he ate without raising his eyes from the table-cloth.

One day he ventured to look up. It was only for a second: Gervais was sitting opposite him, at the adjoining table, watching him.

Jean shrieked aloud. He hardly noticed the other people getting up in confusion on all sides. A mist of blood covered his vision: but his terror overcame his anger and he rushed out bareheaded. He wandered about all day, turning back on his tracks again and again and only stopped when, worn out with fatigue, he sat down on a bench in the Rue des Gobelins. He breathed once more. His anguish had been so great that an icy perspiration still covered his neck and his cheeks. His knees were trembling. Some of the passers-by stopped in pity at his appearance but the cold soon hurried them on again. Jean, drawn and haggard, did not feel the biting wind.

He stared into the distance, riveted to his seat by weariness and the horror of his fear. In the confused coming and going of the street, in the gloomy light, he watched for the man who, he was sure, had followed him. Twice he thought he recognised the indolent gait of Gervais. Then, suddenly, he appeared from another direction and reading a paper as he walked along.

Jean leapt to his feet and could be seen running along by the railings of the *Manufacture*. He ran for some minutes in and out of the neighbouring streets as if he were in a labyrinth, and finally found him-

self in front of the iron gates of the Montparnasse Cemetery. He retraced his steps, lost himself again and went into a church. As night fell, he started off once more. And henceforward the material presence of Gervais continually haunted him. He thought he saw him by the Observatory getting out of a taxi. Later on about eight o'clock he saw him outside a café, near St. Germain des Prés. He was not alone: another man was sitting at the table with him and talking with animation. Jean, leaning against a lamp-post; saw them get up and go off arm in arm in the direction of the Concorde.

He at once started off at a great pace in the direction of the Boulevard S. Michel.

Lost and aching with hunger he prowled about the obscure streets of the Latin Quarter. He did not dare to stop or to go home. In his disordered mind he still retained a sort of middle class reluctance to appeal to the police. Near the top of the Rue Champollion by the fence of a timber yard, a girl of the streets came up to him. He nearly gave way and followed her into the entrance of a neighbouring building. But he kept on and found himself, almost worn out, and without knowing how he had got there, in the Rue de Montpensier by the entrance of the Palais Royal Theatre.

It was the time of the interval. Idle spectators, chauffeurs and hawkers stood round this wild figure whose eyes searched all the recesses of the walls as if he were looking for some invisible being. A motorcar dispersed the assemblage. Jean, who was left alone in the middle of the road, was knocked down. He picked himself up unhurt.

Without even shaking the dust off his clothes he turned to the left along the Rue des Petits-Champs and then to the right along the Rue de Richelieu. He thought he saw the object of his fears in the distance: he turned back again and started off at a run in the direction of Rue Montmartre. Gervais seemed to be waiting for him at the entrance to a cinema. Like an animal at bay Jean backed on to a wall, ready for anything. But the apparition had disappeared: in the square of vivid light there was no one but a policeman in his cape stamping his feet. Jean moved on, looking round him desperately. He could see nothing and plunged into the Rue du Croissant.

Out of breath he finally reached his lodging. The gate on to the street was already shut. Just as he rang he heard the noise of footsteps on his left: the silhouette of Gervais was outlined at the corner of the street against the white shutters of a dyer's shop.

Jean's heart stopped. The man came up with a swinging step and easy pace.

Jean rang the bell.

The man came on. He was only a few paces away.

Jean rang again.

The man came nearer still. A quick click and the gate moved. Jean, in an agony of terror, flung himself into the entrance and with all his strength of his back and shoulders, of his whole body, he shut the door again. Then he listened, his ear against the wood. The steps stopped for an instant in front of the house, then they went off without hurrying, just as they had come.

Jean shouted his name in the darkness, crossed the court yard with a rush, and drawing his clothes closely against his chest, which was soaking with perspiration, he ran upstairs without stopping till he reached the glass door of his lodging.

• • • • • • •

His hand trembled. The flame of the match contended feebly against the prowling shadows of his room. Jean went backwards and forwards . . . where had he put the lamp? At last he got it.

Nothing had changed. The light touched everything with the familiar reflection. The objects round gave him back his courage; they surrounded and protected him.

Then and then only he realised from the disorder of his person the extremity of his terror. His hair gave his ravaged face the appearance of madness: grey locks matted with sweat covered his forehead. He had lost his necktie in his long flight. This boots and the bottom of his trousers were covered with the mud of the gutters.

But what did it matter? Jean was at home! The familiar noises of the fifth story reassured him: One by one the tenants returned noisily home. From one room to another, through the open doors, they exchanged with a gloomy pleasure the disappointments of the day. The last arrivals walked more heavily. Jean sitting near the table under the luminous cone of the lamp, his eyes turned towards the door, watched for the sound of another step. As the moments passed the fear of hearing it grew less. And Jean said to himself that if the night passed without the man coming back he would be saved. What was the good of looking for him? Safety would come with the dawn. This certainty glowed like a night-light in the darkness of his struggling consciousness. He must wait for the dawn, watch the roofs growing blue and the first

smoke go up in the haze of the morning . . .

Gradually the comings and goings stopped and the fifth story went to sleep. Jean alone was awake, attentive to the slightest rustle. He could only hear the faint sound of the flies round the lamp and the ticking of the alarm clock. From time to time the far off hoot of a motor horn came up from the street, or the dull sound of a door shutting. And then nothing more. The flat silence of the night.

How long did this go on? Jean never knew. He had calmed down and yielding to his fatigue he was now in that dulled state, in which the process of recuperation begins to fade into sleep, when an unmistakeable noise roused him from the chair and brought him to his feet.

The portrait, his, portrait, had fallen from its nail and lay in fragments on the floor in a dust of broken glass: in falling it had brought with it the curtain over the door and Jean, petrified with horror, saw, close up to the glass, the pale but calm countenance of Gervais.

What happened to him in the very second that followed he never tried to explain. A jet of blood seemed to rush from his heart through all his being. As on the evening of his first apprehension in the hotel of the Rue Notre-Dame-des-Victoires, he felt himself suddenly strong and full of decision. The terrible visitor was there, thoroughly alive. Here was his chance. Jean was at the door in one bound, drew the bolt and turned the handle with such vigour that Gervais staggered and nearly fell into the room.

The struggle was short and horrible. Not a cry. Nothing but the desperate breathing of two enemies who were trying to strangle the life out of each other. But hatred increased Jean's strength tenfold. His hands, bent like talons, reached the neck of his adversary and stopped as they found the throbbing knot of the throat and felt the folds of flesh. He stiffened, and pressed with all his force until the vertebrae cracked and the sound seemed to re-echo deep in his own breast: Gervais fell loosely on to the carpet. Jean wiped his forehead slowly with the back of his hand.

• • • • • • •

The door had been open during the struggle. Before shutting it Jean looked carefully into the corridor. Not a sound. There was only a cat at the end near the staircase, whose eyes were open and looked like two little green moons.

The numbered doors of the apartments seemed like coverlets over that silence of sleep which is like no other silence. He listened and

waited. A regular snoring could be heard from a neighbouring room, that of the cabman. Then Jean pulled himself together and without haste and with infinite care began his preparations.

To get to the drawing room he had to step over the corpse. He made a careful stride, noticed that he had forgotten the lamp, came back, and finally left the dead man in darkness.

He fetched the small trunk and filled it with linen. Into the pocket under the lid he slipped his jewels, money, some securities, a pencil-holder, some smoked glasses and a few photographs. There was still enough room for a pair of slippers and his travelling cap. He carefully fastened the two locks and did up the straps of the cover. Then he took off his clothes and began his toilet, taking his time like a man in no hurry.

Shaved, powdered, his hair plastered down, he picked up the lamp and went into the other room in which was the cupboard containing his clothes. He chose rather a peculiar travelling suit, from among his original wardrobe, a sort of pea jacket with a leather belt, and a pair of loose trousers. When he had dressed he went back into the drawing room, put the music straight, tore up various papers, shut the piano noiselessly, put the chairs in a row, then always with the same regular step, the lamp above his head, and carrying his valise, he went back to the other room.

Gervais' body, his face already purple, took up the entire floor. Jean looked at him and in order to see him better bent over him, holding the lamp.

The great open eyes of the strangled corpse stared at a corner of the ceiling: his lips were curved in a laugh and a spot of foam lay on his grey mouth. His necktie had slipped up over his collar and altogether he had a look of some malicious puppet, a huge marionette from another world, an appearance which was emphasised by the position of his feet, that were turned inwards and of his right hand which lay spread out over his shirt front with the pompous gesture of a singer at a wedding.

Jean found the spectacle of this ignoble corpse intolerable. He put the lamp down on the mantelpiece and taking Gervais under his arms he dragged him in the darkness to the further end of the apartment where his bed lay.

He felt neither fear nor remorse but merely annoyance at possessing only one lamp. He went to fetch it in order to hoist his victim more conveniently on to the mattress. He took a white sheet out of a cup-

board and stretched it over the body. From the forehead to the point of the feet the stuff fell into that stiff curve peculiar to a shroud as it falls round the body of the dead.

Before taking away the light Jean glanced about him and seeing that everything was in order he went out slowly, walking backwards. As soon as the door was shut he went to look at the time.

It would not be long before it was light. Jean now awaited with composure the dawn that would come in time and shine upon his steady. eyes.

Mechanically he put in order the scattered objects in the drawing room. While he was collecting himself he noticed between the window and the mantelpiece the portrait of Jeanne, an oval pastel, framed in tarnished gold. He took it down. A surprising lucidity dispersed the last shadows from his mind and it seemed to him that for weeks and months he had looked at the portrait with forgetfulness and indifference. He hardly recognised it. It was no longer the melancholy image of his beloved but her appearance in the happy days of their betrothal. One would have said that a touch of joy seemed to animate the colours of the pastel. Jeanne's very expression seemed to have lost its sombre fire and her regard seemed to move over her husband's face with an expression of tenderness and weariness. Jean kissed the glass over the smooth pale forehead. Then he took out one by one the small wedges that kept the cardboard in the frame and after a last long look at it he threw it in the fire. Then he disposed of the medical reports which he found lying in a case of pigeon-holes. He was on the point of opening a desk which contained his most precious souvenirs when he was overcome by the smoke.

He went to the window and opened it. Six o'clock struck. With his elbows on the window sill he listened to the clocks answering each other in the cold still air. Soon after the last belfry sank into silence, Jean noticed a square of dark indigo surrounding the dark lines of two chimneys.

A fresh breeze blew from the invisible horizon and quickly, in the lifting iris-coloured darkness, the entire landscape of roofs, towers and balconies awoke. The whistle of a locomotive rose like a summons from depths still dark. Day had come. Jean Mourin looked a long farewell on the belongings of his humble life, picked up his bag, went out, and, having carefully closed the door, threw the key through a grating into an abandoned attic. The sound of his step faded into the distance and a moment later he was in the street.

II

Where should he go? Jean did not reflect: he obeyed. Since that moment when, cured of his fears, he had taken Gervais by his throat he lived a more intense and concentrated life. His actions, far from escaping from the control of his will, obeyed a preconceived order which he followed coldly with the precision of an actor familiar with his part. Had not his every movement served its purpose? Was it possible to kill more silently and leave fewer traces of his crime?

The question now was to get away. Jean was ready for anything, and drew strength from the very feeling of danger. From the moment when the body of Gervais had grown heavy and relaxed between his arms before collapsing on to the floor, Jean had felt in a sense awakened. The drops of sweat had dried upon his face and without the slightest effort he had controlled all his movements. With the same composure he had arranged a departure, his preparations for which resembled those for an escape.

And now, buttoned into his belted jacket and carrying a trunk stuffed with valuables, he was walking with a firm step along the deserted pavements of the boulevards. At that hour he met nobody but ragmen, sellers of newspapers and a few restaurant-keepers hurrying towards the markets with napkins tied round their necks.

At the corner of the boulevard and the Rue St. Denis a small refreshment shop was open.

"Coffee?"

"Yes," said Jean, "and a railway time-table."

He looked up carefully a slow train which would take him to Sens where, one hour later, he could catch the Geneva express. He thought that in this way he would baffle the first curiosities of the police. But he subsequently reflected that this elementary ruse could only delay and betray him. He decided to leave Paris by the Troyes line and cut across the P. L. M. at Moret. He got there about four in the afternoon and liked the place. Why should he be in any hurry to leave it? He lived at the hotel for two days tasting every minute the delight of regeneration. He did not for a moment believe that the corpse of Gervais could be

discovered. After the affair of his other journey and the observations of the police, the neighbours would not be in any hurry to notify his disappearance. The corpse was under lock and key and could well wait for the waggon from the Morgue. Who knows?

The autumn was nearly over. Icy showers lashed the country. Then the sky cleared. Jean walked along the towing path by the river Loing. Gleams of pale water lay dreaming in the tracks. A few boats moved gently by the willow-planted banks. Over the low houses fluttered the last leaves swept into the wind by the smoke rising from the roofs.

Almost too deep a peace, too wholesome an air! An immense hope swelled in Jean's heart. He was living with all his strength, he walked and breathed in these clear spaces in which he saw the mirage of his future. O to live and go forth!

Should he go to Geneva? No, that would be foolish. There the police of all the world lay their snares. Before he had set foot on the quays of Cornavin he would be tracked, discovered and quietly arrested in the corridor of a hotel. He could see himself going back through the frontier station, between two gendarmes, on the yellow bench of a third class carriage . . . No! not that rat-trap!

Where should he go! A little French town with its cobbled streets, a pension de famille by the ramparts, a shining room where one goes to bed at dusk, what could be a better refuge? Of course! Too near Paris would be defying the police: too far off, he would run the risk of arousing provincial curiosity. He would do best to go to earth and wait, without useless movement, until the case had been put away. Why not here?

He walked on carefully. The sight of a man standing still who seemed to be watching him made his heart shrink: but he mastered himself and forced himself to walk slowly with a natural air. Suppose the crime was discovered! The name and description of Jean Mourin would be circulated to all the police headquarters. Suppose they were looking already for the 'clean shaven man,' dressed in black, in all the stations on the harbour quays, in suspected lodging houses, at Meilles, round the Rue St. Sauveur.

Suddenly Jean heard the sound of voices. At the end of the street which opened out into a square in front of the station, people were standing round a seller of newspapers: others were walking towards the town reading the opened sheets. Jean felt a presentiment: he quickened his steps and came up to the group.

"Give me a paper," he said.

"The *Petit Parisien?*"

"Anything you like."

In the middle of the front page there was a sketch which Jean noticed with a sudden dizzy shock as if it had struck him in the face.

It was his own portrait, the one taken at the hospital, the upper part of his body covered with a white shirt, an anxious expression on his face, and behind him a door loaded with great bolts, the photograph which Dr. Hugues had given him and underneath it the legend:

"Mourin, the supposed assassin . . . or the victim."

He stopped abruptly. Then his eyes wandered towards the heavily leaded heading over the picture and the text. A STRANGE CRIME IN THE RUE ST. SAUVEUR. *Discovery in a lodging of the body of an unknown man whose identity appears to be confused with that of his murderer who has disappeared.*

And Jean leaning against a tree in the square read as follows:—

"A very curious affair, which seems without precedent in the annals of justice, aroused a lively sensation last evening in the Market quarter when the facts were discovered.

"No. 27 in the Rue St. Sauveur is a building of some age, the lower floors of which are occupied by offices or expert agencies. On the third and fourth floors are the modest households of small business men, while the fifth floor, consisting of attics, is inhabited by various establishments of the working class. At the end of a long dark passage which leads from the top of the staircase past the doors of these rooms, there is a small apartment of three rooms whose windows look on to the street.

"On March 3rd last a certain Jean Mourin, 45 years of age, took possession of this lodging which had been transferred to him, together with the furniture, by an employé in the Post Office, one André G——. The arrival of Mourin, who had previously been living in a hotel in the Rue Notre-Dame-des-Victoires, was preceded by that of two large trunks. Subsequently he acquired a piano. Where did this tenant come from?

"The object of the present enquiry is to establish this. It has been ascertained that he stayed only a short time in the hotel in the Rue Notre-Dame-des-Victoires. On the tenants' register he is entered under the assumed name of Thévenet, and is described as being of no profession and coming from Canada. It is probable that this point will soon be cleared up.

"Although of somewhat eccentric character and quite uncommunicative, Mourin who had some independent means, was a man of regular habits.

"According to the reports of the neighbours he played his piano a great deal. It does not appear that, during his residence at the two addresses given above, he engaged in any remunerative occupation.

"The evidence differs regarding his appearance. While the hotel-keeper and the staff assert categorically that Mourin wore a short round beard, and that his hair was grey, the lodgers at the Rue St. Sauveur maintain that they always knew him as clean shaven, and wearing his hair long 'like an artist.' This singular contradiction has a certain importance, as will be seen later.

"Mourin received no letters or visits. From the day on which he took possession up to September 20th, that is to say for a period of six months, so far as was known he held no communication with anyone. On the 21st September, a little after midnight, Mourin was brought back in a taxi by an unknown individual as the result of a somewhat singular incident which took place in a music-hall in the République quarter.

"Mourin having by accident come into the company of the individual in question was overcome by a nervous shock of such a nature that, as a result of the meeting, and for several days afterwards, he remained in a condition which gave considerable cause for alarm.

"The unknown personage, as we have said, having brought Mourin, who was still unconscious, back to his lodging, stayed with him, while Dr. Morelli, who was called in, rendered first aid. When questioned by the neighbours and the doctor, the unknown repeatedly asserted that he did not know Mourin. About the middle of the night he went away, having paid the cab: in any case his presence appeared to exasperate the sick man.

"This person remained long enough in the room for various witnesses to notice and recall his appearance.

"On this point their statements are in agreement: he was of middle height, about 45 years of age, of a good humoured expression, wearing a beard and dressed like a workman in good circumstances: he spoke in a husky voice and disclosed incidentally that his profession was that of a tailor.

"Since that day he has not been seen either in the building or in the district.

"On the morning of Friday the 8th December a lodger on the same

story, Madame Petiot, who looked after Mourin, came as usual and knocked at his door. No one answered. She tried to lift the latch. The door was shut. Madame Petiot was not particularly astonished as Mourin had gone away, in the preceding June, in rather an odd manner, and had returned just as the police-commissary of the district was about to have his apartment opened.

"At the same time Madame Petiot thought fit to let the porter know.

"By the next day, which was yesterday, Saturday, Mourin had not re-appeared. No doubt the other lodgers would not have informed the police at this stage unless one of them, M. Brielle de Chuinaz, had not made an unexpected discovery. In his attic he picked up by accident a key which he recognised at once as being that of Mourin's lodging. Somewhat disturbed by this discovery M. de Chuinaz informed his neighbours.

"By a general agreement it was decided to place the matter before the Commissary of Police, who came round forthwith and entered the apartment.

"A terrible spectacle awaited the magistrate and those who accompanied him.

"In a room which Mourin used as bedroom lay the body of a man half decomposed and covered by a sheet. As soon as the neighbours saw it they recognised it at once: it was the unknown who on the night of 21 and 22 September had brought Jean Mourin home and had never been since in the neighbourhood of the Rue St. Sauveur.

"On his neck were the marks of strangulation and he appeared to have succumbed during a violent struggle. In his pockets were papers bearing the name of Gervais, tailor, without any note of an address. But it would seem that these papers are false. The name is entirely unknown to the employers and workmen's Union.

"The preceding circumstances would appear in no way to distinguish the case from an ordinary murder except that the details now to be related, suggest something strange and disconcerting, something almost in the nature of an hallucination.

"Near the bed on which the corpse was lying the examining magistrate discovered in a drawer of the small bedroom table two photographs which, when compared with the corpse, left no doubt in the minds of the witnesses.

"They were two photographs of the victim. How did they come to

be there? This is the point which the enquiry is attempting to clear up.

"But this is where the mystery begins. On the first of these photographs is the following inscription scratched with a knife on the gelatine of the plate.

"'*Mourin* (Jean); age 42. Fontenay (Vendée); musician. Ob. 1032 Rm. 67. June 11th, 1920.' On the second in the same handwriting, 'Mourin (Jean); age 44; Fontenay (Vendée); musician. Ob. 2815 Rm. 67. August 12th, 1922.'

"It would seem therefore, if importance is to be attached to this discovery, that here is the real Jean Mourin, while the supposed assassin, that is to say the lodger of the Rue St. Sauveur, must be someone else. But there is a further peculiar circumstance.

"When these photographs were shewn to the hotelkeeper of the Rue Notre-Dame-des-Victoires he recognised his old tenant without the slightest hesitation. When confronted with the corpse he did not hesitate for a moment. 'This is certainly the man who lodged in my house until March 6th last.'

"The police were about to reach the conclusion that between the moment when the man with a beard left the hotel and the time when the man who wore no beard took possession of the lodging in the Rue St. Sauveur, there occurred purely and simply a substitution of identity. But at this point a new fact came to light. The police inspectors discovered in a desk a voluminous correspondence and various old photographs proving that the name of the man who has disappeared was in fact Jean Mourin, born at Fontenay-le-Comte (Vendée) on March 5th, 1879. There can be no question of an usurpation of civil status. Consequently the tenant of the Rue St. Sauveur, that is to say the supposed murderer, must be the real Jean Mourin.

"Must it be assumed therefore that the inscriptions on the photographs of the dead man are false and intended to mislead any investigation? No, for the officers at Headquarters who deal with questions of identity at once recognised them as medical photographs which must certainly be authentic. To sum up, we have here a murderer and a victim having the same name, and at different times, the same appearance.

"Indeed, except for this latter point the characters of the drama are exactly identifiable with each other.

"One is lost in conjecture. Unless it is subsequently established that the man who has disappeared is named Gervais—which the correspondence seized makes highly improbable—the astounding hypothesis

must be accepted that these two individuals have the same appearance and the same name. But even if this improbability is admitted the mystery does but grow deeper. Only the arrest of the supposed murderer can throw a little light on the imbroglio.

"One final detail will bring the mystery home to our readers.

"On the night of the crime Mourin came home alone about half past ten. He went out at dawn and walked without hurrying in the direction of the boulevards. In the interval no sound of a quarrel was heard. The concierges, when questioned, assert that on the night in question they only opened the front gate to tenants belonging to the house.

"The magistrate's enquiry is being pursued. The Anthropometrical Section will take impressions of the finger prints of the murderer and his victim. The ablest inspectors from Headquarters are searching for Mourin. Throughout the evening and during part of the night there has been an enormous crowd, in spite of the bad weather, in front of the house in which the crime took place.

"At the moment of going to press we are informed that a hairdresser in the Rue des Martyrs, who had seen in an evening paper certain details about the crime in the Rue St. Sauveur, came of his own accord to see the examining magistrate. He announced that on a certain day which he could not exactly fix, but before the end of April, an individual answering to the description of the supposed murderer came into his shop to get his face completely shaved.

"The hairdresser had been much struck by the excited condition of his customer and by his eagerness to get his appearance altered. The photograph of the victim was shewn to him and he recognised it at once as that of his customer.

"'That's him,' said he. 'I remember his eyes very well.'

"The worthy citizen has been bidden to hold himself at the disposal of the police for a confrontation which cannot be long delayed, for it seems that the police are already on the track of the assassin who, on the day following the crime, took the train for Chaumont. It is thought that he has sought refuge in Switzerland."

• • • • • • •

Jean remained rigid. His hands were clammy, his eyes staring, and his back was cold with sweat.

The last phrase of the article reassured him completely. But he was afraid of moving lest his trembling gait should attract attention. So he

stayed motionless leaning against the tree, his eyes fixed on the paper that he held wide open. But supposing he had followed his original idea and gone to Geneva! He shivered.

Then suddenly he felt a sensation of extreme tranquillity. The sight of the portrait, which was that of the dead man, gave him at one and the same time a feeling of deliverance and of anxiety for his own safety. No one would see that face again. The false Mourin had been wiped out of the world, destroyed: there was no crime in that. It was like a sham suicide, the removal of an impersonation. He had merely strangled a phantom, *his* phantom, the persistent phantom of his own reflection.

And here were the stupid police taking him for Gervais.

They were looking for Gervais whom they had just deposited on the marble slabs of the Morgue. What a sinister farce. He wanted to shout out to all those readers of newspapers who were walking back towards the centre of the town, "I am Jean Mourin."

He pictured the scene, fainting women, and everybody running for the police. And the tocsin ringing at Moret!

"Come," he murmured to himself, "I mustn't be so stupid."

He folded the paper and put it in his pocket, and, as lunch-time was near, he walked slowly in the direction of the hotel, by the Sablons road.

He ate with a good appetite. At the adjoining tables everyone was discussing the astonishing news. There was a general feeling of incredulity and the invention of the story was ascribed to the dearth of news from which the papers were suffering.

"This" observed a tall and serious-looking individual, "is the sort of rubbish that gets all over France instead of proper instruction on economic subjects."

But someone else, pointing to the photograph, objected.

"There are people who knew him, so you will see that there must be something in it."

"Is there anyone?" thought Jean. And the image of Dr. Hugues immediately came into his mind. He never thought of Dr. Hugues without fear. By this time the doctor in Grenoble knew everything. He had read the papers and he would certainly be telegraphing to the magistrates that he was at their disposal.

This idea was so vivid in Jean's mind that he found in the face of the first speaker a resemblance to the learned doctor.

The servant poured out the coffee. Jean lit a cigarette and took the

paper out of his pocket.

He went through it from end to end like an idle person killing time. He was not reading. The lines wandered on, devoid of sense, under his absent eyes. He struggled against a somnolence that was overcoming him. *Theatres, Prices at the Markets, Stock Exchange, Latest News, Exchanges, Sport.* Suddenly, an illumination. His eyes fell upon the following, in small print, at the bottom of a column on the fifth page:

Mail Steamers.

> Long distance mails. French and Foreign. FAR-EAST. *S.S. Maelstrom* (Sw. R. Co.), mails Dec. 10th. Havre for Corunna, Lisbon, Cadiz, Gibraltar, Port Said, Djibouthi, Colombo, Singapore, Canton, Shanghai, Yokohama (leaving Havre Dec. 13th).

Jean wondered later, and never knew, if he had been dreaming. He said the names, all the names over to himself, closing his eyes on the visions they evoked. They passed and repassed in magic cohorts, full of melancholy splendour.

Spain, Portugal, Africa, Ceylon, China. Was it a dream that unrolled this changing panorama of capitals, domes, pagodas, harbours, naked humanity, tropical rivers, tumultuous seas, gigantic freights and silky dragons. Jean was in a little hotel in the Seine-et-Marne, a newspaper on his knees and his eyes shut. A servant who was folding napkins might imagine she was near him, but he was already going forth to those lands of forgetfulness where the traveller thinks he turns his back on his sorrows. Jean on his chair, with his head bent, was no more than a dream of tapering masts and smoke.

O to get away! In a flash he had forgotten everything, his misery and his crime. If he could only escape his destiny that seemed like a curse upon him! He understood now that he hated his fellow men, without reflecting that he had done nothing to get into touch with them and follow them on the way. They had passed near him but they had not helped him. What had he come back to look for in his living death in the midst of a world that was deaf to the mystery of his existence.

What was the use of striving against the eternal powers that dictate the life of human societies and which mortal men obey just as they listen to the throbbing of the blood in their veins? A country is the creation of an epoch. The hearts of its citizens are but a single heart and it

is shut behind a barrier like a wall.

The miracle of Lazarus is but an ancient lie: among the millions of living men there is no place at all for one who has returned from death.

O to get away! Henceforward, he would not look for support among his own kind. He would go to one of those countries where men live and die like insects in a countless swarm.

Beyond the forests and seas there are cities full of overflowing humanity where, under the almighty sun, multitudes of men ceaselessly pullulate, in a gigantic confusion of stench and noise—a cauldron of peoples. O to lose himself in these thronging crowds, deafened by the din of gongs beaten night and day by the hundred arms of gods seated under their crimson roof-trees!

What else could he do? He would depart and week after week leave further behind him the land of his fathers, where by the cruelest of miracles, he was the solitary stranger, a hermit, a leper.

He would set forth to the vast desert of exile where all stand side by side and are equal,—outlaw, settler, fugitive, missionary and soldier. The sea would close, bit by bit, the pathway that the ship had opened. Morning after morning in the same place the sun would rise cleansed from the waves and sink to the edges of the darkened sky into the western sea. After days and days through forests and over seas Jean Mourin would find in the heart of Asia the city where he would give up for ever his search for the key to the riddle and would wait for his death. And yellow men would shut down the earth over the remains of him who was no one and came from the unknown.

Jean shook himself and picked up the paper and made sure of the dates. The date on the newspaper was December 17th. He went along at once to the proprietor and paid his bill. The same evening he arrived at the Hotel de Bordeaux at Havre and requested the porter to book his passage on the *Maelstrom.*

Three days to wait. Jean showed no sign of impatience. And he felt no further sensation of fear. He went from one café to another, mixing with the dockers, the Customs House men and policemen, and took no sort of precautions.

But a singular agitation was troubling his mind. While a secret sense of security strengthened him against the danger of being tracked and taken by the collar, he had to fight against a desire, which increased every day, of taking refuge in the hospital at Grenoble. In the old hospital, with Dr. Hugues and Sister Céline. He pictured to himself the

happy days and silent nights in Room 67, and this with a lucidity that surprised him and gave him the sensation of coming out of a delirium. A thin gleam of light shone under the closed door of his recollections. Everything that Gervais had read and spoken for sixteen years in that room lay in a confused mass in the consciousness of Mourin. Now Gervais was dead, should he not take the place of his own double and thus escape the consequences of his crime? Should he go back to annihilation or go away,—which? He did not know. He was under some unknown direction, now as always.

While he talked to himself and gesticulated as he walked along, some curious passers-by stopped. He quickened his pace and to keep himself in countenance looked up at the clock on the Arsenal. Then creeping along some blackened palings he moved off, away from the railway station and disappeared under a portico, while a hungry dog stood barking at the sky.

III

M. Jean Mourin, first class passenger, walked quickly up the gangway.

The rain drove the black plumes of smoke that rose from the ship into the fog, amid clanging bells and hooting sirens. A few passengers were already walking briskly round the deck. Others, wrapped in rugs, were lying on deck chairs. Everyone, passengers, stewards, bandsmen, postal officials, felt their individuality enhanced by the fever of departure. Only the sailors in their blue jerseys preserved the quiet demeanour of people who were going about their accustomed business.

Jean found his cabin, tried the taps in the basin, and moved the lamp which stood on a shelf and would throw too much light on the head of his bed. A monotonous rain pattered down upon the porthole from the leaden depths of the sky. The vivid white walls gave out a slight odour of tobacco: the door, of which the upper panel was opaque glass, opened on to a thickly carpeted corridor: and the soft shadows of the attendants flitted across the dim square of light.

On the shelf lay an open copy of the *Illustration* displaying on one side photographs of a new steamer and on the opposite page pictures of Paris on a day of festival.

Jean sat down on the bed for a moment. He took out of his luggage a cap, a handkerchief and some gloves: then he began to think about his valuables and banknotes. He stuffed the money into his pocket and left the rest in his trunk which he carefully locked and then, with his hands in his pockets, he went up on deck.

• • • • • • •

The passengers seemed to have increased in numbers. Most of them, in spite of the rain, were leaning against the side of the ship watching the quay where their friends were standing several deep waving handkerchiefs and umbrellas.

Suddenly the siren was silent and the quay slowly moved away. The ship was casting off. Jean hurried towards the bows and stood by a bench at the top of the gangway ladder. He stared at the green walls of the harbour as they passed him. With dry eyes he was starting off on his endless exile. Although he watched with a melancholy fixed gaze the

land as it seemed to turn and subside into the sea, he did not see it with the eyes of the emigrant.

Can the man who has survived death be said to have a country? Can there be a more implacable desert in the world than a man's own country when its inhabitants are unknown and enemies?

The ship was already cutting a track through the stormy plain of the open sea. Jean lowered his eyes and noticed below him, on the third class deck, a man dressed in a shabby suit, carrying a small bundle knotted into a check handkerchief, and leaning against a capstan. He raised his head and Jean saw that he was weeping. It was an unfortunate man who was following his destiny. He wept as he watched two blackened mooring-posts, an iron ring, the square mass of an abandoned landing stage with its old ravelled ropes, pass and disappear into the night. He wept because that paved quay which he would never tread again, which would be washed by the tides and swept by the careless winds of the sea, was for him the end of France. Jean shook his head and went away. Why had not he, like this poor wretch, something to regret?

It was very cold. The date was December 13th, one year, day for day, since Jean Mourin had awakened at the hospital.

• • • • • • •

In the large saloon, the band was playing loudly. Jean, almost alone on the wind-swept deck, passed at regular intervals across the estuaries of light. The sound of the dark waves beating against the sides of the *Maelstrom* made the orchestra seem confused and far off. The windows were clouded by steam and Jean saw and heard, as in a dream, the concert, the black coats and powdered shoulders, the waiters in their white jackets, and the light of a thousand lamps.

Through all her portholes and all her galleries the ship opened eyes of flame into the darkness which surged in upon her in thick eddies. Above, the saloons, bars, smoking rooms, the fantastic glitter of mirrors and lamps: below, the palpitating life of the crew and the engines, as they drove the great mass southwards through the night, like a palace *en fête*. From far off and further off moans of distress and anger came down from the rainy sky: the cries of sirens. The bell rang. It seemed like a summons from those who stood above in the storm, straining their eyes to pierce the blackness of the night.

Nothing but darkness and rain. The great *Maelstrom* moved on pursuing the lights on her bows. The rain grew heavier and the darkness seemed to grow even more thick. Suddenly the lightning flashed from

the sky, hurled like a scythe of silvery blue, and its crooked zig-zag tore apart the velvet darkness.

Jean, blinded, leaned over the side towards the tumult of the waves. Then the need of movement, action, the desire to set his blood in motion took hold of him, and as the night wore away he strode along the decks, leaning against the bulwarks and climbing up and down the ladders.

Sleep? He would not think of it! In the midst of the hurricane he had the feeling of escape from the suffocation of a narrow cell, as if he had slipped out of some closely guarded confinement and breathed at last the free air, the wholesome breeze of the open sky. He shut his eyes and it seemed to him as if he stood on a balcony over a garden on which a shower of rain was beating down. He felt uplifted by this exaltation and walked with rapid steps, making great meaningless gestures, and then stopped, holding on to the rails, and leaning towards the sightless distance as if he expected to see something appear.

• • • • • • •

One by one the passengers went back to their cabins. The bell rang again. The sailors of the watch were going over the ship. Jean was still watching and shivering on deck. The rain beat savagely in gusts against the vessel. Sometimes it seemed to be whirled up to the sky and sometimes driven into eddies by the wind. And all around him in the night were the lamentations of the storm. Jean kept his eyes fixed on the same point: he was waiting for something he could not define—something that would appear. . . .

About the middle of the night the storm seemed to slacken. A harsher, colder wind began to get up. Jean looked towards the left of the *Maelstrom.*

Soon he observed two long points of green light against the blank abyss. He looked at them fixedly. They did not increase in size but grew brighter. The blackness of the sea and the sky seemed to be developing a violet tinge. Were they the double lights of a light-house? They blinked like the two eyes of a cat and came rapidly nearer. The bell on board awoke again as if by magic and from up above in the mist came the hellish screaming of the siren.

The lights of the ship had long since been put out and nothing could be seen in the vast darkness but the gleam of the light-house which grew more distinct as the *Maelstrom* approached. The noise of the waves became clearer and Jean could hear the sound of distant singing. The lights gradually lengthened out into revolving rays like arms which

seemed to be beating down on to the sea.

Jean Mourin went off to his cabin suspecting nothing. The white, carpeted corridor stretched away into the distance. In each door was a pane of opaque glass. A woman attendant in a linen apron was dozing in a chair. Just before he got to his door Jean noticed a narrow tall looking glass with a shelf above it. He looked at himself casually as he passed and saw with horror that his beard had grown. It was gray, the same colour as the overcoat he was wearing.

Jean stopped as if he had run into a wall.

"Where was he?"

Was this his cabin? He raised his eyes: the number painted in red on the opaque glass gave him another shock: 67.

At the same moment he felt someone take him by the shoulders. It was not a sailor. It was a man dressed in blue, wearing a cap with a leather peak. And he heard a voice.

"Now then, Gervais, you have been out again tonight although I said you were not to go. Go back to your room and go to bed."

The hospital! He was in the hospital. He put his hands to his forehead. What did it mean, this horrible return, after his marvellous adventures?

Jean Mourin looked at the face of Gervais in the mirror. Then he passed his fingers over his cheeks and chin and felt his beard.

He saw the calendar on the wall and the large figures of the date: 13 December 1922. One evening. . . .

Just one evening. In the dark re-duplication of his being, the actions and the appearances of life—with the swift hallucination of a dream—had unrolled their confused and shining panorama. A few hours of light and now, for ever, he must return to the black imprisonment of madness.

Dr. Hugues shook his head with the sternness of an old soldier. Francoz was urging his patient forward, carefully but firmly. Sister Cêline, who resembled Mother Petiot, had got up from her chair. Not a movement in the white corridor of the hospital. Flowing arpeggios from an accordion: and from behind the partition the nasal utterances of M. Brielle de Chuinaz. An interminable rain beat upon the window-panes. Jean Mourin rushed into his room with a shriek of despairing laughter.